Liberty Two

Robert Lipsyte

SIMON AND SCHUSTER   NEW YORK

SBN 671-21694-5
Library of Congress Catalog Card Number: 73-20698
Designed by Jack Jaget
Manufactured in the United States of America
Printed by The Murray Printing Company, Forge Village, Mass.
Bound by The Book Press, Brattleboro, Vt.

1   2   3   4   5   6   7   8   9   10

For Marjorie

Liberty
Two

One They finally came for Cable in the spring, just when he had begun to think they had forgotten or no longer cared. They came on a moist Sunday evening that gently hugged the tender green hills north of the city. He was sitting on a high stool behind the bar watching a young couple, their knees touching beneath a red formica table, tourists headed for Oregon, staring at each other over sandwiches and beer. They stirred vague memories in Cable and made him uneasy.

The only other customer, a ranch hand, was staring up at the television set above the bar. "They turned that crazy astronaut loose."

Through the window above the cash register Cable saw the sun leak orange into the valley. A county ambulance, a white panel truck with red crosses, had begun the slow, low-gear climb up the corkscrew road. The ambulance disappeared behind pines, then reappeared, glinting in the dying sunlight. Cable watched it wink on and off along the switchbacks of the mountain road. An old man lies dying in his vineyard, Cable thought, a horse tramp's wife is giving birth in a second-hand trailer.

"The mad moon man himself," said the owner. She stood beside Cable wiping glasses. Her fleshy upper arms quivered as she stuffed a damp rag into a bar glass, then twirled it with the reddened fingers of her other hand. "What's he got to say now?"

"He's gonna wake up America," the ranch hand said.

Cable twisted toward the television set. The face glaring out of the set surprised him, fierce, jutting bones and deep, haunted hollows. He remembered the face fuller, rounder. Cable's uneasiness grew, but he did not know why.

"Don't wake us up too early," said the owner. "I need my beauty sleep." She winked at Cable. She would close soon, they would eat together in the kitchen and go upstairs to her bedroom. Cable thought, I'll have to be moving on.

A news commentator's confident voice: ". . . Defense Department nor the National Aeronautics and Space Administration would comment beyond the official announcement, although sources indicated that . . ."

The county ambulance crunched over the loose gravel outside the restaurant and parked at the front door. Two attendants walked in briskly. They let the outer screen door bang shut behind them, but they left the heavy wooden door wide open. Cable smelled the cool, moist dusk.

"Kitchen's closed, boys," she called.

". . . Although there have been reports that Commander Rice would appeal his forced medical retirement, the former astronaut told a brief news conference today that he had no such plans. Rice said he preferred that history be his final judge and that the American people . . ."

One attendant was black, the other white, both trim, wide-shouldered men with hard, clean features and quick, darting eyes. They wore spotless white duck uniforms and white shoes with red ripple soles. The white man stood near the front of the bar and watched the young couple feed each other bits of sandwich. The black marched to the bar.

". . . Rice eluded newsmen and was driven to the Houston airport by an unidentified man in a rented car. They boarded a flight to New York, where Rice will presumably begin his proposed . . ."

"Bonnie Fuller?" The black pulled a yellow slip out of his shirt pocket.

"Never felt better, Doc."

The black man didn't smile. "Looking for a man came in here about a month ago. Caucasian, a little above average height, thin, full beard. Early thirties."

"We get busy around here I don't even look up." Bonnie snapped off the set. "Can I buy you a drink?"

"He freaked out in your lavatory."

She waved the rag toward the back of the restaurant. "Take a look, maybe he's still in there."

The attendant moved closer to the bar. "He drove in with some hippies in a Volks camper. They bought some beer and you filled their thermoses with coffee. They used your lavatory, this guy passed out and they left him in there."

"You know more than I do."

He put the yellow slip back in his pocket. "We got a call from Seattle, one of the hippies checked in with plague. We're trying to track down all contacts."

The ranch hand looked at Cable, then at the black man and dropped some money on the bar.

"Afraid I can't help you." She turned to Cable. "Ring any bells?"

He shook his head.

The black man looked at Cable for the first time. "About your size. Thinner. Had a beard."

The ranch hand edged toward the door. The white attendant stopped him with a smile and an upraised finger.

The woman's voice rose. "We get a lot of hippies stopping, mostly for gas. They all have beards."

"This guy's got old surgical scars behind his knees."

She pressed her lips together and avoided looking at Cable. "How would you know?"

"Couple of the hippies balled with him nonstop from Tijuana. One of them was the reported case. A guy."

The young couple came up to the cash register, holding hands. They had left most of their food, Cable noticed. The young man said, "We'd like to pay." He was only slightly taller than his girl. They were both very slim and pretty.

Bonnie Fuller waved them out. "It's on the house, kids. Good luck."

"Hey, wow, thanks . . ."

"Forget it. Just go."

The black man turned to them. "We're from the County. Please wait a minute."

Cable thought, so they've finally come for me. Took their time. He slid off his stool and raised a section of the bar counter. The white attendant moved to block the door. His right thumb was hooked over his belt buckle. The front of his white duck shirt sagged forward. Cable wondered if he was carrying a gun.

Bonnie Fuller looked at the black man. "Let him get his gear, it's out back."

"Better burn it, Mrs. Fuller." He took Cable's arm firmly, professionally, and led him out the door. The white man followed them, carefully closing the heavy inner door behind them.

The back of the white panel truck was open. A cot was

bolted to the floor. A narrow bench ran the length of one wall. Cable climbed in and sat on the cot. The white attendant perched on the bench. The black man locked them in and walked around to the driver's seat.

Through the side window Cable made out Bonnie Fuller's large body framed in the doorway. The sun was gone and her face was indistinct in the blue dusk. He began to forget her features as the ambulance started across the gravel yard.

Through the back window he saw a car pull into the space the ambulance had left. Four men climbed out. Then the ambulance jerked onto the mountain road and the restaurant was gone.

"You comfortable, Mr. Cable?" The white man was leaning forward, his elbows on his knees.

Cable nodded. The man offered him a roll of Lifesavers, the silver paper peeled back. Cable shook his head and stretched out on the cot. He noticed he was wearing the soft old moccasins Bonnie had found for him at the bottom of a storage closet. Outside the back window shadows of trees rose and fell as the ambulance rolled smoothly down the twisting road. The night blackened the window.

After a while the attendant said, "You haven't lost your touch, Mr. Cable. Plague and those hippies and she still wanted to give you a chance to go out back and make a run for it."

The driver slid open the metal partition behind his head. "I'll go right out on the runway and back up to the hatch. You better trank him now, Jack."

A dim overhead light clicked on. Jack rummaged in a black satchel at his feet and came up with a plastic box. He lifted out a syringe.

"Sorry about this, Mr. Cable. Which arm?"

Cable lifted his left arm, the arm nearest the attendant. Jack smiled sheepishly and put Cable to sleep.

TWO The room was small and warm and stuffy. There were no windows. The door was closed. Probably locked, Cable thought. The walls were celery green up to a rounded molding six inches from the ceiling. Above the molding, a strip of wallpaper ran the length of each wall. Teddy bears, brown and black and golden Teddy bears, tumbled and skipped along the wallpaper strip. Some of them hopped on one furry leg. Every fourth Teddy bear was juggling three red balls. There were lumps under the strip where the paste had dried unevenly. A wrinkle in the paper had twisted one golden Teddy bear's smile. The paper did not rest evenly along the upper edge of the molding, and in several places it had frayed and split against the ceiling. Some of the Teddy bears were in shadow. Harsh light spilled out over the edges of a frosted glass shield attached to a fixture in the center of the ceiling. The shield was crooked and loose.

"How do you feel?"

It was a man's voice, cool, deep, trained. Cable tilted his

head up from the pillow. The black ambulance driver sat in a chair alongside the bed, facing him. He wore a beige cashmere turtleneck sweater.

Cable let his head sink back into the pillow. He found the wrinkle-smiled Teddy bear, one of the jugglers.

"You'll be on intravenous for a few days until we finish the testing." He stood up. "My name is Sand. I'll be back." Sand knocked on the door and was let out.

When he woke again his mind was clear of the drug but he could not move his legs. He poked his body until he realized he was paralyzed below the waist. The crotch of his pajamas was soaking wet. He felt small and helpless. He remembered the wrinkle-smiled Teddy bear and when he found him, furry golden paws stretched toward the red balls, Cable's eyes filled with tears that leaked into his ears. He did not know why he cried.

He tried to think of something else, and remembered the hippies in the Volkswagen camper. It was as far back as his mind would go. There had been five of them, three boys and two girls. They had found him sleeping on his back in Golden Gate Park in San Francisco. They circled him and one of the girls knelt and tickled him awake with a dandelion.

"See, he's not dead," she said. "Are you?"

He sat up slowly, wary. They seemed friendly.

"Spiritually," one of the boys said. "I didn't mean legally."

"I'm not dead."

"Hooray." The dandelion girl kissed his bearded cheek.

The boys lifted him to his feet and held his elbows all the way to their camper. They fed him brownies and coffee.

"Are you a park person?"

"Just passing through."

"We're going north. Want to ride with us?"

"Why not?"

He climbed into the back with the two girls and sat on a red vinyl-covered bench. The girls sat opposite across a formica table top. The three boys in the front seat put on stereophonic headphones. Two of them clapped their hands and the driver snapped the fingers of one hand while he drove with the other. The camper moved slowly but it seemed to sway to music.

On the other side of the bridge, the girl who had tickled him awake said, "God, it's hot in here," and took off her blue denim work shirt.

Her breasts were very small and the nipples looked soft. They seemed vulnerable, almost poignant breasts.

"Damn little titties make me look thirteen years old."

The other girl said, "American men have a thing about big tits. The mother thing."

"I'd rather have these than some floppy old tits that get in your way all the time."

"They're very nice," said Cable.

"Would you like to touch them?"

He reached across the table and let his fingers brush one breast. Her skin was tight but the flesh beneath it did not seem firm for a girl so young. His hand dropped to the table.

"What's the matter?"

"I don't want to kill you, too."

"What the hell are you talking about?"

"Just leave me alone."

"Oh, shit, another weirdo. Give him a tab, Jen."

The drug hit on the climb up the mountain road, freezing his hands and feet, spinning his head into a child's kaleidoscope of jagged bits of red and yellow and blue, squares and triangles that formed flowers that exploded behind his eyes, explosions that grew larger and larger until they filled his body. Before he vomited and passed out in the restaurant bathroom he saw, at the edge of one of the explosions, a car's steering wheel rising in a lazy arc. A hand without an arm was turning it.

Bonnie Fuller bathed his face. "Some friends you've got. But you're okay now. Trip's over."

A nurse was adjusting his intravenous feeder when Sand came back. He did not know if it was the same day. Sand was followed by a small, soft, older man with carefully groomed white hair. He had a smooth, benign face. He came up to the bed and said, "Do you remember me, Cable?"

Cable nodded. "What about my legs?"

"It's part of the testing," said Sand. "It's only temporary."

"Do you remember my name, Cable?"

"Barrett. Senator Barrett."

The man smiled. "We're glad you're back with us."

"Then why did you wait so long to come for me?"

Barrett smiled again. "I'll be stopping by from time to time to see how you're getting along." He bowed his head to Sand. "You're in good hands with Dr. Moore."

The door opened before Barrett had to knock. A hidden mike and camera, Cable thought.

Sand sat down and lit a little cigar with a white plastic tip.

"Are you a shrink?"

Sand nodded.

"Why were you driving the ambulance?"

"I'm here to help you. We all are."

"How did you find the same wallpaper? How did you know about it?"

"You've talked about it under medication. We weren't able to duplicate the wallpaper, but we came close enough to suggest it. Your mind and the drugs have done the rest."

17

Cable stared at the frosted glass shield. Cigar smoke curled around it and broke on the chipped corners.

"How long have I been here?"

"Time is not always a valid measurement."

"Why am I here?"

"What's the question? Why did we bring you back, or why did we let you go so long?"

"It might be the same question."

"It might be. We can talk about that." Sand rubbed out the cigar on the inside of a small tin wastebasket. The can was gold. A brown Teddy bear, a tumbler, was pasted to its side.

Sand got up and knocked to be let out.

Bonnie Fuller had said, "Now let's see what you look like."

She wore brief, patterned panties and a brassiere that barely contained her breasts. Cable thought they would burst free and flop into the hot, oiled bath water. He was submerged to his neck. She was on her knees beside the four-legged bathtub, her round stomach pressed against the high white porcelain wall. She lathered his beard with quick, circular brush strokes, then shaved him with a straight razor.

"Say, you're not half bad looking without the spinach."

For the first time in months he could not feel his body, no crimp or dull ache reminded him of nights dozing in the cab of a long-haul truck or on the table of a highway bar. The nights had been the worst time, hoping tensely for sleep yet fearful of dreams. The mornings and the afternoons were numbly taken with the need to blunt the pain in his stomach and the need to keep moving on, but then night would come and he wasn't always exhausted enough for sleep.

Once, on a bridge in Cincinnati, a policeman rapped

the iron railing with his nightstick. Cable's head clanged like a belltower and the railing vibrated in his hands. Pain rippled up his arms.

"You got some I.D., pal?"

He turned into the headlights of a passing car. When he could see again, the policeman's face was twisted in disgust.

"Do me a favor, pal, take your dive on somebody else's bridge."

He drummed the railing until Cable let go and shambled away. Too filthy, too cruddy, lousy, matted, scabby to touch, to stuff into a patrol car, into a crowded rummy tank, Cable had thought. I'm only a bar of soap away from thirty days in jail. And they'll find me there.

Bonnie Fuller let some of the water drain out and ran a finger down his chest. "Your ribs look like a washboard. What's your name?"

"Davey." It had been years since he had thought of himself as Davey.

"Where you from?"

"East."

She laughed, a warm, throaty bark. "If you were from west you would of come in a canoe." Her voice changed, became tougher. The urging was in her narrow eyes. "Stay a few days. I'll put some meat on your bones."

He nodded.

Her voice changed again, higher, lighter. "I'm not doing you any favors, Davey, you're going to have to work for your potatoes. This damn place is a three-man job and there's nobody here but me." She ran more hot water and pushed his head forward to scrub his back. "Got half a mind to sell out. My kid sister lives on Russian Hill, her husband's in business. Ever hear of Archie Gorman Associates? They're always after me to come down and live with them."

Sand put a steaming Teddy bear mug on a cork Teddy bear coaster on the scarred maple nightstand. "Chicken soup. No more I.V."

"You're getting more obvious every day."

"We're trying to pop the lid on your head, Cable." He sat down. "Mind if I smoke?"

"I do. There's no ventilation in here, the room stinks after you leave."

It was the first time Cable saw Sand smile. He had Chiclet teeth. Sand tucked the pack of little cigars into the top of one high black boot, then carefully smoothed a flared pants leg over it.

"Was the bed-wetting your idea, too?"

"This is an interesting new technique, kind of an instant psychoanalysis, but it's still time consuming and expensive. Some of the people here want to shoot volts into you."

"Why?"

"Get you back into the field faster."

"That's all over, I'm finished. You're wasting your time."

The white ambulance attendant walked in. "Morning, Mr. Cable," he said cheerfully. He had curly blond hair and a friendly smile. He was wearing blue boat sneakers, a white-and-blue striped polo shirt and clean blue jeans. Cable thought it was the perfect outfit for his beach-boy looks.

"You all set up, Jack?" asked Sand. When Jack nodded, Sand stood up. "Let's go, Cable."

"Where's the wheelchair?"

"You don't need it anymore."

He flexed his toes, then carefully swung his legs off the bed. They were rubbery and there was a gnawing pain in the small of his back, but he could stand up. Jack handed him a white terry-cloth robe and Cable followed the two men through the door into a small living room.

He was surprised. When the nurses had wheeled him out for tests the door had always opened into a long white corridor.

The living room was square and windowless. The walls were off-white. A series of framed Picasso bullfight prints hung above a board-and-cinderblock bookcase. The walls were bright with peace posters.

"Sit down." Sand pointed to an upholstered brown love seat.

Jack switched on a large television set and dropped a cassette into the slot on top. The color picture focused slowly. An astronaut lumbered toward the camera, pitched forward under his backpack, faceless behind a visor that reflected the spidery lunar module.

"The mad moon man himself," said Cable.

"Why do you call him that?" asked Sand.

"I heard it somewhere."

There was a crackle of static and then a voice, distant and uneven but unmistakable.

". . . This is Commander Charles Rice, speaking from the surface of the moon. Tonight I have seen the earth plain. I have seen the purposelessness, the decay, the corruption. I have seen the murderous vanity that hurls us into space, the . . ." There was a click. The picture faded.

Jack laughed. "Last time they ever let anybody transmit live. Now comes the . . ."

"Quiet," said Sand. "Do you remember where you were when you saw this, Cable?"

"No."

"Two months ago, Cable. Just before the . . . accident."

"I said I don't remember." A steel band tightened around Cable's throat.

There was a scraping noise from the television set, then muffled shouts. A voice said coolly, "Keep him on record, announce transmission failure, switch to lunar orbiter."

The band fell away. Cable swallowed. "How'd you get that?"

"We had a staffer in Houston," said Sand. "There's more."

Commander Rice's voice was rising. ". . . manipulating us like puppets, programming our lives, weakening our bodies. The time has come for a second American Revolution, a . . ." There was another click and the tape wooshed on to the end of the cassette. It popped up from the television set like a piece of toast.

"There's even more," said Jack, "but we've never got hold of it. They've got it in a vault somewhere."

Sand asked, "How many times did you interview Rice?"

"I don't remember."

"Do you remember interviewing him?"

"No."

"When we picked you up at the restaurant Rice was on television. You noticed how much his face had changed in the last seven years."

"Do I talk in my sleep?"

"Nonstop."

"You'll have to tell me about it sometime."

"I'll play you the tapes." Sand shrugged. "Look, Cable, it's in your head, that shit's got to come out or your head'll split open like a rotten cantaloupe." He walked out of the room.

Jack, wrapping the cord around the television set, said, "You know, Mr. Cable, it's a real honor working with you. We studied a couple of your assignments in the school." His blue eyes were guileless.

"I'm not working."

"That last assignment was a classic. The way you . . ." He stopped. "I'm sorry. I wasn't thinking."

"Tell them to give up. I'm finished."

Jack carried the set to the door. It opened at a tap of his sneaker. He handed the set out to someone in the corridor and returned with a sandwich, a small bowl of salad, and a glass of milk on a round tin tray decorated with hand-painted flowers. He set it down on a wheeled typewriter table beside the love seat.

"After lunch you can use the pool."

"I don't swim anymore."

Jack smiled sympathetically and walked out.

Cable picked up the sandwich, tuna salad on rye toast. He was very hungry. He took one bite and saw an old black Royal typewriter on the floor beside the cinderblock bookcase. He gagged on the sandwich and put it down. He went back into the bedroom and closed the door. Sitting on the bed he drank the chicken soup, cold and scummy. The golden Teddy bear grinned at him.

That first night at Bonnie Fuller's he had slept on a folding bed in the restaurant. Sunlight streaming through a front window gently woke him. He thought of the hippie girl with the dandelion before he saw the red formica tables and the long mahogany bar and, behind the bar, a pitted mirror reflecting rows of bottles and stacked glasses. A face appeared in the mirror, hard, cold, pale.

He whirled to confront the stranger. Dizzy, he had to sit on the edge of the bed with his head between his knees. When the dizziness passed, he stood up.

He was alone in the restaurant.

The face was his.

Bonnie Fuller clomped downstairs. "Betcha forgot what you looked like. A bar of soap and a razor blade does wonders."

She was wearing a long flowered robe and a man's scuffed carpet slippers, but her hair was brushed and her face freshly made up. "How do you feel?"

"Fine."

"You look like a new man. Yesterday I thought I had a stiff on my hands. What were you scoring on, acid?"

"I don't know. They gave me something in the car."

"Sonsabitches. Well, you're in good hands now. Bill Fuller, rest his soggy soul, used to say, 'Mama, you've put more people together again than the Mayo Clinic.' Never helped him much, you got to want to get put together again."

She reached over the bar for a glass pot of coffee. "It's been heating all night, tastes like hell, but it'll raise your hairs."

He sensed she was afraid to let him out of her sight. She kept glancing at him as she poured the coffee into two mugs. He drank it black. It was hot and bitter, and it cleared his head. She sipped at hers daintily, one thick pinky extended. She wore a gold wedding band on her pinky. She studied him over the mug.

"You were babbling like hell last night. Who's after you? Cops?"

"No."

"I'm not going to turn you in. You running from anything?"

"Just running."

"From yourself, huh?"

Suddenly he wanted to please her. "Just myself."

She patted his hand. "Those damn hippies did you a favor, Davey."

They worked through the morning, mopping and polishing, stacking crates, filling sugar and salt and pepper shakers, sweeping and hosing the garbage bins and the concrete deck behind the restaurant. Leaning on a broom, Cable looked down at rolling green meadows of grazing horses and small, neat ranch houses. The restaurant was perched on a range of camelback hills that grew into snow-

tipped mountains set into soft-focus against a clear blue
sky.

"Bill Fuller used to say, 'It's God's country, only the old
man's on vacation.' "

"You've been out here a long time?"

She pursed her big lips coyly. "I should tell you how
long. C'mon, no work, no grub."

She had a strong body and enormous energy. Cable
pushed himself to keep up. Early in the afternoon she led
him up narrow wooden steps to her bedroom and helped
him into a king-sized bed. Before he fell asleep he saw the
room was paneled in dark wood and lined with shelves
bearing hundreds of figurines, glass and ivory and ceramic
and wood, whimsical animals and children in foreign native costumes. When he awoke she was sitting in a padded
rocking chair, sewing and humming and glancing up at a
musical show on a big color television set. When she saw
he was awake she took off her glasses and snapped off the
set.

"Like some dinner?"

He nodded.

She lifted a plate out of a food warmer beside the bed.
A small steak, green peas, a baked potato.

"I'm warning you, Davey, don't get used to this." She
watched him eat.

It was the best food he had eaten in a month, and he was
hungry, but his stomach was filled before he was half
finished. She poured them each a glass of red wine. They
drank silently.

She shut off the light before she undressed and climbed
into bed with him. Hesitantly at first, then more boldly,
her fingers explored his chest and stomach and legs. She
traced the old scars behind his knees.

Her fingers moved back up, so gently and sure that he
felt no tensing in his groin. She stroked him for a long time.

"You get hurt there, too?"

"No."

"It's in your head, huh?"

"I guess so."

"It'll come back, Davey. No rush. I can wait some more."
She gathered him into her warm body, his face against her
breasts, and rocked him back to sleep.

He imagined his father sitting in the chair by his bed in
the Teddy bear room. "How do you feel, Davey?"

"My legs hurt."

"That's good, Davey, that means you're getting better."

"Where's Mommy?"

"You've got to sleep now."

"I want my Mommy."

His father looked up at the wallpaper strip. "When
you're all better we'll take that down; I saw a really nice
one with trains and ships and airplanes . . ."

"I want my Mommy."

He was four years old.

His father began to cry.

He went into the living room.

He imagined Susan sitting on the brown love seat, her
legs up, crossed at her thin ankles. Her knitting yarn rested
on her swollen belly. Her face was full and glowing, her
eyes bright.

"Did you get good work done, darling?"

"It's moving along. I think I'll be able to take the first
three chapters in next week. The stuff on rent control is
even better than I thought it was. Pure dynamite.

"You're pure dynamite."

He kissed her forehead. "How do you feel?"

"I'm so happy, David. I wish you could feel how I feel,
looking at you over there and feeling you in here."

26

A male nurse took Cable down to the pool in an elevator marked *Staff Only*. Sand was waiting for him.

"We'll take it easy today, Cable. Five laps and a rub."

The water was warm and heavily chlorinated. His eyes stung almost immediately.

Three

Barrett sat behind a wide desk in an office walled by law books bound in red and brown pebble-grained leather. Inscribed photographs of presidents and foreign heads of state were clustered around a window that overlooked the East River. Photographs of his family beamed up at him from under a thick glass desk top.

"We had hoped you would consider returning to the staff," he said.

"I'm not taking any assignment," said Cable.

Barrett did not seem to have heard him. "A very complex situation. We need an experienced correspondent."

"You've got other people."

"Not with your talent. Or with your established credibility with the subject."

"Commander Rice. So he's why you finally came looking for me."

"We didn't have to look for you, Cable, you were never out of our sight. We wanted to give you time and room to come to terms with yourself."

"Did I?"

Barrett's manicured nails tapped an intricate rhythm on the glass desk top. "There's some difference of opinion. Dr. Moore wants more time. I personally think you've had quite enough time to get over feeling sorry for yourself."

Cable lurched out of the visitor's chair and slapped the desk. "You can say that, you've got them all safe under glass, nothing's going to happen to them."

Barrett's lips formed his benign, equitable, political smile, but his eyes were cold. "We'll talk again. Ultimately, of course, going in has to be your own decision."

He nodded at Jack who led Cable back to the Teddy bear room.

He had scarred the maple night stand when he was six, in a cold fury, pounding the butt of an iron cap pistol like a hammer. The gun had jammed and his father, trying to fix it, had broken the trigger spring. The trigger wagged like a dog's tongue. There was no more satisfying click as he lay in bed shooting the Indians crawling through the Fort windows. His father had rushed in at the hammering noise and gently pried the gun out of his hands. They stained the gouged wood together, but it never matched the original maple. His father bought a tiny brown throw rug for the night-stand top. It lay there for years, its fringed corners hanging over the sides, swaying every time he opened or closed the drawer, reminding him of the broken gun, the mismatched stain, that the sad-eyed man was his father and mother.

Cable wandered into the living room. The tuna salad on rye toast sandwich, a bite missing, still lay on the flowered tray on the typing table. Once he told Susan it was his favorite sandwich and she made him one every day for months while he worked on the book. Standing in the doorway to the kitchen she would mimic a trumpet flourish and parade into the living room bearing the tray, unselfconscious of the comedy of her rising belly. He had never told her when he lost his taste for tuna salad.

Cable ran for the outer door and wrenched it open, ready to feint and dodge around the corridor guard. But there was another room there now.

It was a small room, even smaller than his Teddy bear room, and dimly lit by a tensor reading lamp on a black steamer trunk next to a narrow bed. There was no other furniture in the room. One wall was nearly covered with pictures of Malcolm X, Che Guevara, George Jackson, Angela Davis, and the mutilated bodies of Vietnamese farmers and Bolivian Indians. The floor was littered with books, tape spools, scraps of paper. Dust particles fell frantically through the tensor beam onto the bed, unmade and sour-smelling, two mustard Army blankets rumpled at the foot, a stained sheet thrown carelessly over a splitting mattress. His eyes followed the tensor beam to a newspaper photograph taped to the wall over the bed. Five young people were being led down the steps of a brownstone house by a dozen plainclothesmen wearing badges pinned to their windbreakers and golf sweaters. A tall dark-haired girl, smiling defiantly, her head high, strained against the hands on her arms. Behind her, Cable was trying to twist out of a hammerlock.

Cable screamed, "Bastards, you bastards."

He grabbed a corner of the photograph and yanked, but the tape held and the newsprint tore. The dark-haired girl's defiant eyes mocked him.

He threw the tensor lamp against the wall and rushed through the living room, upsetting the typewriter table. A half slice of rye toast skidded over the polished wooden floor. He threw himself on his bed.

And dreamed of the explosion again

This time, Cable is standing naked on his dewy lawn. The morning sun gleams on the freshly painted white shingles of his split-level house. The door swings open and the boy bursts out, tugging Susan's hand as she raises one knee to balance her pocketbook while she fumbles for keys. Cable shouts, Go back, but there is no sound, not even inside his own head. They run down the concrete walk, hand in hand, the boy's curly brown hair bouncing. He is three years old and his face is still pudgy and round, but as he passes Cable the baby fat melts away, the face begins to taper down past a wide, full mouth to a strong narrow jaw, becomes Cable's face. The boy pulls so hard Susan stumbles, laughing as she regains her footing, her shag-cut blonde hair growing till it tumbles silkenly off her shoulders, the tense lines around her sullen mouth vanishing. She grows young as she passes the mute, frozen Cable, a laughing girl with a little boy sockless in blue sneakers. When they reach the red Volkswagen at the curb, Cable begins to run toward them. She is buckling the little boy's safety harness. He is wearing a blue-and-white striped polo shirt and clean blue jeans. Cable is screaming, No, no, but Susan is turning the ignition key and a giant red flower blossoms from the car, jagged bits of red and yellow and blue, squares and triangles growing larger until the giant petals open and fall back to earth. A car's steering wheel rises in a lazy arc. A hand without an arm is turning the wheel. A soft object strikes Cable's naked feet. He does not look down because he knows it is a little blue sneaker, red-speckled.

He woke up screaming.
No one came.
The pillowcase was gray with moisture. His clothes were soaked, they clung to his convulsive body. He jerked over

on his back. The golden Teddy bear smiled down at him, its wrinkle a malevolent leer, You killed them all, Davey, you killed everybody who ever loved you. Mommy and Susan and the boy and Lynn . . .

He sprang at the Teddy bear, clawing at the wallpaper strip, falling back on the sagging bed again and again until his fingernails finally snagged on the peeling paper, ripping it loose from the dried clots of paste. A long tongue of Teddy bears dangled from the wall. He grabbed it with both hands and stumbled around the room, pulling the strip down. He yanked out the nightstand drawer and smashed it against the wall. He overturned the bed. He ripped the cushions off the chair. He hurled the tin wastebasket at the light fixture. The frosted shield shattered, spraying shards. Exhausted, he staggered into the living room and collapsed on the love seat.

Sand was sitting in a green canvas sling chair watching him wake up.

"You had the dream again."

"Leave me alone."

"It's becoming more explicit, less symbolic."

"Just leave me alone."

"Each mind finds its own way to deal with traumatic experience. Yours chose to cork it and bury it, but it's in there, like a pocket of underground gas, expanding, pushing at the walls. We're trying to put in valves to drain it before it blows your head off."

"You should have been a plumber."

Sand smiled.

"I told Barrett I wasn't taking the assignment."

The black man looked interested. "What did he say?"

Cable sat up. "What's so important about Rice?"

Sand shrugged. "I don't know. You've met him."

"That was six, seven years ago."

"You wrote a story for the newspaper?"

"A free-lance magazine piece. On test pilots."

"How many times did you see him?"

"Four or five."

"You were interested in him."

"He was different from the others."

"In what ways?"

"More thoughtful, deeper." He tried to think about Rice. The dream had left his body sore and cramped, his mind anxious and disconnected. He found he could blot out most of the dream by concentrating on Rice.

"He seemed better educated. Philosophy, literature, history. He was very confident without being cocky. He wasn't a white-scarf flyer, he was very serious. He didn't seem to have too many friends, he didn't run with the other pilots. He seemed . . . special. And the others respected him, even though they didn't seem to like him very much. He was different."

"Can you be specific?"

Cable relaxed. He felt comfortable talking about Rice. "He could sit still and think about a question. The others were always moving, their hands, facial expressions, standing up to rearrange things. They used to drive outside the base at a hundred miles an hour tail-gating each other. He never did things like that. I had the feeling he thought he was above that."

"Did you write all this in your article?"

"Some of it. I got a note from him after the piece appeared. That's very rare. He said he disagreed with some of my conclusions, but he thought it was a very professional job. He said he'd like to talk more sometime, to explain some points I'd misinterpreted. I was flattered, but then I got busy on other things and I . . ."

Sand stood up. "Let's go down to the pool. Twenty lengths today."

"Not today. I'm too tired."

"You need the exercise."

He slipped into an easy overhand stroke and drifted into a sweet mindlessness. After awhile he was no longer aware of the other swimmers. When his arms ached he turned over to backstroke, reaching tentatively at first, then farther, until he felt the muscles pull along his sides. He anticipated pain, and when it arrived he welcomed it. How long since he had felt glad to be so connected to his body? He remembered the coach stalking the edge of the pool, his great flat feet slapping at the puddled tiles, Pull, Cable, pull, it's only pain, swim right through it, boy, you'll never know who you are till you get to the other side, hold that kick, pull, Cable, you got to come the distance to find out who you are. . . .

When he finally dragged himself out of the water, Sand was gone. Jack stood at the top of the iron steps offering a hand. The tiles rocked.

"You got a nice stroke, Mr. Cable. You ever swim competitively?"

"A little, in high school."

"That's all? Why'd you quit?"

Cable shrugged. Even if he could remember, Jack would never understand. Rice might.

Jack led him back down the white-walled corridor to a gray metal door that now opened directly into the living room. Sand was on the love seat, his booted feet up on a mahogany arm. He was smoking a little cigar.

"Where's the bedroom?" asked Cable.

"Which one?"

"The one with the Teddy bears."

"You destroyed it. It's gone." He waved the cigar. "Sit down."

34

Cable didn't move. "You've gone to a lot of trouble setting up this little psychodrama, haven't you?"

Sand said carelessly, "If you've got the facilities you might as well use them. Sit down, I've got something to tell you."

"You're wasting your time. You should get Rice in here, he's the one you're interested in. You could turn this room into the lunar module, and that one . . ." He was surprised how his finger trembled as he pointed toward the open door leading into the littered bedroom with the black steamer trunk and the narrow bed. ". . . that's the surface of the moon. And if you ever find the Teddy bear room you can paste up model airplanes and . . ."

"Cable, you've got to want to get put together again."

He thought of the large, pale body. "Bonnie Fuller said that."

"You've been thinking about her?"

"No, I haven't."

"I'll play you those tapes. You're afraid something might happen to her because of you."

"Why should I be?"

"Because that's your pattern."

He felt a cold splash of fear. "Did anything happen to her?"

"We're not sure."

"Answer the goddam question for once. Did anything happen to her?"

"She's gone. She disappeared."

"Where?"

Sand sipped at the cigar. Smoke trailed out of his wide nostrils. "Don't know." He stood up and motioned to Jack, who knocked at the door.

They both left.

There was a telephone on the bookcase. A white princess telephone. The bastards really do a job, Cable thought. He dialed the restaurant's number. There was a faint click before the connection was made. Of course they would tap the phone. A record told him the number was no longer working. He dialed long-distance information for the highway patrol station at the foot of the corkscrew mountain road.

"Private Booth speaking."

"Sergeant Wellbank, please." Wellbank came in once a week for dinner. Bonnie always made a fuss over him.

"Wellbank here."

"Sergeant, this is Jim McElroy from the *Chronicle,* we're doing a follow on that Fuller story."

"Jim who?"

"McElroy, the San Francisco *Chronicle.*"

"What'd you have in mind?"

"Anything new?"

"I'm not in charge of the investigation, you'll have to . . ."

"I know that, but we heard you knew her pretty well. Thought you might be able to give us some human interest, what kind of person she was, you know."

"You boys have raked it over pretty good."

"But we never got any line on what she was really like, a woman running a place like that all alone. Was she a real tough old bird?"

Wellbank snorted. "Heart like a pillow. Give her a sob story, she'd give you the register."

"I need anecdotes. You know, any anecdotes?"

"Some drifter freaked out in her crapper, she took him in, cleaned him up, gave him a job."

"What's he got to say?"

"The only one we found in the place was a wrangler off one of the local spreads. You know that."

"What'd he say?"

"Don't you read your own paper?"

"I'm sorry, Sergeant, I'm cityside features. When the story broke the state desk handled it."

"He died in the fire."

Cable held his voice steady. "The only one?"

"Only body we found."

"The rest were gone, huh?"

"What rest?"

"Wasn't there anybody else in the place?"

"Hold on a minute, Jim, I got another call coming in."

Wellbank was no fool. He'd have Private Booth check with the *Chronicle* or call for a phone trace.

He was right back. "Now, where were we, Jim?" His voice was falsely expansive. Playing for time. Booth is probably calling for a trace.

"Any chance the old lady did it for insurance?"

"We thought about that, the fire marshals poked around, but it just doesn't jibe with the kind of gal she was. Or the bullet in the ranch hand. She could of burnt the place down any time, why shoot a customer? You follow me, Jim?"

"Maybe she had a lover's quarrel and split after she killed him."

"Not that guy."

"What about the drifter?"

"What about him?"

"What's his connection?"

"We got a bulletin out for him, too."

"Any chance it was robbery?"

"Money in the register."

"Find any cars around the place?"

"None. Bonnie's pick-up was gone." There were some muffled words. Booth's trace was working. There was no more time.

"What about the ambulance?"

Wellbank's voice changed. "Where'd you hear that? Jim

. . . Jim . . . Can I call you . . ."

Cable's hand shook as he hung up.

The phone rang.

"Mr. Cable, Jack. I just had to tell you, that was a piece of work. Really pro."

Cable slammed down the receiver.

It had been Wellbank's voice, no doubt about that. He couldn't be in on the psychodrama, too.

Susan always hated to hear him work the phone. Sometimes she would pull her silky blonde hair over her pink clam-shell ears and run out of the room. So sneaky, she'd say, so deceitful. A lesson to you, he'd reply, triumphantly high on a freshly uncovered fact, never trust a newspaperman. He enjoyed working the phone, his voice was better than his eyes at feigning interest, innocence, sympathy. Once, when he came back from an out-of-town assignment, he found the white Princess telephone in place of their standard black phone. It was not Susan's kind of extravagance. A humanizing instrument, she explained. How can you grub and ferret and lie on a little white telephone? How can you use it to make people spill their guts for a crummy newspaper story?

She never understood the joy of assembling a story detail by detail until it was spread whole like a living-room jigsaw puzzle. She called it an imitation of life. You don't participate, she said, you observe. You hide behind your telephone, your pad and pencil, your press badge. You're a reporter because you're really afraid of living.

He was busy enough to ignore what she said. For a year, his last year on the newspaper, he directed the investigative reporting team. He was rarely home, and he never felt so free, a shadow in a hundred other lives, listening with his eyes, moving soundlessly, without footprints, in a dozen other worlds. He rolled with precinct detectives and he drank with small-time hustlers in obscure waterfront bars. He lived three days in a drug crash pad in the East Village, and he worked four days on a high-speed assembly line. He spent a week as an attendant in a mental institution and the series he wrote led to a state investigation and journalism prizes. He ended the year with a five-part series on the connections between local realtors and the mayor's office. He expected the stories to tear the top off the city. But without explanation the series was gutted and cut, printed in two parts as a mild exposé, a three-day wonder that brought some garbage mail and a routine call for a federal inquiry.

Cable raged through the news room until the managing editor called him in and said he'd been working too hard; he needed a few weeks off with pay. He quit on the spot. For two months he sat in the living room, pounding on the old black Royal, eating tuna salad on rye toast. The writing came hard, he had always been a better reporter than writer, but he wrote and rewrote and polished, rarely sleeping more than three or four hours at a time, furious at the paper's betrayal of the facts he had so passionately unearthed.

Susan sat on the brown love seat, swelling, waiting for the book and the baby, smiling as the manuscript pages grew, biting her lip as the kicks in her belly fluttered the cloth of her skirt.

No one would publish the book. It was libelous, they said. Unsubstantiated. People are sick and tired of corruption stories. It won't sell.

The baby was born and they ran out of money.

The Clune Center for American Studies called. The director, former Senator Thomas L. Barrett, would like to have lunch with David Cable.

They ate in a dark wood-paneled private dining room on the eighth floor of the Clune Building, a massive complex on the East River, which also housed the Clune Foundation, the Mary Clune Memorial Research and Rehabilitation Facility of the adjoining Clune University Hospital, the Clune Brothers Fund and the Clune Collection of primitive American art.

Senator Barrett was a virtuoso of small talk, the New York weather, his grandchildren in Connecticut, Douglas Clune's obsession with Indian artifacts. Cable barely kept up his end, realizing nervously that he was being examined and judged. After coffee, although he rarely smoked, he took a cigar to keep his hands occupied.

Barrett leaned back.

"What are your plans, Cable?"

"I'm looking for a job."

"You haven't found a publisher for your book."

"I hadn't realized you knew about it."

"Remarkable piece of research."

"You've read it?"

"Several times. We'd like to buy it and distribute it privately as a Center Report."

"What did you have in mind?"

"You can work that out with our people downstairs. More importantly, we would like you to consider joining our field staff. Do you know much about our work here?"

"No."

"We're a rather small institution. We make grants for research that furthers our basic interest, the phenomenology of social patterns and movements. We also maintain a field staff that operates rather like investigative journalists, except that they are not hampered by deadline pressures, erratic budgets, advertiser interests. I'm sure you understand."

"I'm afraid I do."

"On the other hand, the work is rather anonymous, no bylines, no pictures on delivery trucks, no talk shows. It's difficult and sometimes dangerous work. It sometimes becomes necessary to penetrate a group or a movement for several weeks, even months, to obtain reliable information. You might think about it for a day or two."

Susan didn't want him to take the job: more skulking, more eavesdropping, more hit-and-run history, she called it; at least on the paper you put your name on top, now you'll be completely invisible. She wanted him to go to law school. They could borrow money from her parents; she would work. He was only twenty-eight, and with his mind, his experience, he could make an enormous contribution, an activist lawyer, poverty, civil rights, consumer rights, war protestors. He barely heard her. He kept seeing the massive Clune complex. He would be part of something large and powerful, he would have time and the resources to really dig, to assemble his facts, to solve his puzzles.

He took the job. His first assignment, a series of interviews with religious and educational theorists, was mildly interesting. He turned over his reports to a staff sociologist and never heard about them again. By that time, Susan had used the tax-free grant the Center gave him for the book as a down payment on a small split-level house thirty minutes from the city, and they were busy furnishing it and getting to know the baby. Cable was enthralled by the little boy; he would play with him for hours while Susan tiled the kitchen or made drapes. For the first year, until he began to penetrate, he was always home evenings and weekends.

Sand said, "You never mention the boy's name. Do you remember it?"

"No."

"You've been going back twenty, twenty-five years. You

remember people and incidents around the time of the accident, but not your own son's name."

"Each mind finds its own way to deal with traumatic experience," said Cable.

Sand did not acknowledge the sarcasm. "We've got a lot of work to do."

"I thought you people were interested in Rice."

"Barrett's interested in Rice. I'm interested in you."

"I'm ready to swim now."

"Later. Sit down. Did you name the boy after anyone?"

"What's Rice doing these days?"

"He's right here in New York trying to raise money and get national exposure. Did you name the boy after your father?"

"Why is Barrett so interested in Rice?"

"I don't know, but it's a source of pressure. Barrett wants you to either pick up Rice or leave."

"What do you think?"

"I don't think you're ready for either, but Barrett considers all emotional disturbances defects in character. Indulgences. I think you should see Rice."

"Why?"

"Give us more time here."

"What makes you think I want more time?"

Sand smiled. "You haven't been exactly rattling the doorknobs lately."

"It's been getting interesting."

"If you make any kind of effort, I can probably convince Barrett to put a couple of staffers on Bonnie Fuller. Find out where she is."

"That's not my problem."

"I think it is. If anything happened to her, too . . ." He spread his hands. "Rice would be glad to see you. The government stamped him nut pretty hard, he's having a tough time."

"Where is he?"

"He's living out in Queens with one of his old ground crew chiefs. You believe I just happen to have the number?"

He was not surprised that the corridor door now opened directly into the small, littered room. The tensor reading lamp on the black steamer trunk pointed up at a peeling curl of paint. The ceiling was dappled with shadows and water stains. The newspaper photograph above the bed was gone. The bed had been made, the same stained sheet pulled tight over the thin mattress, the mustard Army blankets neatly folded.

Lynn had always been careless of the room; even after they began sleeping together she refused to make the bed, annoying him by sitting on the sheet in the grimy fatigue pants she wore to demonstrations. He would complain, We lie naked on that sheet, and she would look over the steel frames of her glasses, her high forehead wrinkled in mock thought, I've got it, Dave, let's fuck on the floor. He'd grab the loose folds of the fatigue shirt and pull her up against him. She was a big girl, physically intimidating in her zippered black combat boots, and she became bigger as he undressed her, slipping the shirt off broad, smooth shoulders, away from full, round breasts, her baby-bottle nipples growing harder as his hands moved down her sides to unbuckle the heavy leather belt, to unbutton the baggy pants that covered the firm, low-slung ass and the thickly muscular legs. They always laughed as he struggled with the boots. Naked, she jumped on the bed, impatiently bouncing as he undressed and jumped up beside her.

He'd wrestle her down, pull off her glasses and unstrap her big wristwatch, and yank the hairpins to free her thick, black hair. She was strong and aggressive in bed; sometimes he strained to overwhelm her energy, never entirely subduing her. Afterward, when every other woman he had ever screwed lay calmly beside him or smoked or dozed, Lynn would leap out of bed, recharged, to show him a press clipping, play him a record, bring him food, read him the draft of a new manifesto. He might think of Susan then, gentled by sex, nestled against him, drained and drifting to sleep.

Lynn's revival after sex dismayed him, then delighted him as he watched her strong, clean movements with a possessive pride. He had never expected to fall in love with her, to let the affair get in the way of the assignment. He had almost convinced himself that the affair was part of the assignment.

The last time he had closed with Lynn's tigerish body, Susan was turning the ignition key that triggered the bomb.

He lay for hours on the bed staring at the cracked and peeling ceiling until the curl of paint became a wrinkled leer from another room, another time. They're dead, they're all dead now. What about Bonnie Fuller?

He did not sleep until he decided he would string along a little while longer; he would find out exactly what they wanted.

Four

Commander Rice coursed through the airport crowd. His face was gaunt, his sandy hair gray at the temples, but his unblinking pale blue eyes were as startlingly bold and intense as Cable remembered.

"Cable!"

He was surprised by the warmth of Rice's handshake, and slightly flustered as Rice looked him up and down.

"You look a little . . . compressed." Rice's eyes flicked to the car at the curb. "Is that yours? Mind if I drive?"

The sense of banked energy a hair trigger from full power had not diminished in seven years. Rice made the car an extension of his stiff arms and pushed it away from the curb toward the exit ramp. He grunted approval of the car's response. Jack had personally picked it for Cable out of the Center's motor pool.

"How was your trip?"

"Interesting. They scrubbed me from the parade." Rice's eyes were on the highway; his profile a cold axe. "They must have gotten calls, right across the power axle, Washington, Houston, Detroit, Indianapolis."

"What was their reason?"

He smiled without opening his mouth. "The president of the Speedway said a local department-store owner complained there were too many noncontributing exhibits in the parade. He got one of the big oil companies to back him. That's the official story."

"Do you believe it?"

"Of course not. NASA called. General Motors called. Maybe the President called. They want to stop me before I get to the people."

"What are you going to do?"

"Go. I've got to get out in the country, Cable, see the people, feel the roads, shake down the bus. I want you to see the bus."

"I want to."

Rice's voice became warmer. "It's good to see you again, Cable. What have you been doing?"

"Some free-lancing. Nothing very exciting."

"When you called I thought you might be interested in doing a story on the Liberty Bus."

"I might. Are you all alone?"

"Larry Bruno's my mechanic again. That's it."

"What about financial backing?"

"There are people interested, very interested, but they aren't sure the time is right." He smiled, an electric instant. "But it's the only time I've got."

He turned off the parkway into a quiet neighborhood of small, old houses ringed with elaborate flower gardens, and pulled into a corner gas station, Bruno's Service Center.

Cable followed Rice through the repair bay to an open lot behind the garage. On a bed of scrub grass and rusted auto parts, a snout-nosed yellow school bus sagged drunkenly on broken springs and flat tires.

"The Liberty Bus," said Rice softly, an invocation. "Imagine her silver with red-white-and-blue trim. Wired for public address. A speaker's platform on the roof. Imagine the impact."

"It's only a week to Memorial Day. Could you have gotten the bus ready in time?"

Rice nodded. "A thousand dollars. Isn't that pitiful? All I'd need to get her into temporary shape for the Speedway."

"What about those interested people?"

"Very cautious. Intellectuals, mutual-fund revolutionaries. They don't want me to go to the Speedway unless the Speedway wants me."

Rice suddenly shrugged and touched Cable's arm. "Why don't you come over for lunch? I'm staying with Larry, a block from here."

"I'd like to get back to the city, talk to my agent. I think there is a story here. I'll be in touch."

They shook hands again. Cable left Rice behind the garage staring at the crippled yellow school bus.

He drove into Manhattan thinking about Rice, only dimly aware he was not driving toward the Center. He parked off Broadway on the Upper West Side, and walked down a street of old brownstones. A junkie nodded him along. Two fresh-faced boys wearing yarmulkes played ball against the stoop of a synagogue. A girl stared out a bay window, the mobile dangling from the ceiling above her head turning slowly in the breeze off the Hudson River. The shabby row of gray and brown and dirty pink fronts was broken in midblock by the open foundations of a building under construction. A billboard set in the rubble of the site advertised studio apartments available for late summer occupancy. He stared at the heaps of stone and wood and metal for a long time.

"No more apartments, Mister." A beefy man had come out of the basement of the adjoining brownstone. A dozen keys rattled on the ring he wore on a pants loop. "I keep telling them to take the sign down, people buzz me all day, all night."

"Were you here when it happened?" asked Cable.

"Right across the street. The TV guys were parked in my kitchen for two days, fed 'em, let 'em use the phone, leave stuff overnight. You think I got a thank you?"

"Everybody in the house die?"

"That's what the papers said. You should of heard that blast. My fillings hurt for a week. My kid still has nightmares."

Cable turned away and walked to the Drive.

The park sloped sharply down to the highway and the river. Sometimes Lynn packed beer and sandwiches in her knapsack and they'd find an isolated thicket of bushes above the dog runs. It was a relief just to get out of the house, away from the continual ringing of the phone, the interminable meetings that erupted with screaming dogma and collapsed into clumsy group therapy, the constant tension of police surveillance, informers, the drugs on the roof and the bombs in the basement. They had fallen in love in the thickets above the dog runs. He never thought he would fall in love with her. Or that it would kill her. And Susan and the boy.

He found a phone booth on the Drive. Barrett's secretary took his number and said she'd try to get someone to call him back. He was sitting in the booth, trembling, ten minutes later when Sand and Jack pulled up in a maroon convertible. He gave Jack his keys and told him where he had parked the car. He climbed into the back of the convertible and collapsed on the white leather seat.

This time, Cable is sitting in a lawn chair in a front yard of whitewashed pebbles. The morning sun gleams off the red roof of the Volkswagen he has just finished waxing. Jack comes out to tell him what a good job he has done. Sand will be pleased. Cable feels good. Susan and the little boy come out of the front door. They look very happy. The boy is wearing a toy space helmet. Jack begins to drum on the white plastic helmet, his manicured Barrett fingers tapping the intricate rhythm, his pink Sand palm slapping out the beat. The boy cries and looks to Cable, but there is nothing he can do anymore. Jack and Susan are laughing. Susan asks him for the car keys. He holds out a key in each hand, one for a black Ford, one for the Volkswagen. The boy wants to ride in the shiny new red car. This time, after the bloody petals clatter to the street, the little blue sneaker lands in his lap.

Neither Jack nor Sand was at the pool. A stocky woman with short hair and a round, friendly face blocked the ladder. "Do you have a therapy slip?"

"I'm just going to swim."

"You'll have to wait until this session is over."

He sat on a wooden bench against a brown tile wall. In the shallow end three physical therapists laughed and shouted encouragement as children struggled to thrash with stick arms and legs. The children were silent and grim, only their eyes screamed as the water boiled over their tight lips.

The stocky woman sat down beside him. "The results aren't always worth the effort, but you have to give them the chance."

"Brain damage?"

"Predominantly. The kids are beautiful, they try so hard it makes you cry. Gives you hope for the world." She looked at Cable. "The adult sessions aren't like this at all.

You get the feeling most of them don't want to get put back together."

Her facial expression was bland. Just coincidental, he decided.

Barrett leaned forward across his desk top, his elbows on his grandchildren. "You're sure now he still wants to make that trip?"

"Check with Jack, he taps my phone."

Barrett began to drum. "You're a strange man, Cable. Intelligent, capable, sensitive to nuance, thoughtful, but you lack a certain empathy. There's a curious numbness in you—

"You know Mr. Clune has taken a personal interest in this project, obviously our future funding may be involved, you can see my position. Can I be more candid than that?"

"What more do you need to know? Rice and his mechanic are living on spaghetti trying to raise enough money to buy paint and a new motor for a school bus that can't pass inspection. End of report. End of project. What about Bonnie Fuller?"

"We haven't located her yet. Why is he so intent on going to the Speedway?"

"There'll be a quarter of a million people there."

"What about these people who are so interested in him? Why won't they give him a thousand dollars?"

"From what Rice says they won't touch him until he gets some attention and acceptance on his own. They're more afraid of backing the wrong horse than missing the race."

"What if you gave him a thousand dollars?"

"On what pretext?"

"You got an advance on a magazine article, or a book."

"If the Center finances Rice, don't we become operational? How can we do an objective report on something we're implicated in?"

"That's very simplistic, Cable. He's obviously going to get that money some place. We're merely accelerating the situation. A convenience. For Rice, for us, for Mrs. Fuller."

An icy worm began inching up Cable's spine. An old friend, he hadn't felt it in a long time.

Five

The silver school bus dazzled in the morning sunlight, a grandiose monument in the Speedway's canvas and raw wood boom town. Cable, cramped and aching after the thirteen-hour ride, pushed through the swirling crowds to circle the bus. It was the first time he had seen the new silver skin in daylight; fantastic, he thought, a tank of plastic spray can transform squat ugliness into an impression of dignified strength. Spray the world!

Each side of the bus bore blue letters: LIBERTY TWO. Rice and Bruno had discussed the lettering for an hour yesterday afternoon, their voices reverberating in the service station's locked repair bay. Bruno, his dark face passionately wrinkling, twisting, clenching, vainly turning to Cable for support, had argued for three-foot-high letters slanted toward the rear to give an illusion of speed. Rice, expressionless, had heard him out, then decreed simple block letters eighteen inches tall: This is not a circus wagon, he had said softly. Bruno, unfazed, offered a compromise—the bus could be called LIBERTY 2 or LIBERTY

II. Cable had been aware that Rice was careful not to look at him, to take the chance of creating even momentary alliances. He had been on too many three-man teams.

Bruno had plunged on. "Numbers give you a real space-age identification, you know, Gemini 3, Apollo 11."

Rice shook his head. "I'm all the identification we need. Numbers give you too much sense of continuation. If we do it right this time, there won't be any Liberty Three."

Larry Bruno smiled and surrendered then, his soft brown eyes satisfied that Rice had again proved out wiser, surer and in absolute command. Cable, backed against the garage's concrete wall, felt an intruder in an intimate moment.

"The insignia," said Rice.

Bruno handed Rice and Cable each a bronze medallion as large as a saucer. The thirteen-star American flag—its red and white stripes diagonally slashed by an ascending rocket—was superimposed on the earth as seen from the moon.

"Beautiful job, Larry," Rice had said, finally looking at Cable to demand unanimous agreement. "Bolt them on the hood flaps."

Larry's face darkened in triumph, and Rice climbed into the bus with his clipboard for the final check.

The Speedway crowd barely noticed the bus, it was just another obstacle among the hamburger stands, the decal booths, beer tents and portable toilet sheds that broke the flow of spectators streaming across the infield toward the grandstand. The few who looked up at Rice on the bus roof and tried to stop to listen were quickly swept away. Rice didn't seem to care, his eyes burning with energy and joy as he shouted down at the indifferent heads through a battery-powered hand speaker that muffled and distorted his voice.

". . . is called Liberty Two because it symbolizes the beginning of a second American Revolution, the second time our nation will unite to drive out its oppressors and show the world the promise of a tomorrow in which . . ."

The rest was lost in the clatter and snarl and dying whine of car engines tuning to racing pitch.

"Damn," said Larry. "If only we could of gotten that sound system."

"Wouldn't make any difference," said Cable. "They're just not listening."

"Because they can't hear. That bullhorn's no good. I got a single speaker we can try later. I better get him down now. He's knocking himself out for nothing."

"He looks like he's enjoying himself."

"Yeah?" Larry's eyes flashed. "Look, he kills himself up there you don't get much of a book, right?" He elbowed through the crowd.

The greasy heat had steamed Rice's dark suit into a damp rag. His sandy hair glistened with sweat and his reddening face was slick. With his feet braced on the rounded metal roof and his lean body crouched, he seemed to be imploring the passing crowd, almost begging for their time. If it wasn't for Rice's eyes, Cable might have felt sorry for him, the grounded astronaut, the muted messenger, sunstruck as well as moon-struck. But the pale blue eyes were possessed. There was nothing pathetic about Rice.

Larry reached the bus and clambered up the back ladder. Larry was big, taller than Cable or Rice, and heavily built, shoulders like shelves and a large, hard stomach, a barroom bumper. Atop the bus, dancing for balance and talking with his hands, Larry looked clumsy and bearish beside the knife-blade astronaut. Rice finally nodded, handed Larry the bullhorn and followed him down the ladder. Every Don Quixote needs a Sancho Panza to tell him when to eat and when to piss, thought Cable.

A heavy forearm slammed into Cable's back, pitching him forward against the cloth wall of a souvenir stand. He grabbed a splintery post to save himself from falling.

By the time he righted himself, all he saw were the backs of half-a-dozen faded blue denim jackets cut off at the armpits. The emblem on each jacket was a riderless motorcycle zooming out of a grinning skull. GALLOPING GHOSTS M.C.

Cable watched the hunching pack shove through the crowd. A woman snatched a small boy out of their way, and one of the Ghosts, bearded and earringed, lifted the boy out of her arms and delicately licked his eyes.

The bikers walked around the bus before they joined the crowd moving to the grandstand. Cable thought they had walked too slowly, studied the bus too carefully. As if they were casing it.

Larry was slouched in the driver's seat, sipping coffee from a thermos cover. "Want some?" He was making up.

"No thanks. What's happening?"

"He's going to change clothes and go back up after the race starts."

"You ought to get some sleep."

"This was nothing. One time I was stationed in Texas I drove home and back on a three-day pass I was so crazy for a bowl of Mama's pasta."

"Cable!" Rice called from behind the blue curtain that closed off the back third of the bus.

He found Rice lounging naked on the brown leather rear seat, squeezing a rubber hand exerciser. There was no loose flesh on his gymnast's body. A mat of curly copper hair covered his chest down to his stomach's muscular grid. His legs were thick and corded.

Rice asked, "What did you think?"

"I could hardly hear you."

"I'm not concerned about the message right now. What about the visual impact?"

"You looked uncomfortable up there. Unbalanced. You had to lean over too far."

"I was too high for the crowd. The bus has to be at least twenty, twenty-five feet back from the audience if I talk from the roof." He began nodding his head to the rhythm of the hand squeezes. "We definitely need a permanent platform up there. Lightweight metal. Maybe aluminum. You mind taking this down? Your notebook's fine.

"The platform has to be large enough for three or four people, microphones, a lectern, television lights. A collapsible railing. The key to the setup is a portable tower for the four-way speaker system. Telescope legs might do it. We have to be able to raise the speakers fifteen, twenty feet, whatever it is for standard public address, check that out, then drop them right down to the platform when we're driving along city streets broadcasting from inside the bus. And we've got to be able to get them out of the way when we hook into an established sound system, like a ball park or a carrier."

"An aircraft carrier?" Cable suppressed a smile at the sudden image of Rice atop the bus on a flight deck trying to outshout jets.

"That's the beauty of the bus, flexibility and mobility, large enough to attract attention, small enough to transport by rail or ship or helicopter. I'm really sold on the bus now, practically as well as symbolically. As soon as we get back I want to rip out these seats and make private quarters for myself back here and put in a work area, bunks, a galley and a head up front."

He began bending and stretching unself-consciously, his muscles rippling under his smooth, lightly freckled skin, his penis, thick and alert, bobbing in a ginger nest. Cable looked away with effort.

"Are you going back up again?"

"Yes. About forty-five minutes after the start they drift back to the infield."

"Have you been here before?"

Rice smiled. "Two years ago. I led the parade and I drove the pace car."

Cable watched the start with Bruno. On the second lap a rookie in the last row locked wheels with a car he tried to pass and drove them both into the concrete wall. The crowd screamed as red flags waved the race to a halt; then froze, guilty and silent, as medics, fire fighters, pit crewmen and photographers sprinted to the wrecks. There was applause when both drivers walked away unhurt.

"They're disappointed," said Larry. "Nobody got blown away. Dipshits."

For the first few laps after the cleanup the driving was subdued, then the also-rans in the back began to nudge at the holes. The field loosened as cars made their first pit stops. Larry went back to the bus. Cable watched for another half hour, lost in the grinding monotony of the race.

Rice was on a plank supported by two wooden sawhorses, his back to the bus. He was wearing gray slacks and a short-sleeved blue sport shirt open at the neck. His body seemed relaxed, he gestured easily with a hand mike wired to a speaker on the roof.

"Why?

"I'm going to tell you why.

"Hot iron and cold blood.

"Am I right?"

He had already drawn a crowd of several hundred, catching them between the grandstand and the refreshment tents with money in their hands. They kept enough of a distance from the sawhorses so that Rice could look in their faces by lowering his eyes.

"You know I'm right.

"I've been there and back. I've busted my jeans on every piece of iron you can tie a wheel or a wing to. One-wheel bicycles. Skate boxes. Karts. Stocks and midgets and chopped hogs and jet fighters and the X-15. The Apollo. I've seen the earth plain. And I see you.

"Deaf, dumb and blind."

The crowd stirred, raising eyebrows, grinning, nudging.

"Why are you here?

"I'll tell you.

"They sent you here.

"That's right. They sent you here. They put a tiger in your tank and slapped a piston decal on your bumper and pointed your nose right here. Told you to get it off."

He put his fists on his belt and shook his head and chuckled, a stagy gesture, but the crowd chuckled back, a little nervously. A fat boy near the front punched his buddy's bicep. Cable was struck by the contrast with the morning's stiff performance. Only Rice's eyes were the same, hot and hard.

"Here we are. Just where they want us to be."

"You tell it, mad moon man." Cable realized it was Larry's voice.

Rice nodded before the crowd could respond on its own. "Mad moon man, that's right." He pointed up at the cold, white moon.

"If you stood up there and saw what I saw, the earth plain, you'd be mad as I am. Angry as hell. My life and your life have been manipulated and perverted by values based on corruption and purposelessness and decay."

A column of black smoke rose from the track. Rice lost his audience in a stampede back to the grandstand.

He shook his head but kept speaking. "We have to get it back, our souls, our country, our world. We have to flush out our minds and our homes and our rivers and our governments."

The steady roar of the cars was broken by metallic growls and shrieks as yellow caution flags slowed the race. Rice climbed down and Cable followed him around the bus.

"Hot iron and cold blood wins every time," said Rice.

"You looked comfortable up there."

"I was." He looked pleased. "I had eyeball contact, I had good balance, and that helped my timing. I'm not sure about the tent-show style, it might work on a fair grounds but not in the cities and never on television. Hey, what's this?"

The bus door was jammed shut with two wedges of scrap wood. Rice pried them out and wrenched open the door. Larry was sprawled in the aisle, on his back, moaning. Blood ran down his face.

"Don't touch him," said Rice.

He stepped over the body and unhooked the first-aid kit from the wall behind the driver's seat. His movements were quick but unhurried. He squatted beside Larry, opening the tin box on his knees. He wiped away the blood to find the wound, a gully of torn skin and crushed bone along the hairline of his forehead. Blood seeped up to fill it as fast as Rice sponged it out with gauze pads.

Cable said, "Should I get a . . ."

"Not yet."

Rice opened Larry's eyes with a thumb and forefinger, then began probing his skull, neck, shoulders and back. His cool efficiency fascinated Cable: it seemed as though Rice had done it all before in a dry run through his life.

Larry tried to struggle up, but Rice held him down. "What did they hit you with?"

"Chain." He squinted, trying to focus. "Couple bikers at the gas tank. They must of dragged me in here, I don't remember coming in."

"Galloping Ghosts?" asked Cable.

"I don't know."

"Some Galloping Ghosts were looking the bus over this morning," said Cable.

"Galloping Ghosts," said Rice, rocking on his heels. "Must be local. Or a front."

"For who?"

"Anybody. F.B.I. Defense. C.I.A." He stood up and walked to the back of the bus. From behind the curtain Cable heard a series of metallic clicks, then the sound of a lid scraping open. Rice came out wearing a blue baseball cap and a blue nylon windbreaker. The peak of the cap was pulled low, nearly touching his nose. Rice was pushing a magazine into the handle of a .45 automatic.

"Keep Larry quiet on the floor." He slapped the magazine home with a dry crack.

"Commander?" Larry was on his elbows.

"You'll be all right. Cable, close the door behind me." He was down the steps and out of the bus.

Larry fell back.

Cable pulled down a blanket and pillow from the overhead rack and made Larry comfortable. The big man closed his eyes. Cable wondered if he should keep him awake in case of concussion. Larry was breathing regularly. Cable let him sleep.

The air in the bus was hot and damp and foul. The windows and doors were shut. A fly buzzed frantically around Cable's head, louder and more insistent than the distant roar of the race. He thought of Rice's palm striking the butt of the magazine, the dry crack as it snapped into the handle. He was out hunting Galloping Ghosts without even knowing if they had slugged Larry. Action. The Rices always opt for action. Trial and error. See if it works. Get the show on the road.

Larry opened his eyes. "Commander back?"

"No. It's only been a few minutes. How do you feel?"

"I think I'm okay. He take the gun?"

"Yes."

The dark face relaxed, and the soft brown eyes closed again. For all Larry's dramatic expressions, he had few lines in his face. In repose, he had a sweetly honest, almost simple-minded look. He was in his late thirties, Cable figured.

There was an urgent rap at the door. Cable jerked the handle and a body flew up the stairs and crashed into his shoes. Rice was right behind it.

"Close the door."

The biker scrambled to his knees and Rice pushed the .45 into his left eye. "Relax."

"Kiss my ass." The biker was nineteen or twenty, lanky, bearded in sparse tufts. His boots and jeans were encrusted with oil and dirt and spilled food. His name, Eddie, was stitched on the left breast of his cut-off denim jacket.

Larry rolled over. "That's one."

Rice asked mildly, "You put anything in the tank, Eddie?"

Eddie stared back at Rice. He was either stoned or fearless.

Very carefully, Rice slid the magazine out of the handle and tucked it into his waistband. "I wouldn't want to kill you by accident, Eddie."

He whacked the pistol against the side of Eddie's face. His cheek turned blue. "What did you put in the tank?"

"Suck my dick."

"Here's the plan, Eddie. I'm going to break your wrists, one at a time. Then your ribs, two at a time. Then I'm going to smash your kneecaps and your ankles. You'll be able to tell people you didn't make a curve." Rice's voice was matter of fact, even slightly bored, as if he was reciting a menu. He pushed the pistol into a back pocket.

"You touch me, motherfucker, you're gonna have . . ."

61

He stopped suddenly to catch his breath. Rice was bending the biker's left fist down to meet his wrist.

". . . hey . . . AHHHHHH." The bone snapped and Eddie slumped over his arm.

Rice grabbed his right hand.

"No."

"What did you put in the tank?"

"I don't know. Bucket of some shit, smelled like paint. Guy gave it to us."

"What guy?"

"Some guy. Prez knew him a little."

"How much?"

"A dollar."

"A dollar?"

"A hundred, means a hundred . . . stop."

"That's smart," said Rice. "A hundred to these fools would never be traced."

"Why?" asked Cable. He wasn't sure what his question was.

"It's just the beginning. There's something in the tank now that'll seize up the engine after a few miles. A breakdown on the highway. There'll just happen to be a wire service photographer there. Feature picture all over the country. Make me look ridiculous."

Rice was smiling. He was very pleased. He reloaded the pistol and handed it to Cable. "Be ready to move out fast when I knock on the door."

He was gone again.

Eddie looked up. His mouth was swollen lopsided. "Cocksucker."

"Shut up," said Larry. He stood up unsteadily, blinking and yawning.

"Can we drain the tank before that stuff gets to the engine?" asked Cable.

"We can take the tank off." Larry closed his eyes and

swayed. He held the back of a seat for support.

"What's his pitch?" asked Eddie.

"Just shut . . ." Larry vomited on the seat, his big body heaving and jerking uncontrollably. He collapsed over the back of the seat.

Cable moved into the aisle and put a hand on Larry's back to keep him from falling sideways. Eddie looked at him from the corner of his eye and Cable pointed the pistol at his head. Cable wondered if Eddie could sense he'd never shoot him.

There was a knock on the door and Rice shouted, "Let's go."

"Open the door, Eddie." Cable waited until the biker jerked the handle, then draped Larry's arm around his neck and dragged him to the door. Rice helped them down.

"Get away from the bus," said Rice. He held a thick, four-foot length of chain. He took the pistol from Cable.

There was a fire under the back of the bus.

Larry revived in the outside air and stumbled in the direction Cable pushed him. Fifty feet from the bus they turned in time to see Rice toss the chain to Eddie. The biker caught it in his uninjured hand. Rice shot him in the chest.

Eddie fell backward against the silver bus, his mouth open. He began to slide to the ground in a sitting position.

When the fire reached the gas tank Rice pocketed the pistol and joined Cable and Larry. The silver skin bubbled just before the bus burst into flame. Eddie disappeared.

Cable, breathless, realized Rice was looking at him. He tried to match Rice's relaxed poise. He pointed toward the firemen and photographers storming across the infield.

"Here they come."

Rice nodded. "Here they come."

Six

On the television screen a colossal Rice stood protectively astride Larry's body. His orange face was fierce and vigilant in a nimbus of red flame. The silver bus burned steadily behind him.

Cable sat on a chair between the beds of Larry's hospital room. He searched for his own face in the grotesque picture. He thought of the imperfect coloring of comic-book pictures. He tried to remember the afternoon but the images in his own mind were black and white, and out of focus.

On-screen, the Speedway infield dissolved into Rice perched on a rolling metal table outside the emergency room, surrounded by newsmen. The camera zoomed in on the hollows of his cheeks. They looked deep enough to hold coins. His voice throbbed: "There's no doubt in my mind this attack was planned by the same interests that have been trying all along to stop me from speaking directly to the American people."

Cable turned to watch Rice watch himself. The astronaut sat cross-legged on the spare bed, mesmerized by the orange-faced shade of himself staring grimly out of the screen.

"Let me make this absolutely clear. We're not going to abort this mission. There will be another Liberty Two. There will always be another Liberty Two. They can never stop me."

On Cable's other side, Larry stirred beneath a turban of bandages. "Don't underestimate those guys."

Rice ignored him. "We were lucky," he said to Cable. "The stations had enough time to process the film but NASA didn't move fast enough to censor it."

"Do you really think the networks would let them?"

"Don't forget what they did to me last time. NASA actually released classified film to discredit my moon speech. Every network ran a special on equipment malfunctions."

"The free press," said Larry. "They all said you were drunk on oxygen."

The hospital guard knocked and opened the door. "Man from the Speedway here to see you, Commander."

"I'll be right out," said Rice.

". . . released in his own recognizance pending tomorrow's hearing. Meanwhile, the man he shot, twenty-year-old Edwin Clark of Terre Haute, an unemployed machinist, remains in critical . . ."

Rice turned down the sound. He lifted the telephone. "This is Commander Rice. I want to call Chicago."

Cable suddenly felt rumpled and gamy. He had not showered or shaved since early yesterday morning when he left the Center to join Rice and Larry in Queens. One shirt sleeve was stiff with Larry's blood. His suitcase had burned in the bus.

He went into the bathroom and locked the door. He took his time showering, half expecting a summoning knock—

Rice, Larry, a nurse. He tried to remember the last time he had enjoyed assured privacy in a bathroom. Bonnie Fuller and then Sand had shared the fear he would fall on his head or open his wrists if left alone too long in a bathroom. Before that, on the road, roaches and silverfish had hurried him along. And before that . . .

He tried to break the train of thought but only pushed it past Lynn and Susan into a far, dark tunnel, a boy throbbing and shamed . . .

He burst out.

Flickering images of orange and green from the silent television set cast the only light in the room. A cowboy movie. Larry was sleeping. Rice was on the floor, naked, exercising.

"That was the PR man from the Speedway. They're going to replace the bus. It should be ready the day after tomorrow." He talked through his sit-ups without losing rhythm or breath.

"That sounds like good public relations," said Cable.

"I think they're afraid of legal action, anything in open court that might establish a link between the Speedway and the people who tried to burn us out."

Cable looked for a wink, a smile, some conspiratorial gesture, but Rice's face was tense with physical effort and his eyes were expressionless. The Rice Version was already hardening into fact in the astronaut's mind.

He flipped over for push-ups. "I gave him specs for the platform and the sound tower. That might take a little longer. They'll ship it to us." He stood up, gigantic in the flickering light. Cable had to squint to separate Rice from his shadow.

"Are we going back to New York?"

"We're heading west, into the country. I want the Liberty Caravan to lift off on July Fourth. Houston. The Astrodome. How does that sound?"

"Sounds good. Can you arrange it?"

"There are people who can."

"Your mutual-fund revolutionaries?"

Rice nodded. "They don't know it yet, but they'll arrange it." He climbed into bed and pulled the sheet to his chin. He closed his eyes.

Cable shut off the television set and stretched out on a cot jammed against a wall. Rice had insisted they all stay together in the guarded room. Cable had slept on worse.

Seven Larry drove the bus out of Indianapolis, blinking at the brilliant morning, sometimes shaking his bandaged head as if to clear his vision. Cable watched him uneasily. The staff neurologist had been reluctant to release Larry; he wanted to observe him for at least another forty-eight hours. He said there might be a blood clot.

Rice had said, "We'll have to risk it, Doctor. I can't wait another forty-eight hours, and I'm not leaving him behind."

"Are you willing to assume the responsibility for this man's death? Another trauma, even a mild one, and that clot's on its way."

"I'll take that responsibility." Rice's pale blue eyes pinned the doctor to a white wall. "You don't even know if there is a clot. And I know the country's waiting for us. Look out your window."

The noise of the crowd pushing against police barriers drifted up. The crowd had formed on the courthouse steps while a judge—almost too quickly, Cable had thought—acquitted Rice. Self-defense. The crowd had grown in twenty-four hours to nearly a thousand, curious and friendly. They took pictures of each other posing near the snout-nosed second-hand school bus parked in front of the hospital. City police kept their hands off the fresh silver paint.

Rice walked to the window. The crowd cheered and waved.

"You can sign us out or we'll just walk out."

"I'm not going to sign you out." The neurologist glanced at his diplomas for support.

The crowd trotted after the bus through downtown Indianapolis. Rice knelt on the brown vinyl back seat smiling and waving. Once Liberty Two was on the highway he sank into a corner of the seat and opened a road map. He marked it with a black felt pen.

Cable first spotted the blue station wagon near the Illinois border, switching lanes and running red lights to stay close. The wagon had an Ohio license plate. Cable lost the wagon in midday traffic and decided to forget it. TV had made the silver bus a curiosity.

Late in the afternoon Larry stalled the bus at a railroad crossing. Cars honked. Cable spotted the blue station wagon several cars behind them. Larry restarted as the red warning lights flashed and bells rang.

He stalled again on the tracks as the white barrier arms began to descend. Larry's hands were clenched white on the wheel and his face bubbled sweat. He blinked rapidly.

Cable saw the train in the distance.

And froze, gagging on the scream that couldn't rise through his throat.

Rice moved lightly down the aisle. He wrenched Larry's

hands from the wheel and pulled him off the seat. Rice started the bus and bucked it over the tracks.

The blue wagon swung out of line and raced after them, clipping off a piece of the falling wooden barrier. The locomotive roared past seconds later, whistles shrieking.

Rice eased the bus off the road. The station wagon cruised past. It was packed with young men staring out through aviator glasses. Cable felt a chill.

"Give me a hand." Rice was hauling Larry down the aisle to a rear seat.

Rice drove so firmly Cable imagined he was on a conveyor belt. The dying sun warmed and lolled him. He opened one of the suitcases of clothing and personal effects an Indianapolis department store had presented them and rummaged through it until he found the transistor radio. He dialed a news station to keep awake.

At dusk there was a bulletin: Eddie Clark was dead. He called out the news to Rice.

Rice's eyes never left the road. "They let him die. One less problem. He'll never figure out how they used him. You know they would have killed Larry."

"Why?"

"A warning. That's why I couldn't leave him."

"Don't you think he needs medical attention?"

"Probably. Look, Cable, it's very simple. If you succeed, the end justifies the means. That's a practical and moral reality. People die in a revolution. If you fail, they've died in vain. If you succeed, their sacrifices have been worthwhile."

"Very simple." It came out more sardonically than he had intended, but once it was out he didn't care.

"Most important things are very simple."

He could not tell if Rice had missed the sarcasm or chosen to ignore it. He switched radio stations and let mindless music and the gentle movements of the bus rock him to sleep.

He woke abruptly in darkness. Rice and Larry were crouched at the rear window, peering out at a moon-washed parking lot.

"There are four or five more of them in the station wagon," Rice was saying.

"We could back right into that heap," said Larry. "Kiss 'em goodby."

"Let's find out what they want."

Larry touched his bandage. "I'm not asking any more questions."

They made room for Cable at the window. Two boys circled the school bus. They looked seventeen or eighteen. They each swung a two-foot nightstick.

"If that station wagon's blue," said Cable, "they've been following us all day."

Larry said, "This time shoot first and ask questions later."

The bus door opened and Rice suddenly appeared outside. The two boys jerked to attention, tucked the clubs under their left arms and saluted. Rice solemnly returned the salute and shook their hands.

The driver's door of the station wagon flew open and a stocky, round-faced young man clambered out, jamming the tails of his short-sleeved white shirt under the waist-band of his chino pants. He marched toward Rice with a self-conscious attempt at dignity, but his glasses kept slipping down his short nose. Each time he pushed them back he threw himself off stride. He had big, loose buttocks.

"Porky Pig," said Larry.

Rice met him with an outstretched hand. They talked briefly. Rice pointed to the bus.

Larry cursed and flicked on the overhead light.

The stocky young man followed Rice into the bus.

"This is Captain Bostic of the White Action Force," said Rice. "They've come from Cleveland to join us."

Bostic was in his early twenties, tense and earnest. He pulled his thick-lensed glasses on and off nervously. Without them his weak eyes tended to drift in different directions. His complexion was pasty but smooth, and his features were very small for so round and broad a face. His nose was so sharply tilted that from certain angles his nostrils seemed to be set flush in his face. He did look like Porky Pig.

He politely refused a seat, shifting from foot to foot in the narrow aisle. He said the Force had left headquarters thirty minutes after hearing about the Galloping Ghosts' attack. Bostic's voice was high and nasal.

"We are radical racists, Commander, ready to fight and die in order to return this nation to the freedom-loving white Christians who created it." He spilled it out in a measured breath.

"We want a share in the responsibility and sacrifice of cleansing our nation of the animalistic blacks and manipulative Jews working with the international banking conspiracy to enslave our sons and daughters."

Larry hooted. "How many sons and daughters you got?"

Rice silenced him with a sharp glance.

"What can you do for Liberty Two, Bostic?"

"We can be guards, ushers, we can pass out literature. We can do a lot of things. We can handle trouble. The Force is tough. We pounded some radical potheads last week, they won't be waving their dirty signs so soon. We can do a lot of things."

He became jittery under Rice's silent scrutiny. His soft maroon lips caressed each other nervously. "We can be useful. Guards, ushers, pass out literature."

72

He gestured toward the six boys drawn up outside the bus in a ragged guard mount.

"Bring them in," said Rice.

Bostic bolted out of the bus with a little cry of triumph.

"You got to be kidding, Commander." Larry's face contorted. "They're nuts. They're poison."

The White Action Force crowded into the bus, awed and wary. Rice waved them into seats. They huddled together, a clinic of bad teeth, blotched skin and curved spines. Lank, greasy hair. Dropouts, Cable thought. Four-F's. Most of them wore jeans and boots and cheap patterned shirts. A tall boy with a concave chest began to wheeze. Asthma. A pretty little blond boy fingered the silver iron cross dangling from a pink pierced ear. He reminded Cable of Susan.

Rice looked them over carefully, one at a time, until they all squirmed.

He spoke very softly. "There is no room on Liberty Two for racists, for troublemakers, for the selfish, undisciplined scum of the streets. I don't need boys ready to die, I need men willing to live hard, to work and sweat and sacrifice to lead their country into the second American Revolution."

"Give us a chance," said Bostic.

Rice shook his head. "There is no room on Liberty Two for a White Action Force."

The boys' faces clenched like fists, hard little faces used to being shut out.

"Liberty Two is going to stitch this country together again. When the silver caravan crosses America, I want black shoulders alongside mine, Indians and Mexican-Americans and Japanese-Americans, Jews and Catholics and nuclear physicists and garbage men. There's room for everyone except the pirates and the stowaways."

The little blond said, "Let's get outa here."

No one moved.

"There's no room for a White Action Force, but there might be room for you as individuals, as men, as Americans. If you think you can chop it."

Their eyes narrowed, suspicious of a trick. Cable sensed the melodrama Rice was building, he was amused by it, yet wings fluttered in his stomach.

Rice's voice was clear and sharp, pitched down at the stony-faced boys. "The spearhead of the first American Revolution was a group of patriots who called themselves the Sons of Liberty. They dumped the tea in Boston Harbor. Paul Revere was their courier. They were tough. They knew the streets. But they were disciplined and they judged a man only by his loyalty to the revolution. They had a motto. 'We Dare Be Free.'

"Can you say it?"

Eyes down, a few boys mouthed the phrase.

"Say it!"

There was an unintelligible mumble.

Bostic shouted, "We Dare Be Free. SAY IT!"

"WE DARE BE FREE." It shook the bus.

Their eyes met Rice's, glittering. Cable was astonished to feel his knees quiver.

Rice saluted them. "Welcome aboard, Sons of Liberty."

Eight

Downtown St. Louis.

Cable, adjusting public address wires inside the bus, looked out at a thickening lunch-hour crowd attracted by the silvery dazzle. They looked up at Rice curiously but grudgingly. It was hot, and a stifling breeze blew a fine red dust. The cool department stores were across the street. But they stayed to listen.

"Seeing the earth plain is asking the basic questions.

"About gun control.

"Don't ask if you should turn in your weapons, don't ask if you should register them. Ask your leaders why so many Americans are so terrified of being unarmed."

The Sons of Liberty, scrubbed, clean-shaven, stood in a stiff rank below Rice. Larry sat hunched at the rear of the bus on the first rung of the new aluminum ladder. He was shivering despite the noon heat.

"About the courts."

"Don't ask why they're incapable of justice. Ask why

they're crowded with so many Americans gone wrong.

"About your money.

"Not should I save it, should I spend it, should I invest it. But who manipulates it, who steals a piece of it out of my pocket every year.

"Don't ask the questions they want you to ask, the irrelevant questions that divert you from seeking the information you need. . . ."

Watching the crowd strain up toward the man on the bus roof, Cable could visualize the thrusting angle of Rice's hard, lean body. The crowd melted into a vulnerable mass. Rice is laying the crowd, he thought.

There was a click at Cable's ear.

"Just one more . . . hey, you moved."

The girl was tall and slim. She had a camera at her face and two more dangling from her neck, and a bulging knapsack on her shoulder. Cable thought of Lynn's knapsack in the park.

"Who are you?"

"I'm shooting the crowd." She focused on Cable. Her hands were quick, confident, long hands, bony and delicately veined.

Click. "What's it like to save America?"

"You better get out of . . ."

Click. "Great. I needed your profile for a frame. Good profile." She lowered the camera. Her eyes fascinated Cable. They were small and round and deeply set. He felt he was being observed from tunnels.

"Hey, this bus smells like a lockerroom."

"Nobody invited you in." He immediately regretted his tone. "Eight of us live in here."

"No wonder. What's your name?"

"David Cable. Who you with?"

"I'm free lance." She scribbled in a notebook. "You the bus driver?"

"I'm writing a book about Commander Rice." He anticipated the flicker of interest in her eyes and enjoyed it. "What's your name?"

"Jean Stryker. Who're you writing the book for?"

"Sentry Press."

"Don't you find yourself responding emotionally when your subject's so morally involving?" She looked serious.

"Not really. I'm a professional. I'm . . . I am a camera."

"Good line, but totally inaccurate. I can alter spatial relations, colors, textures, the time of day. And that's just with lenses and filters and angles. In the darkroom, forget it. There's no real objectivity in our business."

She shook a cigarette half out of a crumpled pack and plucked it free with her lips. She fished a wooden match from inside the cellophane envelope and fired it with her thumbnail.

"See you, Cable." She side-stepped down the aisle to the door, long tanned legs flashing under a brief denim skirt. She's vain about her legs, he thought. She wore lightweight blue suede jogging shoes. He wondered if jogging shoes were chic this month or if she was just eccentric. He had been out of touch.

He watched Jean Stryker move around the bus, shooting up at Rice, whirling to catch off-guard faces in the crowd. The Sons pretended to ignore her but struck stern and watchful poses. They're thrilled by the attention, Cable thought. Losers. The same kind of kids who provoke cops just for human contact. Or travel in motorcycle packs. Jean Stryker crouched and bent and twisted gracefully as she shot; her long body was very supple.

She was not really pretty, Cable decided, vaguely bothered. Features are too strong, almost aggressive. Twenty-seven, twenty-eight, he figured. He felt a distant ache. Not really pretty at all. He almost said it out loud.

She backed to the perimeter of the crowd, shooting, then

turned and walked away. He saw her framed by the distant Gateway Arch. A good picture. Her hair, a thick cap of reddish brown curls and corkscrews, bounced as she loped along. He fixed it in his mind.

That evening, on the way out of St. Louis, Bostic showed him a library book entitled *The Sons of Liberty*. He was excited.

"It's all in here. They even had a song."

"You sound surprised."

"I don't know. He could of made it up."

Cable surrendered willingly to the fitful rhythms of the road. He drove Liberty Two, following the station wagon in a loose, southwest weave. Rice drove the wagon, Larry slumped beside him. They stopped for two days in Little Rock to have the wagon painted silver.

The bus was steamy by day and cough-wracked at night. Cable kept the radio loud enough to drown the incessant chatter of the Sons. They deferred to him; he was their link to Rice. Cable slept on the rear seat, the only seat in the bus long enough to stretch out on. He washed first in gas station sinks and led the way through the serving lines of truck-stop cafeterias. They ate most of their meals in the bus, cornflakes and sandwiches and cans of pork and beans. They attached a secondhand hot plate to wires under the dashboard and boiled water for the coffee and soup they stole from supermarkets along the way. Cable said nothing and Rice didn't seem to notice.

The astronaut was remote, preoccupied. He rarely spoke to the Sons when he got out of the wagon at a rest stop, sitting alone or with Larry, scanning and marking his latest batch of road maps, guides, local newspapers. He made four or five calls a day, often from open roadside booths, a hand clamped over his ear to shut out traffic noise. Bostic would lead the Sons in calisthenics and Cable would watch Rice from the bus. He figured at least half the calls were long distance collect. He asked Larry about them, but the mechanic shrugged dully. He complained he was having trouble focusing. Sometimes he saw triple. On the road Cable could see him lounging in the back of the wagon, picking under his bandage at a long, brown, oozing scab, sometimes staring sullenly back at the bus. Larry avoided the Sons and hardly spoke to Cable. He resented their presence, Cable thought. Larry wanted Rice for himself.

Cable lost track of days. The station wagon stopped wherever there was a crowd: a shopping center, a ballfield, a schoolyard, a country auction. Rice would wait until the bus drew their attention before he would step out and climb to the aluminum platform on the bus roof. His speeches were short and rarely the same. He was testing words and ideas, and he was polishing his delivery. His technique improved with every speech, the hand movements better coordinated with the sentences, the pacing more effective, the inflections more subtle. His voice became a flexible instrument. Cable found himself looking forward to each stop for another glimpse of Rice growing, expanding.

"I have seen the earth plain, a ship speeding full throttle across uncharted waters without a strong and honest hand on its helm. I have seen the strength and treasure of this ship stolen by the pirates and stowaways among us.

"The pirates who raid the ship are your politicians, your corporation executives, bureaucrats. Union leaders. They manipulate your money and your minds, they pollute your skies and your waters, they steal your natural resources and your land, and they kill you with policemen and foreign armies.

"The stowaways drain the ship. They're your welfare

bums, hippies, street people. Convicts. They're parasites hidden in the lifeboats living off your sweat."

Cable tried to listen through the words to the master scheme. What is he saying? Where does he want to take the crowd? Why? What's in it for him?

Sometimes the astronaut seemed bemused to Cable, a computer struggling with simultaneous input and output, or a piano player vamping until the sheet music arrives.

For two weeks, the Sons accepted Rice's remoteness. Bostic enthralled them with the stolen library book. At night, under the bus's overhead light, Bostic read to the boys about the original Sons of Liberty. Cable explained words and interpreted phrases and filled in bits of colonial history dredged up from half-forgotten college courses. The Stamp Act. The Committees of Correspondence. Wily Sam Adams and mad James Otis.

Somewhere near Tulsa, parked for the night in a field, Bostic assigned each of the boys the name of one of the original Boston Sons of Liberty. It was a solemn ceremony and the boys shivered in its grip. The little blond became Joseph Field and the tall asthmatic became George Trott. Ben Edes. Tom Chase. John Avery. Henry Bass.

Bostic renamed himself Alexander Mackintosh after the leader of the Boston mobs.

"I am Captain Mack," he cried, swaying in the aisle. "We are hereby reborn in the second American Revolution."

The crowds were drawn by the silvery dazzle of Liberty Two and the beating pawn-shop drums, Captain Mack's innovation. Joey Field blew a fife. But the crowds were held by Rice's intensity, his rays shimmering down from the platform. Now and then there were scrawled, home-made signs—ASTRO-NUT and LUNAR-TIC—but they were pulled down and torn by the crowd after Rice spoke.

The heckling always died when he ascended the platform, the smiles faded, the winking, nudging, gesturing subsided, and the crowd would fall silent and open.

"Welfare is slavery. Welfare nullified the Emancipation Proclamation. Welfare is a raiding tactic of the pirates and the stowaways. Yet there are people who need help, and we are our brothers' keepers. If fifty families in this community each gave one dollar per week to a struggling family, plus extra food and clothes and guidance and friendship, within six months that family would be able to work and produce, to stand on their own proud feet. And there would be fifty-one families, fifty-one dollars a week available to help another struggling family."

Cable saw heads in the crowd nod: Almost makes sense; Been to the moon and back, no dummy, not running for office, not selling anything . . . maybe . . . well, just maybe . . .

Outside Oklahoma City.

At suppertime Rice turned into a roadside Chicken Big's. The Sons perked up. Cable marveled at his timing; he had ignored the boys for days, then, just as their morale was beginning to sag, just as they were beginning to whine about the monotonous food and the grind of the road and the cramped sleeping on the bus seats, Rice descended from the clouds with paper buckets of chicken and french fries and ice cream shakes, the ego food of adolescence. They found a field outside town and camped. Rice moved among them, smiling, chatting easily, touching shoulders.

Mack reintroduced each Son by his new revolutionary name, and Rice nodded approval, draining the sour juices of their discontent. Cable was amused; Rice had never known their real names.

A local police car pulled up and a young trooper sauntered over with that rolling cockwalk they had seen in a dozen towns. The Sons no longer tensed. Rice greeted the trooper and invited him to sit down. Later, the sergeant, perhaps the chief, would drop in; five minutes of talk, an anecdote, a few autographs, and no one would bother them for the rest of the night.

When stars became visible, Rice traced constellations and galaxies. A bedtime story. Little Joey Field snuggled against Captain Mack and blew a melancholy fife. Cable, drifting, let the music and the astronaut's soothing voice slide away. Cable felt a poignancy he could not reach and a rich, brown pleasure in the distant pain of it. He wallowed in that brown place, floating safe from all sharp edges.

"I know just what you mean, Commander." It was Mack's nasal voice. "They didn't put up a traffic light on my corner till my kid brother got run over."

"That's the disaster mentality," said Rice.

"How old was your brother?" It was Cable's voice, urgent. He was surprised by it.

"Five."

"He wasn't killed." He heard himself plead for the boy's life.

"D.O.A. The truck ran him over and dragged him a block."

"D.O.A.," said Cable. He repeated the sounds to himself until they lost meaning. A meditation chant. D.O.A.

Every eighteen seconds a plastic red comet hummed across the twinkling black velveteen ceiling and crashed into a hundred-foot-high sign. WELCOME TO CONSUMERS COSMOS, EVERYTHING UNDER THE SUN. A gigantic golden ball suspended from the roof turned slowly, winking with messages for lost children, unadvertised specials, COMMANDER RICE & LIBERTY 2—ON THE HOUR—JUPITER MALL.

The Sons of Liberty assembled in a single rank alongside the bus. George Trott carried an American flag. Joey Field blew a bugle. Shoppers paused, turned. The Sons wore cheap white shirts, collars tucked out of sight, and dark trousers bloused over spit-shined combat boots. Their long hair was pulled into pony tails. It was Captain Mack's version of a colonial militant costume. Rice had praised his initiative.

Cable slipped away from the bus to a bank of telephones. As usual, Barrett's secretary put him right through.

"Cable. I'm still waiting for your preliminary report."

"We've been moving too fast."

"It's been nearly three weeks, Cable. Mr. Clune is very anxious to see something."

Cable's hand trembled. "I'll have something soon. Rice told me to be ready to go somewhere with him tonight."

"I want . . ."

"What about Bonnie Fuller?"

Barrett sounded impatient. "Jack's been on that, he expects some information any day. Now what about that report?"

"I've got to go, someone's coming." He hung up on Barrett.

It would have been very easy to write a preliminary report about Lynn's group. He had drafted it in his mind a dozen times.

Subject is a relatively small (stable pop: 7) campus-based "pre-revolutionary" activist cell without national affiliation, financial base or effective local leadership. On-going activities such as campus demonstrations, agitation and minor sabotage (switchboard disruption, mailroom fire, slashing ROTC vehicle tires) have been sporadic and relatively inconsequential. Recommend: 1. Withdrawal of full-time staffer, and, 2. Notification appropriate authorities re: dynamite in basement of rented house.

He had known if he filed the report Barrett would have pulled him out of the house, given him a week or two at home, then reassigned him.

And his life with Lynn would be over.

Once she had opened her knapsack and laid out the sandwiches on the grass and casually said without looking at him, "Some of them think you're FBI."

"What do you think?"

"I don't think so. You don't try hard enough. Dave, I don't understand you at all. You could snatch this whole thing if you wanted to, you're tougher and smarter than any of them. You could take over. If you got off your ass."

He had stood up and splashed his coffee against a tree and stomped off, a stagy gesture. He counted on her being too proud to follow him. He was right. On Broadway he found a pay phone and called the Center. Barrett suggested a drug raid to divert suspicion. There were always drugs in the house.

It was a very efficient operation. The police dragged five of them out of the house in the middle of the night. They all got their pictures in the paper. Only Lynn and Cable were held. They refused to post bail. A lawyer from Legal Aid had them released on a technicality two days later, a woman lawyer Cable thought he had seen around the Clune Building.

No one in the house ever mentioned FBI again. And Cable, in love, never thought too much about the raid or the lawyer or the slickness of the operation.

"Individual responsibility creates corporate responsibility.

"How can we expect the utility companies—the motor

that powers this country—how can we expect the utilities to listen to us when we aren't willing to shut off our lights, our washing machines, our heaters, our air conditioners, our power tools long enough for them to hear our voices?

"So the utilities keep pushing appliances they can't fuel on people who often don't need them.

"And they keep raising their prices.

"And they suppress the development of new and cheaper sources of power.

"Some radicals say take them over.

"Some radicals say blow them up.

"That's nonsense. That's the stowaways talking, diverting us. Conspiring with the pirates to keep us away from the answer.

"Make the utilities responsible. That's the answer. Make them truly give power to the people.

"If every one of you was willing to sacrifice—for two days —you would have safe, sure, cheap power forever.

"Just two days. No lights, no stoves, no heat or air-conditioning, no television.

"Think about it.

"Do you dare be free?"

At precisely 7:07 by the clock on the golden ball he came down the rear ladder of Liberty Two. Seven minutes on the button every time. The shopping center manager had insisted on seven minutes top. He said it was just the right rest for footsore shoppers without keeping them out of the stores long enough to break the buying fevers.

"Cable! Let's go." Rice strode across the Jupiter level to an elevator.

A limousine waited for them in an underground car park. Cable saw only the back of the driver's head. The car purred smoothly along expressways into the deserted heart of the city. It stopped outside an office building. The elevator operator stepped out of the darkened lobby to unlock the glass front door and take them up to the seventh floor. Rice walked directly to the only lighted door in the silent, metallic hallway.

"Commander!" A squat man, bald, sixtyish, vaguely familiar to Cable, stood in the doorway. He clapped Rice's shoulder. Cable thought the astronaut shrank from the contact. The squat man wore an expensive suit perfectly tailored to his short bulk. He glanced over Rice's shoulder, registered Cable as an aide, and lost interest in him.

"I hope you've finally made a decision, Mr. Wendt," said Rice.

Cable recognized him. Lewis Wendt had resigned abruptly after less than a year as Secretary of Agriculture. The newspapers had reported that he quit because the President never answered his phone calls. Wendt refused to be interviewed. He had returned to his farm, the largest in Iowa, and dropped out of public sight.

The room was stark and angular, an anonymous conference room. Lewis Wendt motioned toward one of a dozen black leather lounge chairs scattered over the white vinyl floor, but Rice remained standing. Cable took a corner chair. There were two other men in the room. Their faces were also familiar public faces. They rolled their chairs to flank Wendt in a conversational crescent in front of Rice. The chairs glided silently on ball bearings.

A tall man, martially stiff in fine, out-of-style tweeds. General Tyler Knox. He had been retired prematurely, Cable recalled, a brilliant record clouded. There had been rumors of secret reports, suppressed charges.

The third man wore stylish clothes artfully disarrayed. He had shoulder-length gray hair, a deeply tanned, cruelly pitted face. Cable recognized Howard Lefferts from a decade of television appearances and newspaper photographs; Lefferts in the streets, at fund-raising garden parties, marching out of court with fierce little nuns or soldiers or coal-eyed blacks. Lefferts had been Susan's hero, the activist lawyer she had wanted Cable to become.

Wendt, General Knox and Lefferts seemed comfortable together, a team. They looked at Rice as an object; he was clearly not one of them. Cable felt invisible. He noticed several red push-button telephones on the white floor. He thought of blood on snow and hastily buried the image.

"Tyler thinks you're going off half-cocked," said Wendt. His nuances were subtle, Cable thought: it was only Tyler's opinion but he was not necessarily wrong. And the newsmagazines had portrayed Wendt as an earthy buffoon; they called him Farmer Lew.

"Let me expand on that, Rice," said General Knox. He bit off his words and spat them out as if he was impersonating a retired general. "I think you're running around like a Fuller Brush man. You're wearing out your impact."

Cable, off in his corner, was impressed by the relaxed, almost arrogant cock of Rice's body. His hands were at his sides, his feet only inches apart. Cable could not imagine himself facing these three men without bracing himself, folding his arms, shoving his hands in his pockets. It looked like a trial.

"We are concerned," said Wendt carefully, "that you will either burn yourself out in shopping centers or, to be perfectly frank, persuade someone else to mount your campaign in a hasty and ill-conceived manner."

"Then back me now," said Rice.

"Timing," said Knox. "Until the country is ready for . . ."

"Gentlemen," said Rice, "this is my time. The country is ready when it has faith in a leader."

"It's not that simple," said Wendt. "You have no program, you . . ."

"Program? We've been diverted by years of programs. We don't need another program, we need questions and answers. I'm going to raise the questions and the American people will provide the right answers."

Knox snorted. "That's very naive."

"Commander, what do you propose? Specifically." Wendt's voice had endless nuance. It was definitely a hypothetical question, there was no promise in it. And yet . . .

"I want to open my national campaign on July 4, in the Astrodome. There's a double-header that day, it's the network game of the week. I want twenty minutes between games on national television. I'll speak for ten minutes.

"From Houston I'll hit every major stadium and fair grounds in Texas, New Mexico, Arizona and Southern California. I'll start the return trip East from Los Angeles."

Rice spoke matter-of-factly, a young executive, Cable thought, outlining the campaign for a new product. Wendt and Knox listened without expression. Lefferts curled his lips, a hedging half-smile that could be amusement or encouragement or contempt.

Rice's voice softened, deepened. "Imagine a stream of silver, the Liberty Caravan, rolling eastward across America toward Washington with a mandate for a new era.

"A dozen cars and buses and trucks and trailers, then a hundred and a thousand as the people of America fall into place behind Liberty Two. By the time I leave Houston people all over America will be painting their cars silver as an affirmation of the second American Revolution. By the time I leave Los Angeles they will be ready to join the Caravan as it sweeps east across the country, silver planes writing Liberty Two in the sky, silver ships sounding the call off every coast.

"A million vehicles, two million vehicles. From space you would see a thread of silver binding this country together again."

There was a stillness in the room. Cable heard only his

own quickened breathing. He could not see Rice's face, but the three men in front of him seemed stunned. Lefferts' mouth was slack.

After a long time, Knox said, huskily, "They'd stop you."

Lefferts recovered. "No, they wouldn't. They'd paint the White House silver and ask you to address a joint session of Congress. Marcuse calls it 'absorbent power.' I prefer 'permissive manipulation,' although I . . ."

"Howard," snapped Wendt.

"I can't wait for you much longer," said Rice. His voice was matter-of-fact again. "We don't have much money and we're not getting national attention. You saw how they turned that Speedway attack into a simple brawl. I have to reach the people directly, all at the same time."

Rice signaled Cable to stand.

"It's up to you three now. Before I burn myself out in the shopping centers or find someone else to finance me."

He walked out without another word. Cable, trailing, saw the three men rise and draw together, as if for warmth.

Rice was exultant on the ride back. "They're going to come through. They'll argue and they'll run through their scenarios, but they'll come through. They're running scared, Cable. The country's ready for change, they know it, everybody knows it. People are dissatisfied, frustrated, they feel helpless. They see no purpose to their work, to their lives, they've been pulled and pushed, and they haven't gone anywhere at all."

"Why would those three want to back you? What's in it for them?"

"Control. How is change going to affect the people who've been profiting from the status quo? Obviously it won't be to their advantage unless they can direct that change, manipulate the new moods, use it as a safety valve."

"They're going to gamble they can control you."

Rice laughed, a sharp, humorless bark.

Cable sank back into the limousine cushions. In the darkness he felt Rice's eyes on him.

"This is a time for commitment, Cable, total, irrevocable commitment. You'll have to make a decision, too."

Cable turned toward the voice but they drove for miles before highway lights illuminated the astronaut's face. Rice was asleep.

Dallas.

"You can go to any high school in America and ask a sixteen-year-old cheerleader to get you some dope and if she can't the football captain will. But the FBI and the CIA and the police can't keep it out of the country and off the streets.

"Why?

"Because when you're high on dope you can't be high on yourself, high on your family, high on America.

"Because when you're doped you can't ask the right questions. You'll never see the earth plain.

"Narcotics is a prison of the soul.

"It keeps the poor uneducated, unemployable and pacified.

"It keeps the sons and daughters of America on a mind-less trip to nowhere, walking on a treadmill that leads into the corporations and the stores and the factories and the mines."

His movements had become bold without seeming studied, his voice resonant without sounding theatrical. But what does he want? He's not leading the crowds back to God or into a presidential election, he takes no collections and makes no deals. Cable thought, he's either crazy or incredibly devious. Or both.

The black spot on the side-view mirror grew to dime-size, split into four black spots and started growing again. Cable squinted until he was sure they weren't insects or dirt specks.

Cyclists. They roared up to Liberty Two, then passed the bus two to a side. The lead cyclist on the left drew under Cable's window and smiled up cheerfully. Cable recognized the bearded Galloping Ghost who had licked the little boy's eyes at the Speedway. He wondered if this was the one Eddie had called Prez.

He punched the horn to alert Rice, but the Ghosts were already spurting ahead to flank the silver station wagon. They peered in, blew kisses, then thundered away into a heat mirage that shimmered on the flat ribbon of highway heading south toward Houston.

Rice walked back to the bus at the supper stop. Larry shambled along at his heels. Larry had lost weight, his big shoulders sagged, and the barroom bumper of his stomach had collapsed into a flabby beer belly.

"Keep Larry in the bus with you. We're going to drive right on through tonight. Those bikers might be back."

Larry sat pitched forward, his forehead resting on the horizontal chrome bar behind the driver's seat. Cable heard his phlegmy breathing above the rattle of Liberty Two's loose metal bones. The Sons horsed in the back of the bus, playing catch with one of Georgie's boots and mimicking his complaints and his coughs. Joey sucked and tongued his harmonica. Captain Mack made up duty rosters and tried not to stare too obviously at the little blond.

"Cable?"

"Larry?"

"We're never gonna see Houston."

"Sure we will. Just a few more hours."

"Never in a million years. Those scumbags gonna come back kill us all." Larry's voice was dull, resigned. He sounded beyond fear. "Cable?"

"Uh-huh?"

"You know I was the first one the Commander called from the hospital? Before he called his wife even? He called me. He trusts me. Won't let any other crew chief near those engines, just me. Trusts me. I can put my ear against the engine and spot the trouble in a minute. Always fix it in time for the flight. He trusts me."

"He talk about his wife much?"

"Damn bitch thinks he's crazy. It tears him up inside. Why do you think he wants to go to Houston? He talks to me. He trusts me. I know him better'n anybody."

"I'm sure you do."

"Don't give me that shit. You bought your way in with a lousy thousand dollars." He didn't have the strength to raise his voice. Cable slowed the bus and strained to hear. "He doesn't trust you for shit, he told me that."

"Why don't you go back and lie down?"

"Sure, give Porky Pig a crack at me, you'd love that." Larry heaved backwards and collapsed softly into a shapeless sack. He continued talking but Cable could no longer make out the words.

The Galloping Ghosts hit them at twilight on a deserted stretch of highway. They burst out of an unpaved emergency road and wheeled into a rank of four across the two southbound lanes, boot to boot. They faced the oncoming station wagon and bus without moving. They seemed unreal, nightmare apparitions.

Cable glanced toward the empty northbound lanes,

partially hidden by a high, grassy divider. There would be no help there.

The Ghosts charged, low in the saddle, bandanas whipping their white skull helmets. They peeled into two files and screamed past the wagon and bus by inches. Cable picked them up in the side-view mirror. A quarter mile down the road they spun around, reformed the rank of four and roared up on Liberty Two. Texas tag.

A bottle smashed against the rear window, blacking it out with paint.

"Get down," Cable yelled. "Mack, get them down."

The bikers drifted up beside the bus, two on a side, almost casually slinging bottles at the windows, blacking out the eyes of the bus. The bearded Ghost pulled under Cable's window again. A chain snaked up from his hand and shattered the side-view mirror.

Rice jerked the station wagon in the left passing lane and gradually slowed until there was less than a car's length between his tailgate and the lead bike. Cable held his speed in the right lane.

Rice stopped.

The bearded biker's reactions were superb. The instant the wagon's brake lights glowed he threaded the narrow alley between the wagon and the bus and roared ahead to safety.

The second cyclist slammed into the back of the wagon. His body catapulted over the length of the wagon and landed on the highway. Rice ran him down and left him a flopping rag on the road.

The Sons began to cheer. Georgie jumped up and down, waving his arms. A wrench crashed through a window, spraying slivers of glass. One of the Sons shrieked, "My eye!"

Mack was in the aisle pushing them under seats.

The three remaining Ghosts dropped out of Cable's

sight. Steel spikes clattered on the highway.

Liberty Two shuddered and fishtailed and sagged back. The rear tires were blown. Cable lifted his foot off the accelerator and tapped at the brake, slowing the bus. The rear wheel rims screeched on the stone highway. He eased the bus to a stop.

Rice drove away.

The Ghosts roared up, hunched shapes, half man, half machine. One of them leaped off his bike and clambered up the rear ladder. He began to stamp his feet on the aluminum platform. The violent rhythm echoed in Cable's teeth.

Larry's fingers dug into his shoulder.

Cable heard his own voice. "Keep calm, just take it easy now."

Mack echoed, "Keep calm. Get your sticks. Prepare for action." His voice was shrill.

The boys crawled and stumbled in the dark under the mocking dance. Cable looked out the open driver's window. The two Ghosts on the road clapped and cheered the dancer, an ironic parody of Rice and the crowd.

Larry's fingers tightened. "Here he comes, here he comes."

Rice hurtled toward them at a hundred miles an hour, bright beams freezing the bikers on the road.

Larry screamed, "Kill them."

The bikers wheeled behind the bus with yards to spare.

The bikers pushed out, facing north, waiting for Rice to return. They cackled and slapped palms. There was no sound from the roof.

Rice's headlights appeared, cats' eyes, then blazing rays. The station wagon raced at its limit. The bikers mocked him with their quick machines, spinning out of danger. The biker on the roof threw a handful of small spikes in front of the wagon.

"God, Momma, they're gonna kill him." Larry moaned and hugged Cable's shoulders.

The bikers wheeled out again, almost lounging in their saddles now. The stomping dance began again.

Mack's voice, crackling at the edge of panic: "Stay calm, be ready, Sons of Liberty. Dare be free."

The tailgate lights glowed. The wagon slowed, turned for another pass. In the distance, Rice's headlights were pin holes in the black cloth of the Texas night. Alongside the bus the Ghosts twisted their handlebars until their bikes snarled and bucked with bursting power.

"Mary, Mother of God, help . . ."

A black Ford rammed the motorcycles from behind.

Running without lights, its engine noise drowned in the bikes' roar, the Ford hit the Ghosts before anyone was aware of another car on the road. The bikers were flung sideways, one against the bus, the other over the grassy divider into the northbound lanes. Their riderless machines jumped forward, collided and fell.

The Ford spun out of control and rolled over, landing on its roof off the highway.

Captain Mack screamed, "Whiiiiite Ack-shun," and pounded down the aisle. Cable opened the door. The boys spilled out of the bus yelling and waving their nightsticks. Cable followed them out. They trapped the fourth biker on the rear ladder and clubbed him to the ground. The station wagon screeched up. Rice leaped out. He sprinted to the black Ford and yanked open the door. Cable helped him lift out the driver.

They stretched him out on the grassy shoulder of the road. Rice dropped to his knees and put his ear to the man's chest. "Get the kit."

Larry was on the floor of the bus, moaning.

By the time Cable returned to Rice with a flashlight and the tin first-aid box, the highway was quiet again. The boys were drained. They stared silently at the beaten biker splayed out on the road unconscious. The motorcycles were a tangled heap of hot, ticking metal.

Cable aimed the light on the driver of the black Ford. He was trying to sit up. He wiped the blood out of his eyes and grinned.

Jack.

Nine

Cable called Barrett the next morning from an outdoor booth near the motel. The senator accepted the collect call himself.

"Are you all right? How's Jack?"

"What the hell was he doing there?" Cable's fury tore out of a dry, tense throat. He had not slept.

"How badly is he hurt? The UPI . . ."

"Just answer the goddam question."

"Don't shout at me, Cable. What about Jack?"

The words rushed out, a liberation. "You sent him down without telling me, what kind of a cripple do you think I am, you and Sand and those fucking rooms and those fucking drugs, put me together again so you could set me up, you can shove those Teddy bears up your ass . . ."

"Cable!"

"The Center's operational, it's always been operational, you lied to me from the first day—rather a small institution, grants for research—bullshit, Senator, you're in the business. I always wondered why an old machine hack like you left politics, you didn't leave, you're up to your neck in dirty tricks . . ." He gasped for breath.

"Call me later, Cable. When you're in control of yourself." Barrett's voice was firm but not angry.

"This is the last call. You wire my back pay to the main Western Union office in Houston. This morning. I'll wait for it."

"We need you more than ever, Cable."

He was desperately tired. He turned his back on the rush-hour traffic and sagged against the phone. "You don't need me anymore. Jack's in the hospital but he's all right."

"We need you, Cable." His voice was soothing. Cable imagined his soft finger pads stroking his glass desk top. "We sent Jack down to work under you. He may have saved your life."

The fury was spent. "Why didn't you tell me he was coming?"

"We only decided after you reported on the meeting with Wendt. You didn't call again."

He realized he wanted to believe Barrett. "They scraped four guys off that highway. Two dead. Another one had his genitals sheared off."

"We didn't plan it that way, Cable. Jack was trailing you, he was looking for an opening to get in."

"He found it. And I'm through. Send my money."

"We've traced Bonnie Fuller. She's in Sacramento, apparently well, in the custody of a local agency working with Army Intelligence."

"How can I believe you?"

"Would you recognize her voice?"

"I think so."

"Hold on."

The Houston sun was pale yellow over the flat marshland. Cable's eyes stung and his tongue was thick. His right hand throbbed. He had not noticed the dried gash across his knuckles until dawn, after the police had escorted them to the motel. Rice had refused to leave the highway until the wrecker arrived to tow Liberty Two.

"Cable?"

"I'm right here, Senator."

Bonnie's voice, whispering:

". . . real bad shape, like something terrible happened. He used to hold on to me for hours, sleep like that, if I moved around he'd hold tighter. He was afraid I was going to leave him. We never had sex, he couldn't do it. Just hold me, for hours, and sometimes he'd wake up calling for his mother . . ."

"Is that her?"

"Yes."

"Jack's theory is that the army followed you after the accident. They had an agent in the house."

"How'd you get the tape?"

"Better talk to Jack, he's up on this project."

Cable felt empty. "Send my money."

"Of course. It's yours. You've had a bad time, no one can blame you for wanting to quit. You've done a good job, Cable. I don't want to lose you again, but the decision is ultimately yours. The money will be there before noon. Good luck."

Barrett hung up.

Rice was in the motel parking lot surveying the damage to the bus. Cable watched him wriggle under the sagging rear end. The bus was canted back on its ruined wheel rims. One side window was broken and Rorschach blots of black paint obscured several others. One silver side was dented where the biker had been flung against it. The bus had looked worse on the highway in the stabbing shaft of police searchlights, surrounded by orange warning flares like death candles.

Rice crawled out and wiped his greasy hands on a rag. He looked amazingly fresh, bright-eyed. "Couldn't sleep either?"

"No. I walked around."

"You handled yourself very well last night. You were steady."

"You sound surprised."

"No, but I've learned never to judge a man until he's been tested. Some of you quiet, detached guys are just holding yourselves together by your fingernails. Did you know they had to tranquilize one of the astronauts in flight?"

"I never heard that."

"Of course not. Bad for the image. We were all supermen." Rice touched his shoulder. "Enough ancient history. Listen. The media's been on the horn since dawn. I've scheduled a press conference for noon. I want you to make sure every paper, magazine, radio and TV station knows where we are. I'll give you Lefferts' number. Fill him in. Ask him to come in tonight and bring cash. We'll need a mechanic for the bus. I want the work done here. Check the hours at the hospital."

Cable tried to frame an escape but he was transfixed by the eyes, demanding, including.

"Cable, do you remember in Oklahoma I said you'd have to make a decision, a committing decision?"

"I remember."

"I know you made it this morning. You could have kept walking, right out of here. But you didn't. I'm glad you didn't."

He turned back to the bus.

Cable knew he would stay.

The Sons staggered out of their rooms, sore, bleary, touching themselves in physical inventory. Once they were convinced they had survived intact, they began to swagger and talk too loudly. Cable arranged for a rear section of the motel coffee shop screened off for their meals. He felt a brisk confidence.

Georgie chattered with his mouth full of scrambled eggs. "Did we ever whomp the shit outta those greasers, hadda pick 'em up with blotting paper."

"They was screaming like cunts," said a bandy-legged boy called Tom Chase. "Big deal Hell's Cunts, riiiight? Messed with the wrong studs this time."

Captain Mack beamed. He asked Cable, "The Commander say anything?"

"He said he was pleased by the way you handled yourselves."

The boys swelled. Cable thought: He has made me his extension, his transmitter. His power flows through me.

Rice trooped the hospital rooms, a general visiting his wounded after a victory. Larry was in intensive care, tubed and wired. The blood clot would have to be dissolved or removed. The others were in satisfactory condition. The glass had been picked out of Johnny Avery's eye. Ben Edes' arm was in a cast. He had probably broken it scrabbling under a bus seat but he gazed at it as if it were a medal. Rice asked Jack why he had risked his life to help them.

Jack shrugged and flashed his ingenuous grin.

"I was heading home. The surf's up. They were in my way."

"Did you recognize the bus?"

"Not until I was real close. Look, Commander, I'm not one of your pony-tail patriots, I'm just a guy hanging loose.

It was drive through 'em or drive around 'em, and I've got another sixteen hundred miles before I hit the beach."

Rice nodded. "You'll stay with us until your car's fixed. I'll pay the bill. If there are any charges against you we'll take care of that, too. Your motives are your own business. But, thanks."

Rice led the Sons out. Cable closed the door behind them.

Jack said, "You know, I think Rice might've done it all by himself. He can really push iron. I was watching for a while. Sooner or later those clowns would've gotten careless or tired. If they were serious pros they wouldn't have fooled around, they would have trapped the road or come up shooting. Did I play Moon Man right?"

"Sure. He's taking anybody these days. I talked to Barrett this morning."

"Was he pissed?"

"Why?"

"It was a little sloppy. Barrett's an aunty on rough stuff. One time Sand got caught in a riot, a cop started spraying mace and one of the brothers pulled a gun. Sand punched out the cop so he wouldn't get shot. They arrested Sand, and Barrett chewed his ass to the bone. He'd rather the cop got shot."

"I thought Sand was a psychologist."

"He is. Old Superspade. Got a Ph.D. and a black belt in karate. He was a chopper pilot in Nam. He can do it all. And he lets you know it. One time we . . ."

"You better get some rest." Cable felt uneasy.

"Just a little rubbery, that's all. I'll get sprung tomorrow. Is that okay?"

"Take it easy. We've got ten days to the Fourth."

He was at the door when Jack called. "Mr. Cable? Seriously. I'm really glad to be working with you. Did I ever tell you we studied . . ."

"You told me. See you later."

It wasn't until he caught up with Rice in the hospital lobby that he remembered he was going to ask Jack about Bonnie Fuller.

The newsmen were fascinated. He was an astronaut, he had killed two men. He was obviously possessed. And they sensed a continuing story.

"Commander Rice. After the Speedway incident you were quoted as saying the motorcyclists had been paid to shut you up. What about last night? Was that a paid hit, or do you think they could have been just out for revenge?"

Rice frowned thoughtfully at the question. He stood between a thicket of microphones and the scarred flank of Liberty Two. Coppery threads glinted in his close-cropped hair. He was wearing the trousers of his dark suit and a wrinkled white shirt open at the neck. The rolled sleeves were smudged with grease. Cable wondered if he had planned to give the impression that he had been caught in midflight, busy, intense, careless of appearance.

"Three weeks ago I thought the Galloping Ghosts were just a pack of semipro hoodlums who fire-bombed our bus for kicks and a hundred dollar bill. But last night's attack was so well-conceived and executed that I have to believe it was part of the conspiracy to keep the American people deaf and dumb to the source of their deep discontent."

"Do you think the government was involved?" A reporter pointed to the mike of a tape recorder.

Rice hesitated, as if weighing repercussions. "Yes."

The reporter pressed forward in the crowd, mike high. "That's a serious statement. Can you back it up?"

His voice was young and challenging. Cable, on the periphery of the crowd, stood on his toes to see him. The reporter had hair to his shoulders and a full, untrimmed beard. The new breed, Cable thought, all hair and noise.

Rice answered smoothly. "I can't back it up right now without more information. I'm counting on you people to do your jobs."

"Commander!" A woman waved frantically. "How do you feel being back in Houston?"

There were scowls and snickers at the turn in the interview, but Rice nodded at the question. "I chose Houston to launch the Liberty Caravan because this city is very important in my life. I spent a great deal of time here, my wife and friends and colleagues are here. There's an old saying, Home is where you start out from."

The woman fell back on her heels, triumphant. Cable marveled at the subtle change in Rice's expression and posture. The stern hardness had melted into relaxed sentiment. An angle for every typewriter and film editor.

"Back to your charges against the government." New breed again. "Don't you think that's paranoid?"

Rice's voice turned harsh. "Paranoid? I have four men in the hospital. One of them has a blood clot on his brain." He gestured impatiently at the jacked-up rear end of Liberty Two. Four work shoes stuck out. "Is that a delusion? We've been chain-whipped, fire-bombed, and almost wiped off the highway.

"I'll tell you why.

"Four months ago I touched my thumb and forefinger and made a ring around the planet. Believe me, that's a very profound experience.

"When I stood on the surface of the moon and saw the earth plain I understood how small we are in the universe, how desperately we need to be free from manipulation and fear and disease and war. We dare not step into the vastness of space if we cannot rule ourselves. I called for a second American Revolution because I believe our country can, and must, show the way again.

"They said I was crazy. Paranoid. I was quarantined.

"When men first returned from the moon they were quarantined until scientists were sure they hadn't brought back any organisms that might infect the people of earth.

"I was quarantined because I brought back an idea. The pirates were afraid I might infect the people of our world with the hope they can finally dare to be free."

He paused. "That's all I have to say now. I'll have further statements about my plans in Houston later in the week. If any of you have special needs please contact David Cable, the man in the tan suit to my left."

Rice walked briskly toward the motel. A few reporters detached themselves from the crowd and hurried after him. Most stayed to compare notes. The television cameramen filmed the reporters before they capped their lenses.

"Dave? Dave Cable?" The bearded young reporter extended his hand. "Remember me? Mike Vogel? From New York."

Cable reluctantly shook his hand.

"When you did that series on the Graymere Home I was a copyboy on the paper. When they let you quit a lot of the younger guys in the city room kind of gave up." He touched his beard. "I look a little different now."

Vogel was no more than twenty-two or three. Cable imagined his sharp, dark face without the beard. He didn't remember him.

"Who you with now, Mike?"

"I'm stringing for a chain of suburban papers." He wrinkled his nose. "The desk fights over who gets to butcher my copy."

Other reporters pressed around them. Several wanted private interviews with Rice. Cable took their names and promised to call.

"Listen, Dave, you're busy now. Can I call you later? I'd really like to get together. I could use some advice."

"Sure, Mike. I'll be here." He watched Vogel walk away.

He rarely forgot a name or face, but neither fit in the city room.

Most of the other newsmen were still interviewing each other. Vogel walked to a green Ford GT parked near the motel office. He must have come early to get that spot. A suburban stringer paid by the column inch should have barreled in late with a notebook full of other interviews. Driving a secondhand Chevy. He dismissed the thought. Rice's paranoia is infectious.

"Mr. Cable?" The woman who had asked Rice about Houston tugged his sleeve. She was short and buxom with the long, coyly sweet face of a llama. "Could I see the Commander right now? Alone."

"I don't think he . . ."

"I interviewed his wife this morning. He might want to comment on some of the things she said. Or at least hear them before we print them."

"Just a minute, I'll see." The llama's face disguised shark's instincts. The old breed.

She followed him through the lobby. Captain Mack and Georgie Trott were escalating their heroics for several radio reporters. They lowered their voices as Cable passed. Rice's door was closed.

He knocked. "It's Cable."

"Come on in, the door's unlocked."

Rice was on the bed, his hands under his head, staring at the ceiling. The drapes were drawn against the sunlight.

"There's a woman outside, she said she interviewed your wife this morning."

"Bring her in."

Rice did not change position when Cable returned. His eyes flicked over the woman. "*Houston Tonight.* Betty Barker. I thought I recognized you out there."

"That's very flattering, Commander." She lowered herself to the edge of the other bed and lit a cigarette. Her hand trembled as she reached for the night-stand ashtray.

"What did Cissie tell you?"

"Let me be absolutely frank, Commander. A very nice young man from NASA picked me up at home this morning, bought me breakfast, and drove me to your house. Cissie was waiting for us. Her bags were packed. She said she was leaving Houston for a while. The nice young man taped my interview and took pictures of me and Cissie. She cried. I felt I was being used, but it is a story."

"I appreciate your honesty." Rice sounded disinterested.

"I realize this may be very painful for you. I still remember the day we spent shooting the cover story. You two seemed so close. I was jealous."

"NASA flew me back from the Cape just for your story. It was the first full day we spent together in almost two months."

"She said something happened to you in space. You came back changed. This is a quote." She flipped open her notebook. "'Chuck didn't come back from the moon. A stranger came back in his body. But I still love him very much, and I pray for his return. Chuck needs help, he's sick. I can't reach him and I can't bear to be here seeing him like this and feeling so helpless.'" She closed her notebook carefully, as if not to disturb the words.

"Open your notebook, Miss Barker." Rice might have been dictating a letter. "My wife is a drug addict. She started taking pills when I entered the program. She's been institutionalized twice. You can check that out. We haven't been husband and wife in nearly two years. I'll take most of the blame. I was too involved in the program to help her." He turned his head. "Tell me this, Miss Barker. Did the very nice young man tell you I was scrubbed off Apollo 11 because NASA was afraid she'd commit suicide? They didn't consider that fitting for the first man on the moon."

Betty Barker stood up. "I'm very sorry, Commander."

She looked at Cable. The llama nose and mouth were quivering. Cable followed her to the door and opened it. She hurried down the corridor. Cissie's quote would never appear in *Houston Tonight,* Cable thought.

Rice had rolled over on his side, facing the drapes. Cable tiptoed back in, snuffed out the cigarette in the ashtray, and locked the door on his way out.

His own motel room was similar to Rice's: small, neat, inconspicuously furnished. The twin beds were narrow, the brown carpet clean but pocked with cigarette burns. The only attempt at pure decoration was a large bronzed eagle spread on one walnut-papered wall. The eagle's dull finish was flaking. The beak had been miscast; it was slightly twisted, giving the eagle a pathetically defenseless look. He wondered if the owners had bought out a warehouse of factory-reject eagles and slapped them up as a final touch, unaware or unconcerned that the shoddy emblem diminished their rooms. They probably just didn't care. The highway police had suggested the motel, accessible, convenient, and rarely busy these days because of new bypassing highways. It had seemed like an excellent location, but now, feeling sour, Cable decided the police had steered them for kickbacks. Cable remembered Cissie.

Willowy, graceful, a mass of blond hair framing small, lovely features. He had met her briefly, seven years ago. She had come into their living room while he interviewed Rice, pouting silently because Cable was making them late for a dinner party. Cable became uncomfortable and hurried through his questions. He knew the Rices had little time together. Rice had sensed his discomfort. He suggested they meet again, this time in his cramped office at the airfield.

An addict? Rice, with his steely discipline, would call her an addict for a few bottles of ups and downs. Susan took sleeping pills, she never abused them, but he had resented the deep sleep that shifted the responsibility for the baby at night to him. He made her promise never to take them when he was out of town. He said he was afraid if the house caught fire she wouldn't wake in time to get out. She promised. But he was never sure.

He remembered something about his son.

When the little boy first learned to pee into the toilet, Cable would kneel beside him, one hand bracing his back, the other holding his pudgy hand to his pencil-stub penis. Sometimes the little boy would pee on Cable's hand, a warm golden trickle that made Cable laugh until tears filled his eyes.

He told Susan it was incredible that he could actually enjoy someone peeing on him.

She understood.

They were all subdued at the evening meal. The Sons were talked out. Rice picked at his food. The newsmen were gone, the mechanics had left for the day, a few families and couples on the other side of the screen were absorbed in themselves. The Sons were spinning out coffee and dessert when Howard Lefferts swept into the coffee shop. The lawyer's shoulder-length gray hair swirled dramatically around his pitted face. Without Wendt and Knox he seemed larger, more assured. He ignored the boys and nodded perfunctorily at Cable as he sat down next to Rice and began talking in a voice too low and deep for the others to hear clearly. He balanced an attaché case on his knees, opened it and withdrew a pen and yellow legal pad. The case was crammed with sheafs of typewritten onion-skin paper. He used the case as a desk to make notes as he talked. He flourished his silver-nibbed pen.

Cable signaled the boys to follow him out. In the lobby Captain Mack asked, "Isn't that the big Commie lawyer?"

"He's generally called left-wing."

"What's the Commander want with him?"

The red message button on Cable's phone was lit. He considered disregarding it. Another request for an exclusive photograph of Rice like all the other photographs, another interview with the same questions. But he had nothing else to do. He called the desk clerk. A message from New York: Please call Sentry Press—urgent. No name.

He strolled casually out of the motel. Through the coffee-shop window he saw Rice and Lefferts, head to head. The Sons were sprawled on metal chairs around the small pool, idly watching a seven-year-old girl back flip off the diving board. Cable took a circuitous route to the outdoor phone booth.

Barrett's secretary read him the name of a downtown Houston hotel, and a room number. She repeated it and hung up.

First he saw smoke curling toward the ceiling. Sand sat on the only chair in the tiny single room alternately sipping at a little cigar and a highball glass. Cable stood in the doorway until he had willed himself numb against all props waiting in psychic ambush.

"Relax," said Sand cordially. "I just dropped by to say hello."

"You were in the neighborhood," said Cable dryly. "Did you fly down in your own helicopter?" He walked in.

Sand raised his eyebrows. Cable had never noticed before that Sand's hairline was receding in an even curve. It made his smooth brown face seem rounder than it was. "Helicopter?"

"You're a modest man. You never told me you were a helicopter pilot, a karate expert, a . . ."

"Jack talks too much," said Sand mildly. "How are you feeling?"

"Not glad to see you."

"That's real. Have a drink."

"What's in it?"

Sand poured from an open bourbon bottle into a glass of half-melted ice cubes. He's been waiting, Cable thought.

"How's it going?" asked Sand.

Cable sat on the bed and faced him. He saluted with the glass. "A-OK, as they say. But astronauts never say A-OK. Did you know that?"

"Skip that noise," said Sand. "I didn't come down for a report. How are you?"

Cable swung his legs up on the bed and leaned against the headboard. "I'm all right. Was Barrett angry about this morning?"

"Do you care?"

"I don't think so."

"Do you care what Rice thinks of you?"

"Rice?" He realized he said it too sharply. He took a long drink of bourbon. It was smooth.

Sand said, "Rice threatens you. His positive energy, his willingness to be his own subject, object and instrument. His demands on you. His expectations."

"His wife's a pillhead."

"Do you think Rice would have just split after his wife and son were blown up? Or do you think Rice's wife and son would never have been blown up?"

Cable turned to the window, sealed for air-conditioning. New white buildings were outlined against a gray dusk.

"Cable, I told you once, it's all got to come out. We've got to get it out and deal with it. Before it tears your head off."

Cable drifted but was not aware of passing time. The buildings disappeared. Neon signs glowed in the night. Sand's voice came to him from a dark distance.

"Were you going to leave them for Lynn?"

"No."

"You were going to let things ride as long as you could, cheat on them, cheat on the Center, cheat on Lynn. . . ."

"Lynn knew."

"She knew you had a wife and child?"

"She knew everything. The Center, everything." He turned for Sand's reaction.

Sand tried to blow a smoke ring, failed. The broken circle drifted to the ceiling and was crushed. Puff on that, you cool omnipotent bastard.

"Who do you think planted the bomb in your car?"

"Someone in the house. They were always talking about doing something like that."

"Lynn told them who you were."

"No. She never would. The others resented me, I had her and I was taking over." It began to spill out easily, liberation again.

"They followed me home that night. I thought someone was following me but I was sure I lost them. I drove around for hours to be sure. The next morning I told Susan to use the Volks. I told her I needed the trunk space in the big car to pick up some things. Lynn and I were going to get away for a couple of days, think things out, and I didn't want to use the same car I was using on the assignment. I was still in the house when Susan . . ." The words dried up.

After a while Sand said, "You told me you were screwing Lynn when the car blew. Face it, man, Lynn booby-trapped the car, she did it to get rid of them so she could have you to herself."

"No."

"And then she couldn't cope with what she did and she went down to the basement while everybody was asleep and she pulled a pin. Goodby house."

He tried to get up, even roll off the bed, but he couldn't move. Sand's voice droned on.

"You killed them, Cable, you killed Susan and the boy and Lynn and you're going to kill Bonnie Fuller and you can't do anything about it because you kill everyone who offers you love. Like you killed your Mommy."

His insides gushed out. "I killed them all," he said. He thought Sand wanted to hear that. Sand was all he had left.

"Maybe you did, maybe you didn't," said Sand. "We don't really know. But it doesn't matter. We have to deal with what's in your mind."

This time Cable is inside the red Volkswagen, helplessly watching Susan's fingers turn the ignition key. The car explodes and the falling metal petals, the pieces of glass and bone, the sneakers rain down without touching him. The steering wheel rises in a lazy arc, turned by a hand without an arm. This time the hand wears a ring, a gold wedding band on its outstretched pinky.

He awoke alone in the room. A brilliant wedge of sunlight cracked the window drapes. He sensed the ebb tide of alien chemicals in his brain. He got up and washed his face. The only traces Sand had left were two rinsed glasses on the bathroom sink and a litter of white plastic cigar tips.

It was late morning. He found a cab outside the hotel. He asked the driver to take him to the main Western Union office and wait.

The Western Union clerk checked his identification.

"You'll have to answer a question, Mr. Cable. Final verification. What is your son's name?"

He fled into the street. The driver honked as he ran past. He stopped. He had the driver take him to the outdoor booth near the motel, but after the cab left he changed his mind. No hurry. Think it through. We can both play games. The feverishly warm streets undulated. He felt dizzy. He watched an orange Porsche careen through a screaming U-turn and brake alongside him in an explosion of grit.

"Hey. David Cable."

The car had ski racks and New York plates. The curbside door opened and a head of chestnut curls poked out. He recognized the tunneled eyes and the strong features immediately, but he looked at her blankly.

"Jean Stryker," she shouted. "The photographer in St. Louis. You were afraid I was going to hijack your bus."

He walked to the car.

"Want a lift? I think I'm going your way. Eagle Motel, right?"

He climbed in.

"Fasten your belt, I've been driving all night. I just got in. I was in New Orleans; I saw you on television. You're his press secretary now. No more I am a camera?" She pulled into traffic. At a red light she peered into his eyes. Hers were brown, yellow-flecked. "You look awful. God, you must have been through hell. That must have been a nightmare on the highway."

He began to laugh to himself, lips clamped over chattering teeth, a silent insane laughter that roiled his stomach and whistled through his nose. Nightmare? I am the hero of a nightmare, a serialized nightmare, sets by Sand.

"Are you all right?"

"I'm fine." He forced a smile. "Just beat. Here we are."

They were all standing in the parking lot watching the mechanics mount a new bus axle. The Sons grinned and nudged each other when Jean stepped out of the car. Her wrap-around skirt barely covered her crotch. Jack pretended to wipe sweat from his gauze bandage and fling it away with a limp wrist. Rice was coldly watching Jean shrug her cameras and knapsack onto her shoulders as Cable walked up to him.

"Cable, your personal life is your own concern, but next time you treat yourself to a night out let someone know. I won't waste time worrying about you." He finally looked at Cable. "I wanted you. Lefferts is setting up an appointment at the Astrodome. Larry needs specialists. The national magazines have been calling. And you're . . . out."

His voice was icy and his eyes were pale blue stones.

Ten

The Astrodome surprised Cable. Approaching the great beige blister he anticipated a plastic insult, a raucous pizza parlor ballpark. But the stadium was light and gay, an air-conditioned playroom. Rings of terraced seats ascended to a carpeted promenade. A peripatetic cocktail party of sleek men and women trailed laughter and oil talk as they ducked in and out of privately leased rooms disguised as Oriental tea parlors and French boudoirs.

"It's gorgeous," said Jean. "It transcends vulgarity. I thought it was going to be sterile, a super fallout shelter, but it's absolutely gorgeous. Do you think this is the future, all of us living in air-conditioned, color-coordinated domes with synthetic grass? Maybe under the ocean?"

"On Sundays they'll let us walk outside," said Cable. "Five dollars a head."

"Except that everything would be dead outside, or maybe like a Brooklyn slum, or a really grungey Indian reservation. Hey, Cable, stand right there, behind the boys. I'm going to circle around for a wide-angle."

Rice and Lefferts were ushered off to the executive offices. Jack and the Sons settled into royal blue seats to watch the baseball game far below. A Houston player hit a home run and the scoreboard exploded with bucking horses and fire-snorting bulls with American and Texas flags sprouting from their horns. The sound system crackled with lowing herds, bugles, the hoof beats of a cavalry charge, a fusillade of bullets. Ben Edes winced and hugged his cast at the recorded shots.

A new pitcher ambled to the mound. Cable wondered if Rice and Cissie had ever come to a game at the Dome, wandering into private rooms with drinks in hand, proud of the excitement their appearance stirred. Rice might have thrown out the ball to start a game. He thought of Davey and his father in the dank upper reaches of Yankee Stadium, over polite, Davey eating too many hot dogs, his father stiff in a dark overcoat and hat among the car coats and windbreakers, pretending interest, self-consciously cheering, relieved when it was finally time to descend again to the subway for the long rattling ride back to the empty apartment.

"Hey, are you a baseball freak?" Jean reloaded a camera, a cigarette waggling in a corner of her mouth. "Reliving old glories on the gridiron? No, that's football. The diamond. I thought you looked like a tennis player."

"Swimmer," he said without thinking.

"Me, too. And basketball. My brother made me stand under the damn backboard for years while he practiced dribbling around me. One day I finally knocked the ball out of his hands and sank a jump shot from the corner. He never played with me again." They laughed together.

An usherette touched his arm. "Mr. Cable? There's a call for you. You can take it over here."

Rice's voice was low. "They're complicating it. I'll be here for a few hours. Why don't you go back now, hold the fort. Don't leave until I get there."

He resented the implied rebuke. "I'll see you back at the motel."

Jean was at his elbow. "If you're willing to risk it I'll give you a lift. Just one more shot."

He nodded. Jack was on his feet, cheering. Cable touched his shoulder.

"I have to get back. You can stay as long as you like."

"Helluva game. Say, you never told me where you picked up that long number."

"Enjoy the game."

"You, too."

In her car, Jean asked, "How did you get together with Rice?" She drove with one hand and hunted for a cigarette with the other in a leather box between the bucket seats.

"I did a magazine piece years ago when he was a test pilot. When this thing started I thought he'd make a book. Nobody's really done an astronaut inside out. What are you doing?"

"Oh, sort of serendipping around. I got tired of illustrating other people's ideas. I'd like to do something really meaningful, a long photo essay. I'm trying to sort of capture the American experience in visual terms, the similarity of experience in different parts of the country among different kinds of people. That must sound awfully vague and pretentious to you."

"It could be very effective."

"I think it could work if I find the right thread, something everyone has to react to, but not something obvious like love or death or kids. Actually, right now I'm trying to work up a portfolio. I'd feel a lot more confident if I had a publisher, or at least some interest. Do you think your friends at Sentry might go for something like this?"

He glanced at her but she was watching the road. "I'd be glad to ask them."

"I'd appreciate that."

She drove into the motel parking lot. A crowd surrounded Liberty Two. Tom Chase, surly at being left behind, circled the bus, warning their hands off with his night stick. The motel manager had hung a sign above the office door: HEADQUARTERS OF LIBERTY II.

"Hey, I have a great idea. Want to take a swim? I've got to run downtown to check out darkroom space, but I'll be right back. The pool isn't exactly Olympic size, but it's wet."

"I don't have a suit."

"I'll get you one. What size?"

"Thirty-two."

"I'll call as soon as I get back."

The red message button was lit. The clerk had a handful of telegrams and green message slips. Cable spread them out on his bed. Associated Press, UPI, the Washington *Post,* local talk shows, university student unions, names, please return call, urgent. He sorted them into piles—obvious interview requests, speaking engagements, possible personal calls. One name registered, Marnie Quarles. He recalled society-page pictures of a formidable beauty who entertained presidents and royalty in a Frank Lloyd Wright mansion surrounded by thousands of acres of grazing land.

He returned the news media calls first, setting up tentative interviews. The desk clerk interrupted with more slips. Cable asked for a typewriter and left the door ajar. He started on the speech pile.

He heard soft footsteps and without looking up waved the desk clerk toward the bureau. When he finally turned, Jean was standing on one foot in the middle of the room, balancing a gift-wrapped box on her head. He shrugged and pointed at the piles of slips. He covered the mouthpiece. "I'll call you later." She made a face, dropped the box on a bed and tiptoed out. For the first time he noticed the lines around her mouth and eyes, the lines of a woman who laughed and cried and made faces. Susan had tried not to let her emotions register on her face, she was afraid of lines. She had even told Cable not to frown so much while he was writing, the wrinkles on his brow would become permanent.

Late in the afternoon, most of the slips spiked on a dried-up ballpoint pen, a three-page summary of calls typed, Cable opened the box. The bathing suit was conservatively styled, white with blue piping, boxer trunks with a built-in nylon supporter. A functional suit, comfortable enough for swimming laps, long enough to wear around the motel without feeling half naked. He might have bought it for himself. Her taste pleased him. Susan would have bought tiger-striped briefs that strangled his groin. Lynn would have hacked off the legs of his Levis, or dared him to swim bare ass. He thought of calling Jean to thank her, but a faint dread held him back.

Rice returned from the Astrodome with schedules and diagrams. He looked tired. "They're very efficient up there, all smiles, but they keep saying they have to check with the County Authority and the Baseball Commissioner and the network. I'll have to get Wendt to apply some pressure from the other direction." He ran his finger down Cable's lists, paused at Marnie Quarles, then hurried on. "Good job."

"Some of them ask about a speaking fee."

He thought for a minute. "They can make a contribution to the hospital for the Lawrence V. Bruno Memorial Fund." He nodded at Cable's unspoken question. "About an hour ago. They couldn't dissolve the clot."

"Couldn't or wouldn't?"

"No, I believe they tried. The clot must have broken

loose on the highway." He shook his head. "We had to take the risk."

Four motorcycle troopers escorted Liberty Two to the airport. The Sons manhandled Larry's casket out of the bus into the cargo hold of a chartered plane. Joey Field blew taps. Chills rippled through Cable's body. Jean Stryker shot with a long lens from a respectful distance, but the newspaper photographers and the television cameramen swarmed over the tarmac like maggots. They jostled for better angles as Rice walked slowly to the hatch and held up two long silver jewelry chains. From each dangled a charred metal medallion.

"These medallions, designed by Larry Bruno, were salvaged from the burnt wreck of the first Liberty Two." The round plates gyrated slowly at the ends of their chains. Sunlight touched the tiny silver rocket streaking across the red and white stripes of the flag.

Rice leaned into the hold. The cameras pressed closer as he placed a medallion on the casket and looped the chain around the handles. He hung the other medallion around his neck.

"I will wear it until the second American Revolution is a reality instead of a vision, until Larry Bruno's sacrifice is justified by history."

He saluted the casket, turned and strode through the photographers. They scrambled out of his way.

Jack climbed into the hold and shut the hatch. He would accompany the body home. The bolt thudded into place.

The red message button was always lit. Cable submerged in administrative details, arranging interviews and transportation, screening all calls, paying bills from a strongbox filled with the cash Lefferts doled out. Cable began to anticipate Rice and make decisions for him:

no commercial endorsements of any kind; Captain Mack could recruit new Sons for the Astrodome show. He hired security guards to patrol the corridors against the photographers, the souvenir hunters, the occasional teen-aged girl.

He missed Jean Stryker for almost two days before he inquired at the front desk, overcasually. She hadn't checked out but her bed had not been slept in. He felt a vague loss, then consciously dismissed her, another disconnected girl using journalism as an open ticket. Capture the American experience. She could rattle around in that for years.

When she reappeared one evening in the coffee shop, he could not suppress a welcoming smile. She loped toward him, her eyes deeper than ever, ringed with dark circles. She smelled of tobacco and chemicals. She handed him a fat envelope and walked away before he could open it.

Her photographs were clean, direct and simple. She had stopped time. The fever of Rice's possession, the angular thrust of his body on the platform, the willing vulnerability of the crowds. The Sons, their crabbed faces and miscast bodies quickening with pride. There were pictures of himself he had not realized she had taken—staring at Rice with the hungry intensity of a prospector for gold.

He went to her room. The door was open. She was on her knees sorting negatives, pretending absorption. She wasn't a very good actress, which pleased him. She tried to look startled by his knock but her anxious eyes betrayed her.

"Hey. Did you ever get that bathing suit wet?"

"Not yet. I haven't even had a chance to thank you for it. It was just right."

"I'm glad." She sounded glad. "Come on in."

"Jean, your stuff is great, you really caught it. There's a shot of Captain Mack, you've got him as a pompous Porky Pig and a scared kid at the same time. It would take me a thousand words if I could find the right ones."

"Oh, Cable." She hopped across the room and kissed his cheek. He backed out.

"Hey, I don't bite." She sounded hurt.

"I've got to run. Really. I'll show these to Rice. Maybe we can work something out. Can you ride with the Caravan for a while?"

"I'd love to."

"It could be the thread you're looking for."

Cable fled.

He rarely saw Rice eat and wondered if he slept. Rising early, he might meet Rice returning from his dawn run. After dark there was always light leaking out from under his door. The Astrodome speech. They talked on the fly, in each other's doorway, in cars. Rice would nod mechanically, his eyes glazed, as Cable read from his lengthening lists. At first he thought Rice was simply no longer concerned with the daily routine, he had stepped into another dimension. Then he slowly realized that Rice trusted him. His decisions grew bolder. The Caravan would accept the gift of an Airstream trailer if there was no public announcement or ceremony attached; Jean Stryker of New York had been appointed official Caravan photographer.

CDR. RICE INVITED
TO AD CLUB FÊTE

"I charge every man and woman in this room with murder. You've slaughtered millions on the highways in unsafe cars you've sold on a phoney promise of glamour and speed. You've poisoned America with worthless and, sometimes, lethal food, with liquor and drugs and cigarettes. You are responsible for the seeds of slow death planted in unborn babies, for the contagious lies that cripple minds.

You represent some of the most brilliant criminal brains in America. I charge you with premeditated murder for money."

Driving away in the silver station wagon, Rice asked, "What do you think?"

"You were very strong," said Cable. "I was watching their faces. At first they liked it, they thought you were pitching them their style, but once they realized you were serious they got mad. You didn't make any friends tonight."

"You sound like Wendt. I don't have to make friends, I'm not running for office."

"Is Wendt in town?"

"He's hiding under a haystack. But he's on the phone with Lefferts three times a day. He wants me to walk the line until after the Dome. Don't antagonize anybody, tell them what they want to hear."

"What does Lefferts say?"

"Lefferts is a lawyer. Underneath all that hair and philosophical peanut butter is a very old-fashioned steel-trap mind. Now that we're getting our way at the Dome, he's screwing down every clause and comma. He's playing it to the hilt. I'm not sure he's looking forward to stepping back when Wendt comes out of hiding."

Cable laughed. "You don't miss anything, do you?"

The city loomed up and surrounded them. It was nearly deserted, the streets washed in pools of sickly yellow light. The buildings tilted eerily, a hodge-podge city of old mission sandstone and tall glass, vacant lots and modern white cubes. Hurtling through the dead city he felt very close to Rice. Crewmates in space. For one hot moment he wanted to tell Rice about Susan and the boy. But Rice had never even asked him if he was married.

"Sunday night I'm going to the Quarles. I'd like you to come. Bring Jean if you want."

"Is it a party?"

"I'm not sure what it is. But I have a feeling Cissie's going to be there. They're going to use her to get at me."

Cable thought of Bonnie Fuller for the first time in almost a week. "Is she in danger?"

"Only from herself."

Rice jerked to a stop near the motel entrance and jumped out, leaving Cable to park the station wagon in front of Liberty Two.

Jack rapped on the door, waking Cable. "Just got in on the red-eye. Four days to blast-off. What's up?" He was irritatingly cheerful, but he had brought coffee.

"How'd it go?" Cable sipped the coffee black as he dressed.

"Larry's mother took it very hard." His voice became duly solemn. "He was the youngest son, the baby. She had this picture of Larry and Rice in front of a test plane on her mantelpiece. She smashed out the glass and tore it up. Then she picked up the pieces and held it against her chest and started moaning. I had to get out of there."

"Barrett have much to say?"

"Not too much. Superspade had plenty. He's very interested in Jean. Made me run a check."

"And?" Cable was surprised at his sharp annoyance.

"Jean's clean," said Jack quickly. "As far as any affiliation goes. Her private life . . ."

"Not important," said Cable. He didn't want to hear it from Jack.

"I understand," said Jack. "One thing interested them. Rice isn't getting much attention back East. A couple of paragraphs in the *Times*, a minute here and there on the network news. What does Mr. Paranoia think? The lid's on?"

"Rice thinks everybody's waiting for a consensus on the

Dome show before they jump on the bandwagon."

"That makes sense," said Jack.

The silver Airstream appeared without fanfare, a sleek apartment carpeted and cushioned in bright reds and blues. A small card read: The Greater Houston Association of Recreational Vehicle Dealers wishes Commander Rice and Liberty Two a successful mission. Lined up behind the silver station wagon and the silver bus, the Airstream made a caravan, a small one, but for the first time Cable could visualize a dazzling stream rolling across America.

He had it scanned for electronic devices. It was clean, too.

Quarles sent a two-engine plane for them. Rice was preoccupied throughout the flight. Cable imagined him programming the computer for Cissie. Input scraps of bitterness and tenderness and unresolved questions. Jean shot a few portraits of Rice in rare repose, then, sensing her intrusion, retreated apologetically. Cable had nothing to say to her. Her private life. . . .

From the air, the Quarles's compound was a jumble of odd boxes among swimming pools, tennis courts, a small golf course and a riding ring. Driving in from the airstrip it became a graceful cluster of glass and stone and redwood molded to the contours of the land. Wade Quarles, big and meaty, came out to meet them. "Chuck!" He shook their hands warmly and gathered Cable and Jean in his long arms as Rice strode ahead stiffly. They followed him through high, glass-walled rooms splashed with paintings and prints. A tall, handsome woman waited for them in the middle of a grand hall.

"Here they are, Marn."

She kissed Rice's cheek. He stared over her shoulder.

At first Cable was aware only of movement at the top of

the great stairs, white cloth swaying like a curtain at an open window, then the whisper of cloth. Silk? Cissie Rice descended slowly, a wounded princess, vulnerable but proud. Her back was straight but her head tilted forward, the small chin almost touching her black sweater. Strands of blonde hair lay scattered over her small, high breasts. Rice stood frozen at the foot of the stairs.

Wade Quarles touched Cable's arm. Marnie Quarles was already leading Jean into another room. Cable looked over his shoulder as he followed them. Cissie's long legs were outlined inside her loose white pants. Her eyes smoldered in an ivory mask. Rice had not moved.

The Quarles were a smooth team. Wade steered Cable to a teak bar. Marnie arranged herself on a couch and patted the leather for Jean to join her.

Jean clutched the shoulder straps of her camera. Her voice was angry. "That was an ambush."

"It was the only way, dear," said Marnie gently. "Please sit down."

"This is what friends are for," said Wade. "What are you folks drinking?"

Jean looked at Cable for support. He felt challenged.

"We've been in Houston a week," he said. "Not one call from anyone at the Space Center, everybody who ever worked with him is conveniently unavailable to the press. NASA produced her for Betty Barker, and then got her out of town. When that flopped they . . ."

"She's been staying with us, Mr. Cable," said Marnie. "It's been very hard for her. She loves him very much."

"If she loved him she would have been with him," said Jean.

"She's been real sick, honey," said Wade. "She's never been what you call a strong woman. When Chuck cracked up she just fell apart."

"I know you're friends of Chuck, we care about him,

too," said Marnie, "but you don't know the half of it. They were two perfect people. When Chuck and Cissie walked into the room the music stopped. It was breathtaking. People expected so much of them, they began to expect too much of each other. Did you know they had a child? A poor little . . ."

"Marnie!" Wade looked at Cable. "You said bourbon?"

"Are you enjoying Houston?" asked Marnie. "We don't get in so often anymore, it's like a new city every time. Wade likes to tell visitors that he came back from lunch one day and his office building was gone."

Jean turned her back on them as Wade picked up the routine. "So I just went back for a second cup of coffee. Give 'em time to put up the new building." He winked at Cable. "True story."

"Of course, Wade's lunch was in Beirut," said Marnie brightly. A trouper all the way, Cable thought. He could not bring himself to dislike them. "Have you seen much of Texas, Miss Stryker?"

She turned around slowly, her jaw set.

Cable said quickly, "We haven't had much time. I was impressed with the Astrodome."

"Now that's a piece of work," said Wade. "The feller who put up that . . ."

"Cable!" Rice stood in the doorway, expressionless. "We're leaving. Right now."

They left the Quarles staring at each other.

A tiny muscle twitched under Rice's eye. His knuckles were white. They were aloft before he finally spoke. Then the words rushed out.

"They offered her a deal. Two hundred thousand dollars, tax free. A damage settlement. I'd sign a paper I had hallucinations on the Moon and the contractor would announce he found a fault in my pressure regulator."

He seemed smaller, somehow compressed, as if vital juices had boiled out.

"The administration's behind the deal. They're worried. They should be. The people know I'm not crazy, once they've heard me they know I've seen the earth plain, right through the confusion and the lies.

"They used her. She wants me to take the settlement. She doesn't understand at all. She said we could be together again. Start fresh, another city. An industry job, a university. Just the two of us again. . . ." His voice trailed off.

Just before they touched down, Jean said, "It was the dirtiest thing I've ever seen."

"The Quarles were never my friends. We went to their parties, all the astronauts did, but I never had much to do with them. Marnie always took an interest in Cissie. They went shopping together in Dallas, once they went to Paris while I was at the Cape. I hope they take care of Cissie now."

"Why did you ask us to come?" Jean's voice was soft and tremulous.

Rice watched the runway lights rise to meet them. "I'm not sure. I think I didn't want to leave that house alone."

"We're your friends," said Jean. She reached out as if to touch his arm, then pulled back. She understands, thought Cable. Rice is not a man for small comforting.

By the time the plane taxied to the general aviation terminal Rice seemed in full control again, juices replenished. But he let Cable drive the wagon back to the motel.

The young reporter, Mike Vogel, called Monday morning. He sounded upset. He said he had quit his job. He wanted to see Cable before he left Houston. Could they meet for lunch? Cable stalled him. In forty-eight hours the Caravan would break camp for the Dome. Time was closing in. He promised to call Vogel later in the day. He made another note on a crowded list.

He spent most of the afternoon on the phone with the Governor's office in Austin. It was a shifty, ultimately inconclusive series of conversations. One of the Governor's aides said that a high state official, perhaps even the Governor himself, might be interested in a private meeting with Rice. Depending, of course, on public reaction to the Dome speech. Cable was noncommital. He said he wasn't sure if Rice could squeeze it in.

He went to Rice's room to report. The astronaut opened the door while Cable was knocking. He was swollen with energy.

"Forget the Governor. By Thursday morning we'll have Wendt and Knox on our hands, the White House'll be calling, we'll have to charter a press bus." He paced the room. "I'm almost finished with the speech. Cable, it's going to knock this country on its tail."

"When can I see it?"

"I want you to hear it fresh on Wednesday. Everybody's going to react out of their own hopes and fears. I'll need an honest, objective evaluation. You're my true scale."

Cable smiled, as if complimented. He felt a twinge of guilt.

"Cable, I'll never forget the look on your face when you saw that beat-up old bus behind Larry's garage. Never fly, no way. We've come a distance since then, haven't we? And we've hardly begun. I'm only sorry Larry won't be with us."

"I'd better get back. The vehicles have to be . . ."

"You've come a long way yourself. You've shown me a lot."

Cable felt high.

"Take the night off, unwind a little. It might be your last

chance for a while. Jack's taking the boys to that amusement park near the Dome. Blow off some steam. Have you gotten a chance to talk to Jack? He's all right. There's more there than he'd have you think."

"Jack talks too much."

Rice smiled. "Why don't you buy that girl a drink and a steak. She deserves it."

Cable said he would.

The phone was ringing as he walked into his room. This time Vogel sounded scared. He suggested a back-street chili parlor. Cable said he'd be there at nine. Vogel told him to be sure he wasn't followed.

He debated calling Jean. Why bore her with some tales of bush-league intrigue? Vogel probably offended the wrong people in town; he was running scared from a libel suit or a good beating. But she might enjoy it. He liked the idea of having her with him.

She came breathless to the phone at the photo lab.

"I love chili. Would it be all right if I met you there? I've got the darkroom till nine, I want to be up to date before we leave. I'll try to make it earlier, but nine-thirty for sure. Is that all right?"

He was glad he had called.

The cab dropped Cable at the downtown bus depot. He bought a Coke and a Houston paper, and settled down on a curved wooden bench to read Betty Barker's column. There was still no mention of Cissie, only a paragraph about Rice: "A number of Space Folk, including one of Chuck Rice's 'moon-mates,' have been trying to contact their old friend during his current local orbits. But Chuck simply refuses to see them or even return their calls. One quipped to me, 'Chuck's in his own world.'"

That nice young man from NASA again.

He strolled to the men's room, leaving the paper open, the Coke container half full, as if he planned to return. No one seemed much interested. The grimy depot was quiet. A few black women dozed against their shopping bags. Teen-aged boys cuffed the pinball machines and watched the doors. The ubiquitous sailor and his desperate girl. Cable slipped into the dusk.

He walked shabby, repressed streets, past beer cafes played out from their week-end blasts. A man ambled along with a rifle in the crook of his arm. A dark-skinned girl sucked her lips at him from a hallway leading up to rooms over a shuttered locksmith's shop. Clap or a mugger waited upstairs. The mild exhilaration of playing spook in the bus depot evaporated. He had spent a dim month walking these streets in a dozen cities.

He was five minutes early at Chili Red's. Vogel was sitting in the back picking his beard.

"Thanks a lot, Dave." He banged the table with an empty bottle of Mexican beer and held up two fingers. An albino Negro with a rusty Afro and dark glasses threw back a cool O.K. sign.

"I'm leaving tonight."

"Where are you going?"

"I'm not sure. I've got some friends in a commune near Boulder, I might crash there a while. I never worked at the paper, you knew that. I could tell."

"I didn't remember you. What's it all about?"

"It's stupid, so goddam fucking stupid, they played me like a banjo." He tapped his heel while Red dropped the beer bottles and glasses on the table and sauntered away. "I got fucked up in college. A dealing rap. I panicked. When the narcs offered me a way out, I . . ." His mouth opened and closed.

"Okay, you informed," said Cable. "Are you still working for them?"

"I don't know who I'm working for. I got passed around. Look, let me lay it right out. Lynn was my sister."

Cable started to pour beer to keep his hands occupied but they were shaking too hard. "Vogel. She said Byrd wasn't her real name. Her little joke."

"She was straight. She loved you. I know you didn't kill her. They said you did, but I knew they were lying."

"Who?"

"I don't know. I swear I don't."

"Could they be Army?" asked Cable.

"Could be. I really don't know. They turned me every way but loose. I wanted out, I really did, but once you get tangled with those guys . . ." He settled down. "They know you're working. That's all they know."

"I'm writing a book."

"Look, you don't have to tell me anything. I don't want to know, man."

"They put you on me."

"That's right. But I can't hack it. Lynn really loved you. She wanted to go away with you, dump that whole scene. You were going to leave your family. You were." It was a question.

"She told you I was working. You told them."

"That's all she told me." His lips were nearly covered by hair, but they seemed full, almost too ripe for a man. Lynn's lips. The dark hair and eyes were hers, too.

"Who booby-trapped my car?"

"Oh, no, no, I had nothing to do with that, I swear that on my mother, I never did anything like that, I was strictly information. That was horrible." He closed his eyes and shook his head until his lips quivered.

Cable reached across the table to squeeze his shoulder. *I'm consoling this little rat, I should kill him. Rice would kill him.* "What about Rice?"

"They never said anything about him. I don't know."

"Who's your contact?"

"It's all phone now. I threw the number away." His lips flapped shut.

"Bonnie Fuller?"

"Who's that?"

"Forget it."

"Hey. Am I too early?" Jean dragged up a chair and plopped down. "Hi, Mike."

"You two know each other?"

Vogel looked apologetically at Cable. "I did a little feature on Jean. For the chain."

"Did you bring me a copy?" she asked.

"When I told her I had been your copyboy," said Vogel carefully, "she started interviewing me." A warning? "Wow, look at the time." He jumped up. "Back to the boondocks. Nice running into you, Dave. Jean. See you at the Dome." He almost ran out.

"Do we look like we want to be alone?" Her expression was almost coy. "Hey, are you mad at me?"

"For what?"

"For pumping Mike about you. You're such a private person, I'm afraid to ask questions. Sometimes I think you're positively poised for flight."

"What would you like to know?" He tried to give her his full attention but he kept seeing Lynn, so strong and assured, confiding in her soft kid brother.

"How you knew I loved chili." Her gaiety was a little forced, he thought.

"Let's get out of here." He tossed several dollars on the table. Chili Red hurried over to count them before they reached the door.

They ate in the red plush and black wood steakhouse of a downtown hotel, facing their reflections in a smoked rose mirror. Her presence beside him on the banquette disturbed Cable. Once he looked up to catch her regarding them soberly in the mirror. She looked away. A pink flush stained her high-boned cheeks. He wondered if it was only the wine.

"What did Vogel tell you?"

"What a great reporter you were. How you . . ."

"What else?"

"He told me about the accident. I cried for all of you, Cable." She poked at her meat. "How long were you married?"

"Five years. How did he happen to tell you about it?"

She shrugged, uncomfortable. "I kept pumping him. I don't think he really wanted to tell me. I asked him if you were married."

"What did he tell you about the accident?"

"What happened."

"What happened?"

She looked bewildered. "She was driving your son to school. A truck went out of control."

The dead woman in his mind had brown hair like his own, wind-blown in a summer mountain sun. A vacation snapshot cracked and curling in the night stand of the Teddy bear room. Her body lay in snow.

"It's still so hard for you, isn't it?" Her hand was on his arm, the fingers long and graceful, the nails clipped short.

"You were married," he said.

"How did you know?"

"I don't know. What happened?"

"We didn't make it. We couldn't help each other. We were very young and when we changed we didn't change together." It came out easily, she had said it all before. "I've been thinking about Rice and Cissie. Have you?"

Cable relaxed, grateful she had turned the conversation. "A little. I never knew they had a child."

"Wade didn't want Marnie talking about it. What do

you think happened? Do you think it died, some horrible way, leaving all sorts of guilt and recriminations?"

"It must have happened some time ago. Since he's been in the program he's lived in a fishbowl. He never mentioned it when I interviewed him, it's never been in one of his official biographies."

"I'm sorry I blew up at the Quarles'. But I hate it when a woman lets herself be used like that."

"Like what?" He glanced at the mirror. Her eyes were down.

"Weakness and sex. It's not fair to the man. It's so underhanded. And it degrades a woman, it makes her less than a real person."

"People use the weapons they have."

"People do terrible things to each other," she said.

They finished their meal in silence, quickly, separately, and drove back to the motel in her car. Cable excused himself from·Jean at the front desk to collect the latest green slips. He was still looking through them, stalling until he was sure she was in her room, when Jack and a dozen Sons burst into the lobby, laughing, their arms filled with three-foot dolls and Teddy bears.

"You really missed it, Mr. Cable," said Georgie Trott. "Jack wiped 'em out. The greatest shooting you ever saw. They wanted to throw us out of the place, but we would of maimed 'em."

Jack winked at Cable. "When you're hot, you're hot."

The dress rehearsal was flawless. Cable kept track of the allotted twenty minutes with clipboard and stopwatch. The nine-ton steel door behind centerfield rolled up and Georgie Trott, cock-proud behind the American flag, led twenty black-booted Sons out of the tunnel and under the Dome. Captain Mack drove Liberty Two thirty feet behind the marching ranks. Rice followed the bus. The procession reached the curve of outfield grass behind second base as a doughnut-shaped gondola loaded with light and sound equipment descended from the roof.

Rice mounted the rear ladder.

"Testing. Testing. One, two, three, four. This is Commander Charles Rice speaking from the Astrodome. Jack?"

A white handkerchief fluttered out of the gondola.

"This is Commander Charles Rice speaking from the Astrodome. Jean? Cable?"

A strobe light flashed from the sky-box level. Cable raised his clipboard.

"Scoreboard, please."

Lights blinked into words: WELCOME TO THE AS-TRODOME, CHARLES RICE, COMMANDER, LIB-ERTY TWO.

Rice turned slowly on the aluminum platform, sweeping every curve and corner of the hushed stadium. The stands were empty except for a few maintenance men. Cable wondered if Rice was already imagining the ball park swollen and throbbing, waves of sound crashing down around him, shafts of light pinning him to the dazzling silver roof.

"Cable. Signal me at plus two."

Rice looked down at his honor guard.

"Sons of Liberty. In less than twenty hours we will stand here again with all America watching the start of the second American Revolution. Your children will read about tomorrow as you read about the Boston Tea Party or the signing of the Declaration of Independence. Your names will be as familiar to history as the names of those heroes who put themselves on the line two hundred years ago.

"In twenty hours you will be part of the history of America. The history of the world. You will be the standard bearers of a new era. You will march to the drums of destiny. The world will recognize you as men and heroes. Dare be free."

The boys stood spellbound. The flagstaff never wavered in Georgie's hands. The flag stirred in the mile-an-hour air-conditioning breeze.

Cable held up two fingers.

"The Revolution has begun. On to Liberty."

Trott stepped out smartly on cue, leading the ranks in a wheeling turn that would bring them back to the center-field door. Rice braced as Liberty Two rolled forward.

Cable followed them down to the entrance tunnel. Rice was clattering down the ladder.

"On the button," said Cable. "Do you want to check out the TV control room now?"

"I'm sure you've done it already." He walked to the vast doorway and surveyed the empty field. "Well. Any comments?"

"Just the music," said Cable. "I still think there should be exit music."

"That's diverting," said Rice. "I want to leave them in absolute silence, for the first time in their lives facing the truth."

He dozed intermittently until dawn when Rice's door opened. He heard the astronaut jog down the corridor. He took a long, hot shower and went back to bed, but his muscles were still tight. Early light touched the flaking finish of the bronzed eagle on the wall.

He had not studied the eagle in days. The miscast bird of prey seemed fierce now instead of pathetic. Once he had thought the twisted, factory-reject beak had doomed it forever to just miss its target without knowing why. But this morning the beak was a killer's edge set for the strike.

Eleven

A dozen small television screens flickered in a gun-metal console; a pitcher shaking off his catcher's sign, faces in the Astrodome crowd, the scoreboard. Cable's eyes skipped among the blue windows searching for Rice. In front of Cable, the director, in a double headset, snapped into his mikes, "Camera Five, stay tighter. On the split screen, Three, you'll be on the left with the runner."

Cable found Liberty Two, snowy and blurred. Toy soldiers milled restlessly around the bus. The six original Sons stood apart. Captain Mack inspected their spit-shined boots and new collarless white shirts.

The two color monitors set on the far right of the console showed an identical picture, as they had throughout the ball game except during commercials. The top monitor was the picture transmitted from the Astrodome; the other, the picture going out over the network.

The control room door opened with a hermetic suck. A burst of crowd noise was choked off as the door sighed shut. The room seemed as insulated from the world as the

cabin of a spaceship. The producer squeezed past technicians and lifted one of the director's phones to whisper in
his ear. The director nodded without looking away from
his screens, but Cable thought he straightened in his swivel
chair.

Ninth inning, two out. One man on base. The game
could be over any second now. Then the centerfield door
would roll up for Liberty Two. Cable's thighs were damp.

On a monitor the Sons fell into ranks and snapped to
attention. On another monitor Rice strode along the concrete tunnel. He was wearing a navy blazer, gray trousers,
black shoes. A blue shirt and a dark red tie. An old uniform,
Cable thought. The only thing missing is a NASA mission
patch on his breast pocket.

The producer touched Cable's shoulder. "Some of our
brass just got in. Fantastic interest. The New York switchboard's a Christmas tree. We're going to pop the charts."

A camera swept the steel-webbed underside of the dome.
A trim figure jogged along a catwalk toward the gondola
snugged to the roof.

The director called, "Mr. Cable? On nine. One of yours?"

"Jack Lynch."

"Right. You want to come up here now?"

The producer pointed Cable to the empty swivel chair
beside the director.

"Stay with the runner, Four. Sharpen your focus. Cable,
the girl on seven?"

She was caricatured on the flickering screen, long legs,
bouncing curls, the knapsack bulging with lenses.

"Our photographer. Jean Stryker."

"Okay. On the split screen . . ."

The batter bounced a grounder to the second baseman.
He tagged the base, ending the game.

On both color monitors the players trotted off the field.
On one of the blue screens the Sons of Liberty stood at

parade rest behind Georgie Trott. On another, Captain Mack was climbing into the bus. Rice stood alone, head bowed over the medallion in his hands. In a corner of the screen Jean crouched to shoot up at him. The gondola was descending. The crowd was rising, heads craned toward centerfield. The scoreboard raced through the game's final statistics.

"Sharper, One."

An announcer was talking on both color monitors. Cable tried to read his lips. Astronaut . . . American Revolution . . . Liberty . . . Cable was not sure if the words were the announcer's or his own. The announcer faded off the color monitors. On the network monitor he was replaced by a baseball player shaving. On the local transmission the centerfield door rolled up.

The director leaned into his mikes. "Okay, tigers, this is it. On your toes. Nobody in the country's going to blink for the next twenty minutes."

Cable's eyes roved the console. The flagstaff jerked erect in Georgie's hands. Captain Mack flashed an O.K. sign from the driver's window. Rice let the medallion fall against his chest. The steel door rolled out of sight.

The commercial faded. The network monitor was blank. "Camera One. Beautiful."

A long shot. The scoreboard welcoming message. Georgie Trott, the massed Sons. Liberty Two glinted behind them.

The network monitor was still blank.

"Number Six, panning."

The procession moved onto the field. The console glowed with overhead views, side angles, a close-up of Rice marching triumphantly to his own drumming pulse beat.

Cable was aware of technicians scurrying behind him. The producer sidled in between the swivel chairs. "It's got to be them, not us." He picked up a red phone. "You got less than two minutes to find it. Yeah, he'll be on."

The network monitor: PLEASE STAND BY.

"What's wrong?" asked Cable.

The producer shook his head. "We're feeding New York perfectly."

Liberty Two stopped under the gondola. Rice mounted the ladder.

"You got less than a minute." He covered the mouthpiece. "Must be a break somewhere. It's not going out on the network. But our feed's perfect, they're close-circuiting it to the White House."

"Four and Nine. Steady, tigers."

On Four Rice reached the center of the aluminum platform and took his thrusting stance. Nine aimed down from the gondola, head, squared shoulders, spread feet.

PLEASE STAND BY.

The producer was muttering, "Come on, come on."

Rice began to speak. His lips moved, his hands clenched and rose.

"Turn up the sound," said Cable.

"Jesus. It's dead."

His stomach flushed ice water. They're killing him, sons of bitches, dirty bastards, motherfuckers pulled the plug. A scream gagged in his bilious throat. A truck skidded down the icy hill. He could not move or speak. Red petals burst into morning glory.

Faces in the crowd frowned, turned to each other. The Sons looked up at Rice. His arms were spread like eagle's wings. He exhorted the deaf sound booms. He was the only person in the country who didn't know they were killing him. That he was dead.

Cable jumped up. His swivel chair spun away and crashed into a machine.

"We're doing the best we can." The producer grabbed his shoulder.

"You pulled the plug, you dirty bastards." He found

himself struggling in someone's arms. A hand came around his head and clapped over his mouth.

"Please, Mr. Cable."

PLEASE STAND BY.

"Get him out of here, we got enough problems."

The door sucked open, arms shoved him out. He was in a tunnel. He ran on feet cased in lead. His steps boomed. He passed the exit ramp. The Airstream hooked to the station wagon was surrounded by a dozen riderless police motorcycles balanced on their kickstands.

He slowed to a walk and caught his breath. He pressed his forehead to a wall until his heartbeat slowed. He was drenched in sweat.

Jean was on her knees at the centerfield door, shooting. Laughter crackled through the stadium, jagged slivers among the deeper shouts and catcalls.

Rice was still speaking, unheard, a mad pantomine, a parody of himself.

"Jean, they killed him. He doesn't even know it."

"He knows. Look at him, Cable, he defies them. They can't stop him, he won't let them. Don't you see? They made it so he can't be heard, but he's showing them they can't shut him up."

The procession had turned, it was coming back toward them. The Sons marched raggedly, flinching under the jeering barrage, glancing over their shoulders at Rice.

He stood braced on the platform, shoulders back, face angled toward the skylight roof, a poised axhead. Cable felt small and shamed. Faithless. They can't stop him. Burn, shoot, blackmail, pull the plug. They can't stop him.

"Oh, God, look at him, Cable." Her camera was against her wet eye, clicking.

Cable stood beside her, suddenly tall with a surge of joyous power. They can't stop him. They can't make him run and hide. And I am part of him.

Twelve

The police motorcycles dropped away at the Houston city limit and they were suddenly three cars and a trailer and a secondhand schoolbus heading slowly west in the holiday traffic. They drove with their lights on to indicate a procession, and tailgated to prevent other cars separating them. Cable, alone in the station wagon towing the Airstream, felt his brief surge of joy slip away, leaving him drained, and then gloomy. A funeral procession, he thought. The Airstream was a silver coffin. In the Astrodome tunnel Rice had climbed down from Liberty Two, marched stolidly to the trailer and locked himself inside without a word. Now Cable imagined him lying on the rear bunk staring at the ceiling as if it were a sky filled with stars.

Cable squinted against the descending sun and tried to ignore the shouts and questions from passing cars. The station wagon had no air-conditioning, but he rolled up the window to close them out. He turned on the radio. The faces in the other cars were friendly and curious. They know who we are but they don't know what happened to us. In a few hours the faces will be mocking, or, worse, sympathetic. What do I care? But I do.

Cable's eyes moved tensely from the road to his side mirrors. He tried to prejudge every light and curve and railroad crossing for the trailer and the bus and the Porsche and the Ford. His neck and back ached with the strain of the lead, his hands, too tightly clenched on the wheel, stiffened. The tip of his spine was sore from the springs working up through the lumpy upholstery. He had to urinate badly, a pressure that swelled until it obliterated all his other little pains. He decided not to stop until his gas tank was nearly empty. By then it would be dark and there would be fewer people to see them.

A six o'clock newscast blandly reported the network's account of a power failure compounded by an engineer's error. By eight it was a feature item. One national commentator considered the technological irony of what he called Rice's dumb show. He solemnly announced that the second American Revolution had ended with neither a bang nor a whimper, but a silence as awesome as the silence of space. Cable sneered at the dial. Even school kids know that space is noisy. He wondered if Rice was listening to his obituaries.

Cable turned off the highway and found a large gas station with enough pumps to service them all quickly. In the men's room he gasped at the painful ecstasy of his urine's burning rush, then felt depleted, as if the anticipation of this relief was all that had kept him going. His joints ached, there was a crick in his neck. Coming out, he passed the seven boys waiting in line to use the bathroom. They were quiet and bewildered. He could think of nothing to say to them. Mack wiped his glasses with his shirt tail, his eyes drifting aimlessly.

Jack came out of an outdoor phone booth. "Barrett wants me back in New York. He's got something else for me to do."

"What did he say about me?"

"Just keep in touch." Jack offered his hand. "I'm really glad we had a chance to work together, Mr. Cable."

Cable shook his hand. "I guess he'll be calling me back soon, too."

"Say goodby for me, will you?" Jack nodded toward the locked trailer. "I feel like a rat deserting a sinking ship."

"Sure."

Jack waved as he gunned the black Ford into the darkness.

Cable drove another mile to a small restaurant with outdoor redwood tables. There were few customers. The boys jammed together on the benches of one table and ordered food without enthusiasm. Cable joined Jean. They both ordered coffee. She lit one cigarette from another.

"Did you tell him Jack left?"

"Not yet. Were you listening to the radio?"

"It made me mad. C'mon, let's go talk to him."

"He might want to be alone."

"At a time like this? Wait a sec." She ran to her car. He wondered if she would leave, too. She came back with a bottle of cognac.

He followed her to the Airstream. She knocked. Rice took his time opening the door, but he seemed glad to see them. His tie was loose and his sleeves were rolled above his elbows. "Come on in."

Jean found three paper cups in a galley cabinet and poured the cognac. "This is from my personal preference kit, Commander."

Cable winced at the space jargon but Rice smiled and took a cup to one of the front sofa beds. Cable and Jean sat on the other, facing him across a formica table cov-

146

ered with maps, felt marking pens, a drafting compass and a ruler. Rice hadn't been staring at the ceiling. He had been charting routes.

Jean raised her cup. "To Liberty Two."

The cognac was sharp on Cable's tongue but it spread smoothly through his body and relaxed him. In a moment of awkward silence, Cable said, "Jack left."

"I saw him talking to you," said Rice. "Was he afraid I'd try to persuade him to stay?"

"Would you have?" asked Jean.

"No. The only decision that has any commitment is the decision you make by yourself. I won't cajole."

"What about those poor boys in the bus?" she asked softly.

"Especially those boys. Carlyle wrote that a man cannot lead flunkies and parasites. He can only show the way to other free men. I've always believed that."

"Thomas Carlyle?" Jean made a face. "I did a paper on him once in college. Are you the hero-king?"

Rice smiled. "Hero-king. That's a little gaudy these days. Messenger, perhaps. A man who has come back from the infinite unknown with a message for all men. A man whose words are unique. A man who can see through the appearance of things to the things themselves. A man who can see the earth plain."

Jean swallowed her cognac. The rose stain surfaced on her cheeks. "Did you have a revelation on the moon?"

"That's a religious term. It connotes visions and voices. Nothing came to me. Something came out of me."

Cable said, "I've read about the breakaway phenomenon in high flight. The sense of detachment from all human limitations. A sense of omnipotence."

"That's just another way of saying I was drunk on oxygen. Let me try to explain. I think you two will understand."

Rice was at ease, he seemed to be enjoying the company and the conversation. He waited while Jean refilled her cup and Cable's. He had not drunk any of his own cognac.

"Imagine a computer programmed for a progression of logical accidents, a schedule of causes and effects created to find the one card in a billion with a punch-hole for every circuit. Every other card will be rejected, a missing bit of information, faulty data, an unacceptable series, a rip or a crease. Just one card makes it through the machine. Mine. Why?"

Rice lounged on the sofa, an elbow hooked on the square back cushion. He stared at the trailer ceiling.

"Two memories from my childhood. Watching my father stunt at an air show and listening to my mother give a piano recital in Philadelphia. They were talented people, beautiful people. Childish, incredibly selfish people. I've realized all this only lately, since I've been on the moon. My parents never had to grow up. The three of us were children together; we had no ordinary worries about survival, no moral decisions to make, no abstract uncertainties, no compromises, no cynicism, no sense of the limits of our possibilities.

"We lived in my grandfather's house, my mother's father. He was the mayor of the town, the bank president, the biggest land speculator in the county. He was ahead of his time. He bought a plane to romance investors and he hired the hottest pilot he could find, a barnstormer named Willie Rice. My dad. They called him Wild Rice.

"The old man was a father to the three of us. He used his money and his power to keep the world away from us, to create a world of his own. I had a horse before I had a bicycle and I soloed before I could drive a car. I had a tutor. I sat in that big house and read Aristotle and Aquinas and Voltaire and Carlyle. In a vacuum. I had no frame of reference beyond that house and the meadows and the sky. There was a gym in the basement. I worked out for two hours every day. A boxing teacher came up from Philadelphia three times a week for a couple of years. I never played baseball.

"I don't know that the old man had anything specific in mind for me. He never talked politics in the house, and he never talked business. He was autocratic but we all knew he loved us. And we existed to delight him with our accomplishments.

"I was nine when we got into World War II. Willie was overage but he wanted to go. He had flown with the Escadrille. The old man wanted him to stay home. It was the only time I ever heard them argue.

"Wild Rice went. He was the only one of the three of us who had ever had a life outside that house, he had the framework for rebellion. He just disappeared one day. He was killed in a flight-training accident. The old man wasn't surprised, just angry. The order had been upset. For me, I think for my mother, too, it was like losing an older brother. There was more pressure on me to perform for the old man, and my mother became even more of a child, a beautiful, precious simple child.

"She was very slender, she had long blond hair and dark eyes. After my dad died she played the piano for hours at a time, mostly Chopin, and she got younger and smaller and more beautiful until she died, too. They said it was pneumonia. My grandfather waited a day and a half to call me at college because he knew I was taking a final exam. It's taken me twenty-two years to forgive him for that.

"The old man didn't consult her when it was time for me to go to college. He didn't even consult me. M.I.T. The future was science and engineering, he said. M.I.T. was another insulated world. I interrupted it for Korea. That was a little world, too. An air war has nothing to do with killing people, it's a competition of expertise and I was very, very good.

"I went back to M.I.T. on a navy program. The old man died. I went back to the big house for the funeral and I stayed for the reading of the will. There was very little money left. I don't know what happened to it, if he was cheated out of it, if he spent it, if there had always been less than we thought. He left me a note: 'You have everything you will ever need.'

"I got a master's at M.I.T. I became a test pilot. I married Cissie. We had a baby. It was severely brain damaged."

Jean touched Cable's leg. He didn't look at her. He was mesmerized by the expression on Rice's face, calm, reflective, unchanging.

"Neither of us could cope with it in any real way. I rationalized it as some sort of a test. Cissie refused to acknowledge such a thing could happen to her. She wanted to put the baby away. I insisted we keep it, force ourselves to love it, to train it. The burden was hers, of course. I was never home. The baby died. It stopped breathing one night. I've always believed Cissie smothered it, but I never said that to her. She wouldn't have another child. She started drinking. She graduated to pills. Another test for me.

"I went into the space program. My card was moving right through the machine. Nothing could stop me. Another little world to conquer. Then they picked Neil Armstrong to be the first man on the moon, and I just collapsed. I stayed in bed for a whole weekend. When I got up I realized this was another test.

"When I finally got to the moon I saw everything plain for the first time. I saw all the corruption, all the enslavement, the manipulation, the forgeries and false trappings. I saw it all because I had lived in innocence. I had been obedient to evil, I had been served by evil, but I had never known it was evil. Until that moment. When I spoke from the moon I was actually thinking out loud.

"My card had come up."

It was a long time before Cable realized he was in the trailer, that the images of Rice were flickering behind his own glazed eyes. He closed his mouth with a startling click. He opened his hand, wet with cognac. He had crushed his paper cup.

Jean expelled a long breath.

Rice stood up. "We'd better get going. We still have a way to go tonight." He opened the trailer door for them.

The boys were waiting in the bus. Mack's arms were crossed on the wheel, his chin propped on his wrist. Joey Field and Georgie Trott slouched in a seat behind him. The others were bunched together toward the rear, heads close. They all sat up as Cable and Jean stepped out of the Airstream. The roadside restaurant was closed and dark.

Cable started the station wagon and led them all back to the highway. The circuits of his mind felt overloaded.

The motel clerk shook his head at Cable's teletyped confirmation. There had been a mix-up in reservations, he said. Very sorry. There were only four rooms available instead of eight, and they were scattered throughout the building instead of in a block on one floor, as promised.

Rice, standing in the doorway of the Airstream, was not surprised. He pointed up at the blank message marquee on the motel's neon highway sign. "I expected something like this when I didn't see 'Welcome Liberty Two' up there. They think we're finished. They don't understand. We've just begun."

Cable said, "Do you want to drive on?"

"It's too late, you all need rest. I'll sleep here in the

trailer tonight. Give Jean a room, put the boys in the other three."

Cable waited for Rice to tell him where to sleep, but the astronaut turned away and closed his door.

In the lobby, Cable distributed room keys and watched the boys shamble off. He helped Jean upstairs with her camera equipment and suitcases. At her door, she said, "Come on in for a minute. There's some cognac left."

He sat in a chair beside the double bed while she unwrapped two plastic bathroom tumblers and poured an inch of cognac into each.

Jean handed him a tumbler. "Doesn't that story just blow your mind?"

"If you believe it."

"Believe it?" She sat on the edge of the bed. "What are you talking about? Just because you didn't read it in *Life* Magazine?"

"It might be true. I'm sure he believes it."

"Oh, Cable." Jean sipped cognac. "What do you believe?"

"I believe it was his way of binding us all closer together," said Cable. "Cajoling us to stay."

"Cable. That's so . . . cynical."

He shrugged. "Tell me why you call me Cable."

Her long hands enclosed the cup. She leaned forward. Her skin was close-grained and smooth. A tiny broken capillary near the tip of her nose, a stitch of red thread, diminished the nose's aggressive angle and made her seem more vulnerable.

"What would you like me to call you?"

"I just wondered."

"What did your wife call you?"

"David."

"You're not really a David. You're too private and secret. Sometimes I think you keep secrets from yourself. You're a

Cable. It fills your mouth if you say it slowly. KAY-bull. If you say it fast, Cable, it's a tense, vibrating wire. Just like you. Do you like Jean?"

"Jean's clean."

She laughed, throaty with cognac. "Hey." She touched his hand.

"You're clean. Long, clean lines and honest and direct. Fresh and alive. Like your pictures. Stryker. Is that your maiden name?" When she nodded, he said, "I'm glad."

Their knees touched and their fingers played on the junction.

She said, "It's late. Let's go to bed."

"I've got to go."

She looked bewildered. "Where?"

"The trailer. I have to stay with him in the trailer tonight."

He left before she could speak.

The Airstream had been unhitched from the station wagon. He's making it easy for the boys, thought Cable. Or is he just trimming his crew? The door was unlocked. Rice was already asleep in the rear. Cable made up a front bunk. He wondered if Rice would be disappointed to see him in the trailer in the morning.

He purposely didn't tell me where to sleep. He was giving his tacit approval for me to sleep with Jean. Cajoling us to stay. Binding us all closer together.

There was movement in the night. Rats's paws scurrying across a tilted deck. An engine whined. Tires squealed.

Rice was out jogging when Cable awoke. The silver station wagon was gone. Mack, Joey, Georgie and Jean were staring at a smear of rubber the wagon had left on the surface of the parking lot. The four boys had been in a great hurry to get away.

Cable joined them. Jean smiled at him but he imagined hurt in her eyes.

She said to Mack, "Are you going to call the police?"

"Even if I wanted to, I couldn't," he said. "The car wasn't registered in my name. It's very complicated."

"They couldn't chop it," said Georgie halfheartedly.

Cable asked Mack, "Why did you stay?"

Mack looked at Joey and Georgie, received no response, and shrugged for them all.

Only Rice had appetite for breakfast. "We'll be heading toward El Paso," he said to Cable.

"Straight through?"

"No, we'll be stopping to talk to people along the way."

Joey mumbled, "Right back where we started."

"Not at all. We've learned a lot about the country, about ourselves, about what we're up against. What we have to do."

A fleshy man in a green polyester suit strode up to their table. Two deputy sheriffs, tall and grave, trailed him.

"Commander Rice?" He spoke rapidly. "The insurance company's canceling the policy on the Airstream. They can't indemnify a vehicle that may be used in civil disorders or incitement to riot." He fumbled a business card out of his wallet. "I'm just a local salesman, Commander, I got nothing to do with this."

"Of course," said Rice mildly. "I understand. Let me finish breakfast and then I'll clear out my gear. You can start hooking up."

"Sure, sure, take your time, Commander." The man's voice rose, he was vastly relieved. He placed his card alongside Rice's plate. "Would you mind? My boy's a real space nut. His name's Chip."

Jean snorted and rolled her eyes at Cable.

Cable leaned over to see what Rice was writing on the

back of the card. *For Chip, may he see the earth plain, Good Luck, Charles Rice.*

"Thanks a lot, Commander." The man backed away, carefully tucking the card into his wallet. "Now you just take your time, hear? Enjoy your breakfast. I'm real sorry about this."

Rice shrugged. "It's just a piece of hardware." He was looking through the plate-glass window at the highway slicing west.

Thirteen

Liberty Two felt heavy and unstable under Cable's hands, a wounded machine wobbling through space. He drove cautiously, unsure of the bus's response. The land was flat and the roads taut ribbons, but he imagined that the bus might shudder and die at any moment, just turn off the road seeking its grave or roll backwards, gathering speed until it struck a stone marker or a clump of shin oak, and tumble on its back, helpless wheels whining like grindstones. Cable was tired but not sleepy, physically linked to the clumsy machine.

The three boys clung to the bus. They were reluctant to leave it, bickering over whose turn it was to go out for food. They rode mostly in silence, Mack's eyes glazed, Joey beside him like a kitten. Georgie sat across the aisle, his knees drawn up to his chin, staring out at oil rigs, jerking skeletons nodding at their passage.

Jean followed so closely Cable often could not see the front end of the Porsche in his mirror.

Rice sat on the back seat, marking maps and brochures and local newspapers. Early in the afternoon he told Cable to follow the signs to a petrochemical plant, a grove of steel-stone towers firing gray plumes into the pale blue sky.

They met the day shift hurrying out. Cable, adjusting the sound from inside the bus, did not have to hear what Rice was saying to sense he had lost the fine edge of his delivery. The aluminum platform creaked under his shifting weight. The plant workers were indifferent. After a moment of curiosity and a few minutes of desultory heckling they hurried on to their cars.

The motel near Odessa demanded payment in advance and a two-hundred-dollar overnight deposit against damages. Rice, stony-faced, ordered Cable to drive on. They would pull off the road and sleep in the bus. Joey bit his lip until blood seeped up. Toward midnight, Cable found an abandoned quarry site. The last thing he saw before falling asleep on the wheel was Jean curling herself into a ball in the back of her Porsche. Then her interior lights blinked off and he was left with the rasp of Georgie's asthmatic breathing and Joey's muffled sobs.

Jean was gone in the morning. No one mentioned it. Cable felt both loss and relief. He decided he was glad she was out of it, saved from the limping, whimpering, pathetic end. Just five misfits now, lost in space.

They drove to a large shopping center and Rice spoke with a dogged desperation, but the crowd was meager and unresponsive. Joey's bugle sounded tentative. Cable bought the newspapers. The syndicated columnists were taking their last predictable snap shots before moving on to fresh outrages. One speculated that a Pentagon censor, monitoring the speech with a delay switch, had erased Rice because he was disclosing classified information. Another suggested poetic justice—the network had tried to make money on a freak show and was rewarded with a debit.

A syndicated cartoon: A spaceman peers out his rocket's porthole and exclaims, "What a terrific view! You can really see the earth plain from up here!" His partner replies, "We haven't left the ground yet."

They had killed him and buried him. Made him a crazy, then made him invisible. Only Rice didn't know it yet.

Cable called the Center for contact. Barrett's secretary let him dangle on hold for a long time before she connected him with Jack.

"Hi, Mr. Cable. We thought you dropped into a hole. How's our lunar leader holding up?"

He resented Jack's breeziness, but he needed to keep talking, to be connected to something more substantial than that stricken silver ship.

"He says he's encouraged that the government was worried enough to pull the plugs on him."

"We checked that. It looks like just what the network says. A screw-up. Cost 'em a bundle, too. Did he say anything about my leaving?"

"Four of the boys left, too."

"Let me guess who stayed. Porky, Pussy and the Stork. Nowhere else to go. Bet Jean's still there. She's got her eye on you, Mr. Cable."

"What about Bonnie Fuller?"

"I'm flying out to the Coast tomorrow to poke around. They moved her but we've got a fix. Where are you now?"

"Somewhere between Odessa and El Paso."

"Keep in touch."

He was sorry he had called. The Center seemed even farther away now, the cord stretched to fraying.

The orange Porsche was parked beside the bus.

"Hey, Cable, give me a hand." She was unloading a steel tow cable, two hooks and a gray fabric car cover.

He just looked at her until his pulse slowed again. She blushed.

Mack and Georgie helped Cable attach the hooks and remove the ski rack. They shrouded the Porsche. Jean boarded the bus with her camera equipment and her suitcases. Rice looked up from the rear and smiled as if he had been expecting her.

Her presence gradually lightened the mood inside the bus. She was determinedly sunny, mindlessly sunny, he thought. Her easy chatter with the boys irritated him. His own depression had been easier to bear when the bus was sullenly overcast. Her brightness exposed raw edges, shafts of morning on cracked vinyl and peeling electrician's tape and chromed seat bars worn to black streaks.

She lured the boys out of their shells with tricky equipment, a motor drive shooting four frames per second, an electric eye firing a remote strobe, a row of filters like tinted monocles. Joey responded first to the new toys, then Mack. Georgie took longest, but became the most interested. He said he once had a job as a darkroom helper in a portrait studio,

"Terrif," said Jean. The word grated on Cable. "You can help me process some film, it's really piling up."

"I don't think so. I didn't learn anything. I got fired the third day."

"Why was that?"

"I spoiled some pictures. A wedding."

Cable turned on the radio and their voices dropped beneath the processed twang of Country-Western music.

The next morning she handed Cable her wallet. "There's two hundred dollars in cash in here and my gas credit cards. I've got some travelers' checks in my suitcase."

"We've got some money left." He had counted what remained of Lefferts' money. Enough for another week. At most.

"Look, you're towing my car, I would have spent money driving it. And I have no motel bills." She couldn't resist a comic's gesture: A hand at the tail of her spine and an exaggerated grimace of backache. They were all sore from sleeping on the bus seats.

"Why don't you give it to Rice?"

"I don't know. He seems so wrapped into himself right now, it would be like . . . I don't know, just sort of gross. Besides, he might not take it from me."

She was an intruder, he sometimes thought, a light slithering under the doorways of his blackened rooms, a fingernail snagged in his splitting seams. He imagined her gone again, but the thought of the bus without her depressed him even more.

They drove on. The shopping centers all looked alike.

Rice appeared beside him, supporting himself on the vertical bar behind the driver's seat. He held a marked map. The astronaut's eyelashes were crusted, a sty was blooming on one lid. This first sign of Rice's physical decay sickened Cable.

"There are Indian reservations outside Albuquerque. I'd like to be there day after tomorrow." Rice left the map on the dashboard and returned to the rear, stopping twice to steady himself against a seat.

Cable tightened his grip on the wheel until the tension chewed up to his shoulders and rewelded him to the bus.

Cable held the plastic clipboard for her as she signed the gas credit slip. "You've been making friends with the boys." In his awkwardness with her it came out harshly, almost an accusation.

"They're scared. They were willing to go anywhere with him, but now they're afraid they're going nowhere."

"What do you tell them?"

"That something's going to happen. Something's going to happen to turn it all around for him."

"Is that what you really think?"

"I really do. He's sent out so many positive vibrations one's bound to hit and come back."

The Indian women and children were shyly interested, circling the silver bus with shuffling side steps that loosed puffs of baked brown dust into the clear, dry air. The men hung back. For a weekday morning there were too many idle men among the clustered adobe huts.

The older men stood stiffly in doorways without thresholds. The dirt roads simply continued into their front rooms. The younger men leaned on the sagging wooden porch rail of the community center and trading post, or against the fenders of rusted pick-up trucks. Dogs yapped. Cable had anticipated poverty and suspicion, but not such a gulf of time between the men bound to their arid land and the space traveler poised on the platform.

Rice waited as the last bugle notes died too slowly in the hostile air, stirring tortured ghosts. He plunged into speech.

"We've heard a lot about humane punishment. What does that mean? Kill criminals on the installment plan, five or ten years at a time? Lock them up with television and barber classes instead of bread and water and concrete mattresses?"

Cable cringed for Rice. He should never have come here, intruded on these people. The men did not respond, the women and children seemed more interested in Jean strolling among them shooting pictures, and Georgie, who trailed her with the knapsack. The thrusting angle of Rice's body was less severe than it had been before the Astrodome, his hand gestures, once so surely choreographed, seemed grabs for balance. The crowds he had once so sharply penetrated had leaned out of his range and he struggled to reach them.

"Wake up. See the earth plain. A criminal has to be rehabilitated or exterminated, prepared to return to active citizenship or thrown out with the garbage. Teach him a trade he can use. Settle him in another part of the country if environment's his problem, alter him physically or psychologically, we have the instruments and the drugs to do it.

"But if that doesn't work, kill him."

Two wiry boys began to mimic Jean and Georgie. One rolled the flapping front tails of his oversized Army shirt above his belly and followed her with prancing leaps. She smiled good-naturedly. She was wearing a blue work shirt knotted to expose her long waist above dungaree cut-offs.

Georgie scowled at his little shadow. The Indian boy craned his neck and stumbled around in a marionette's herky-jerk. The Indian boys ignored the scolding women for the young men's snickers.

"That's right. I said kill him. We don't have the room or the resources to carry stowaways. It's a smaller world than you think. I've held it in my hand."

Rice was met at the foot of the ladder by several of the younger men. Cable moved in beside him. The leader of the group was short and slim, no more than twenty, Cable judged. His eyes were so bright with furious mischief they seemed tacked onto his muffin face. He wore his black hair much longer than the others, in a single braided rope down his back. His fingers were studded with turquoise and his shirt and jeans embellished with bead mosaics.

Rice offered a hand. "Hello. What's your name?"

The Indian ignored the hand. "You got to be crazy, man, come out here with that insane genocide number."

"I have something to tell you."

"Sure you do. You have come from face in night sky," he drew extravagant paths in the air, "over mountains through rivers, from great glass tepee to lay on the terse verse."

The young men behind him nudged each other. Others drifted across the dusty road and pressed in. Cable smelled the heat of bodies.

"I'm talking about revolutionary change for all Americans. I don't have a Black speech in one pocket and an Indian speech in the other."

"Native American is the phrase."

"Wake up," snapped Rice. He was losing patience. His infected eye was watering and he had difficulty meeting the Indian's bright black buttons. "We're being divided and manipulated. Only together, as a . . ."   •

"One big American stew. With a little Redskin sauce."

Rice blinked as the Indians crowded in on him. "Who are you speaking for?"

"Billy Fox. Who are you speaking for?"

A brown clod hit the bus with a moist *thap*. Rice's head jerked.

Cable caught Jean's attention and pointed toward the open bus door. She nodded and pulled Georgie's arm. Mack and Joey followed them.

"I'm speaking for all Americans. Can't you see?" The pleading in Rice's voice startled Cable. He was unraveling. "You have to see. They've set us against each other like dogs."

He reached out to Billy Fox. The young Indian tried to back away but the men behind were pushing forward. Rice's hands touched the beaded shirt. Billy Fox was jostled into Rice's arms.

"Start the bus."

Cable's shout froze the Indians, but at the engine's growl

they swarmed forward, pinning Rice to the ladder. The bus lurched ahead. Rice and Billy Fox tumbled to the ground, embraced.

They rolled apart and bounced up. Cable started toward Rice. He was tripped by a leg thrust between his ankles. He kicked it away and grabbed Rice's shoulders, shoving him through the crowd. Cuffing punches bounced off Cable's back and neck. He ran Rice to the door and boosted him up the high steps. The door thudded shut. Jean gnashed gears into motion. A rock clanged against the platform, then Liberty Two was rushing down the reservation road, bouncing through ruts and crushing beer cans. Jean half stood at the wheel, her lower lip between her teeth.

Rice raged, "You damn fool, they would have seen, I would have made them see. You panicked, Cable, you got scared . . ."

"He pulled you out just in time," said Jean.

"Now I've lost them." He sagged against the windshield. His steam was gone. "I hold you responsible, Cable."

Cable steered him down the aisle. The boys looked away as Rice passed. Cable wished they had left with the others. For their own sakes.

Rice fell onto the rear seat. He was exhausted. "That's okay, Cable. Don't worry about it." His voice dropped to a murmur. "Next time."

Cable returned to the front. Jean was driving so earnestly he thought it would be an insult to take the wheel from her.

"When we get to the main road turn right, west toward Arizona."

She brushed damp curls off her forehead with quick backhand swipes. "What do you think's going to happen?"

"It's over."

"He doesn't think so."

"He'd be the last to know." He flopped into the seat behind her.

"How do you feel?"

"I feel sad." The words, unexpected, drew a spongy ball up his throat.

Her shoulders twitched, but she said nothing. He felt a great warmth toward her, he wanted to touch the back of her pale neck, run a finger along the downy shallow groove.

At the Arizona line a uniformed man flagged them over for a fruit and vegetable inspection. He sauntered up and down the aisle, then called in other officers. The boys glared at them, but Rice, sitting almost catatonically in a corner of the rear seat, seemed unaware of the inspectors. They made no pretense of a search, rubbernecking at Rice and whispering. One of them set himself for conversation with Jean.

"That a sports car you're towing?"

"Actually," she said sweetly, "it's a very sick orange. We're hoping it'll recover in Phoenix."

"Now that ain't called for," he said seriously.

The inspectors took their time and left reluctantly when traffic began to back up at their stations.

Jean stripped gear teeth storming away, and drove stiffly until Cable said, "Now that ain't called for." They began to laugh, soft little bursts at first, then, triggering each other's release, long, loud peals that bewildered the boys. Rice never looked up.

"Hey, that felt good," said Jean. "Where to?"

He looked at the map. "We'll be hitting Six-sixty-six soon, it leads north to Interstate Forty. We better head south, the less people right now the better. We'll find a place to stop and sort things out."

"He'll want to go on, won't he?"

"He needs rest," said Cable.

"Tell me how you feel about him now."

"What do you mean?"

"The way you helped him. So tenderly. And I watched you while that Indian boy attacked him. You looked very dangerous."

"Billy Fox? Your friendly neighborhood militant." Or a government agent, he suddenly thought.

"You really have a knack for not answering my questions."

"Watch the road."

"Okay." She drove silently for a few minutes, then asked, "What about the boys?"

"They can crawl back under their rocks."

"Why do you have such contempt for them? They're really part of all this, it's as much theirs as yours. Did you know Joey was an addict? He told me Mack sat by his bed for thirty-six hours straight while he . . ."

"Do you know what they called themselves?"

". . . went through withdrawal. That was only a few weeks before they left Cleveland. Joey hasn't touched anything since then, he hasn't so much as smoked a cigarette in more than eight weeks. He told me he's high on the Sons, it's all he needs now."

"The White Action Force. They're somewhere to the right of the Ku Klux Klan."

"They told me everything. They're different now. Isn't that what Liberty Two's all about? And Mack, God, what a life he's had. For starters, his mother was fifteen when he was born, he never even knew . . ."

"I'll drive now," said Cable. "You're wandering all over the road."

In the early afternoon he stopped for gas at a huddled outpost of sand-scoured stone buildings. He honked twice before a heavyset man came out of the general store, wiping his hands on a blood-smeared white apron.

The man filled the tank before he said, "Saw him on TV."

"That's right," said Cable warily.

"Been havin' a rough time?"

Cable shrugged.

"Lookin' to lay up?" He nodded toward a six-unit motel. "Nobody bother you here. Put the bus out back, can't see it from the road. Steak tonight." He nodded toward a low building with a weathered wooden sign: *Cafe*. "T-bone, home fries, salad, rolls, coffee, ice cream. Five bucks. Can't beat it. Rooms are nine-fifty. Free coffee in the morning."

"Why do you want us?"

The heavy man deliberately hooked the gas nozzle into the pump with a square hand that joined his thick forearm without a defined wrist. "Saw him on TV. Saw him talk on the moon, and I saw him after he come out of the hospital. Saw him at the Speedway and I saw him in the Astrodome. Maybe he's crazy, maybe not. But I figure they been giving him a hard time because they don't want me to hear what he's got to say. That's it. You want rooms?"

"We do," said Jean. Cable had not seen her walk up.

The man looked at Cable. "Got three vacant."

"Okay," said Cable. He was weary of movement. We might as well end up here—nowhere—as any place else.

"Beryl Petty," said the man extending his hand. When Cable shook it, Petty said, "Be an honor."

Cable parked behind the motel. He led Rice into an unexpectedly cool room and lowered him to a bed. He pulled off Rice's shoes and opened his belt and waistband. Rice rolled into a baby's tuck and fell asleep. He breathed shallowly through a slack mouth. His eyelids were cracked ajar exposing deathly scars of white eyeball. Corpse eyes. An old rhyme haunted: He was dead and didn't show it, he was too far gone to know it. Cable fled the corpse eyes.

Jean was next door, bedding down the three boys with

a mock sternness for which they were pathetically grateful. The last layer of Mack's transparent dignity had sloughed off, leaving a flabby, weak-eyed, dependent lump. Joey crawled under a sheet and purred. Georgie pulled a folding bed out of the closet and fell on it without bothering to take off his boots.

Jean blew them a kiss and closed the door. "I'm dying for a beer."

"Me, too."

They walked into a large dim room curtained against the sun. Empty tables were scattered on a stone floor. Beryl Petty was arranging glasses at the bar beneath a flintlock rifle mounted on polished longhorns. He raised a frosty beer can as they settled on bar stools, and when they nodded he popped two rings and filled wet steins. The beer was so cold and fresh it tasted like mountain spring water until it hit Cable's empty stomach and rose to his head in a giddy mist.

Distantly, Petty asked, "How is he?"

Dead and doesn't show it, too far gone to know it.

Jean said, "They'll all sleep for hours." She fired a wooden match on her thumbnail and lit a cigarette. Smoke drifted past Cable's eyes.

"You folks be all right here."

"You believe in Rice, don't you, Mr. Petty?" said Jean.

"There's a fella comes down, Duwayne Stockton, most likely you'll see him tonight, he got nothing to do Monday to Friday but run his dozer and read his books and figure things through. He says you see all these far-out characters on the TV shows, they let 'em get on so they can hang themselves, show how crazy they are. But when the government and the TV try to shut somebody up, well, maybe he's got something we should be hearing."

Cable motioned Petty to refill his stein.

"The man was an astronaut!" said Petty. "Been somewhere we're never gonna go. Saw things we're never gonna see. He had it made. All those astronauts got into big business deals, set themselves up. Not him. How come?"

"He's different," said Cable.

"I figure he got to be sincere," said Petty. A bell rang at the pumps outside. "Excuse me."

Jean whispered, "How do you feel?" She slid off the stool and swayed.

They walked out into the feverish day, shoulders touching. Petty was gassing a patrol cruiser. Cable trusted him. He would say nothing about Rice. Nobody would bother them here.

At her door, Jean fumbled the key out of a pocket of her cut-offs. He took the key out of her hand and stabbed at the keyhole. The key snicked in.

Their lips barely touched through a moist film, their eyelashes brushed. Her bare waist was hot. Her body thrust into his until he felt his own hardness grind into his thigh. He reached around her to unlock the door. They stumbled into the room holding each other. He jerked out the key and kicked the door shut. Her hands were under his shirt pinching the spare flesh of his back.

They toppled on a bed and rolled to face each other. She sucked air out of his mouth. He worked a hand between them and popped the metal button of her shorts, then hooked a forefinger on the zipper and separated the tiny teeth with worrying strokes. Her urgent body slowed to his gentle rhythms.

He slipped his hands beneath bikini underpants, palms kneading her low-slung melon cheeks, cool and firm. His fingers stretched into a warm marsh. Her fingers feathered the downy hairs below the tip of his spine and drove him against her.

They swam on each other in a creamy trance, each button an exquisite puzzle, peels of cloth caressed away, until their damp skins touched and slippered free and sucked and stayed. They took their time, curling around each other, stroking, grazing. Her bush was sparse, a light brown puff above swollen pink lips, baby's ears that hardened into a tender ridge. They tasted sweet and new.

His tongue ached at the roots but could not stop, inspired by the gorging flesh, tongue tip to throbbing button, circling, teasing, steady, demanding response from the long supple body; she stiffened, arched, thrust against his tongue. Her thighs shuddered and she gave herself up. A long deferred cry. She had crested when he finally slipped into her, was enclosed by her burning tightness. He plunged, died. They fell asleep connected, enwrapped.

They woke, shy, pleased, tracing figures on each other's slippery skin. He turned her over to touch that downy shallow groove of her neck, kissed it, dragged his tongue slowly down her spine, up again until the cool melon cheeks rose and parted. Her back was smooth, the ribs and shoulder blades carpeted by firm flesh, the bumpy column of her spine pressing out as her back arched.

He kneeled between her legs and held her breasts loosely. He moved inside her for a long time, she was larger, wetter, the explosion this time was muffled, diffuse, but they collapsed together. She turned in his arms and slept with her face sunk into the joining of his shoulder and neck. Her cheek was hot against his.

He woke alone between warmly rumpled sheets, sweaty, aware of a dull ache in his groin. A shower hissed. For a chilled moment he could not remember who he was with. Susan. Lynn. Have to call in. Barrett's waiting for a preliminary report. He sat up too quickly and felt dizzy. From the bureau top, the glass eye of a metal cylinder stared at him. A telephoto lens. Jean Stryker. He had slept with Jean Stryker, the first time he had made love since the explosion.

Four months ago. Only four months? Four months already?

He felt self-conscious in the stark bathroom, put off by the humming fluorescence and the lemony disinfectant and by Jean at the steamed mirror, polishing her teeth with a jeweler's absorption. He side-stepped carefully past her flushed haunches into the shower stall. Under the spray he regretted the loss of their mingled smells. It had been so easy with her, so natural. It was the first time in four months he had desired a woman, only the second woman he had actually held. He had been grateful to Bonnie Fuller, he had wanted to please her, but her mothering flesh had suffocated desire.

He dressed silently. He rummaged through the snarled litter of his clothes, reluctant to put them back on. But he was unwilling to go next door for his suitcase and risk Rice's corpse eyes. He watched Jean dress, slip farther away from him inside sunburst briefs, a pale blue shirt-waist dress that clung to patches of damp skin. She brushed her tangled hair into a springy chestnut helmet and made up her eyes from a plastic kit of brushes and color cubes. Finishing, she sensed his mood and kissed him, a long, reassuring kiss that stirred him again.

"You're all dressed up," he said.

"For you." She took his arm and let him lead her out to the cafe. The late afternoon sun still commanded the sky, but it had lost its savage lick. There was little warmth left in the bronze light that bathed the buildings and the plateau. A jagged mountain range crouched in waiting to puncture the sun on rusty peaks.

A ranch family celebrated quietly at a long table, the children scrubbed, the mother carefully groomed, the father's benevolent pride touching Cable. A few middle-aged couples and a construction gang in clean jeans spun out their meals. Beryl Petty was behind the bar, talking with two men in plaid shirts and stained cowboy hats. Mack, Joey and Georgie looked up as Cable and Jean entered. The boys were still sluggish from sleep. Joey smoked. Mack waved tentatively. Cable was glad there was no room for two more at their table. He waved back and steered Jean toward a corner table near enough to the boys to avoid seeming rude yet so placed that they would not have to look at the three puffy, uncertain faces.

A plump blonde woman in an apron came over and introduced herself as Margaret Petty. "The steak dinner?"

"Both medium rare," said Cable, remembering their dinner in Houston. "And a bottle of red wine."

She backed away with a sentimental smile. He was grateful she didn't start a conversation, that she respected their mellow cocoon. He dimly remembered another couple in a country restaurant, their knees touching beneath a red formica table, feeding each other bits of sandwich. But he could not place them clearly and let them drift away.

Beryl brought the wine. "How's Commander Rice?"

Cable realized he had not even thought to look in on him. "He's still sleeping."

Beryl wrenched out the cork and poured two brimming glasses without ceremony. "Sure hope we get to talk with him tonight. That fella I told you about, Duwayne Stockton? He's over there at the bar. The big one's his partner, Carley. Real anxious to meet the Commander. Couldn't hardly believe he was here."

Cable and Jean turned in to each other, toasting with small secret smiles, but Beryl did not leave. "Duwayne says if them soldiers at the missile site get their way it'll spread like the plague, but if they ain't bluffin' . . . boom."

"What are you talking about?" asked Cable, annoyed by the intrusion.

"Been on the radio all afternoon. That missile site in the desert outside Las Vegas. Some soldiers took it over, and they're holding their officers hostage. News'll be on soon." He gestured at the television set over the bar. "Enjoy your meal." He finally left.

"I wonder what that's all about," said Jean.

"They probably want longer marijuana breaks," said Cable. "How's your wine?"

"Don't be so flip. It could be very serious."

"I can only think about one fiasco at a time."

She picked a cork crumb out of her wine. "What's going to happen to him?"

"I don't know. We can rest here for a few days until he gets his bearings."

"Then what will you do?"

"We'll have to see," he said, wondering what he would do, what Barrett would tell him to do. "What about you?"

She shrugged. "I wonder if he is still sleeping."

He swallowed enough wine to protect what was left of his glow. "I'll go see."

Rice had turned toward the wall. He was breathing regularly. Cable tiptoed back to the door.

"Cable? Where are we?" His voice was fogged.

"In a motel in Arizona. Northeast of Phoenix."

"What time is it?"

"Almost six."

"Morning or evening?"

"Evening. We're all having dinner."

"Would you turn on the light."

There were patches of flaky white skin alongside his nose. The crusty eyes squinted. His cheeks were covered with a sandy beard stubble. He sat up slowly and swung his legs off the bed as if anticipating pain. Cable felt tender toward him. He was beaten and brittle.

"Can I do anything for you?"

"No. Go on back to your dinner. I may join you."

He left Rice staring at his socks. They had wrinkled down below his shiny anklebones.

"He's awake," said Cable.

"You look upset," said Jean.

"I feel sorry for him."

After a few bites Cable had to stop for breath.

"Me, too," said Jean. "I thought I was starving. Cable? Can I ask you a question?"

He laughed at her.

"No, really. I know I talk too much, but I mean a real question. About the night in San Antonio. Why did you leave?"

He juggled neatly packaged answers. Rice was waiting in the Airstream. He had been very tired, afraid of performing poorly and disappointing her. She might even believe that one, it rang of painful honesty. But he did not want her to believe a slick lie. He teetered on the edge of truth, but there was no truth unless he told her everything: the Center, Lynn, the explosions, his flight across country, Bonnie Fuller. He could not tell her the truth. He suddenly placed the other couple, the young tourists headed for Oregon. Did they ever get there?

"Cable? Don't think up something to tell me. I'd rather you said nothing than something you think I want to hear. Okay?"

"Okay."

Petty turned on the big color set. The missile site story led the news. An on-camera reporter standing among military vehicles parked against a cyclone fence read his notes with professional indignation. All but four of the hostages had been released in return for the area commander's promise that a television crew could enter the compound to film the mutineers reading their grievances. But a general flown in from Washington had canceled the deal. Now the mutineers demanded a phone call from the Secretary of Defense. Communications between the compound and the troops massed outside had broken off. While military spokesmen were refusing to comment publicly, one of them had speculated that the four hostages were already dead. The specific grievances were still unknown, although the freed hostages, before they were whisked away by helicopter, told reporters they concerned working conditions and alleged harassment.

"Why doesn't the Secretary of Defense just call them up, hear them out?" asked Jean.

"The chain of command," said Cable.

"They could have valid complaints, they've probably been brushed off every . . ."

Rice was at their table. He had shaven so closely his skin glistened. His eyes were bright between raw, crustless rims. For the first time since the Astrodome he was wearing a tie and blazer and gray trousers.

He sat down. "You've heard the news." His voice was surprisingly strong. "If we get there fast enough we can pinch it off before those fools let the site blow up."

It took Cable a moment to make the connections. "They won't let you near the place."

"We'll get inside. There'll be a way. There's always a way."

Petty hurried over, towing the two men in cowboy hats. "A real honor, Commander. I want you to meet a couple fans of yours."

Rice turned, smiled, started to rise.

"Don't get up, Commander." Petty shook Rice's hand enthusiastically. "I'm Beryl Petty. This is my place. This here's Duwayne Stockton, and his partner, Carley Carleton."

"I'm glad to meet you," said Rice. He glanced over the three as he shook their hands. "I'm going to need your help."

"You got it," said Stockton. He was a short man, hard and windburned. Cable thought of a small piece of leather, tightly stitched.

"How well do you know this area?"

"Worked it thirty years."

"I want to get to Las Vegas as fast as possible."

The three men were electrified. Stockton recovered first. "I got my own maps in the jeep." He hurried out.

Petty said, "Can I get you some food?"

"Sandwich and coffee," said Rice.

"What kind of sandwich?"

"Any kind." Rice turned to Jean. "What kind of shape is your car in?"

"We used to rally it. And I just had the . . ."

Cable said, "You need rest, you have to . . ."

"We lost momentum and crashed," said Rice. "I've crashed before. If you don't go right back up you're finished."

Petty rushed back with coffee, his wife trailing with a sandwich. The three boys drifted over and stood at a respectful distance. Rice ate methodically until Stockton returned with a tattered map.

"We cleared some of these mountain roads to bring in mining equipment," said Stockton. "They're real rough. I'll drive you."

"If you would, I'd like you to drive Liberty Two. You can take the long way and meet us in Las Vegas tomorrow. There's only room for three in the Porsche and I want Cable and Mack with me. Petty? Will you unhook the car? Gas and oil it."

Stockton signaled to his partner, a tall man with a horse face. "Give 'im a hand, Carley."

Rice sipped his coffee black. "Jean. Clear the rooms, we won't be coming back." Color had seeped into Rice's cheeks.

"I been waitin' for you a long time," blurted Stockton. He suddenly seemed embarrassed.

"And you were ready," said Rice. Stockton swelled.

Rice stood up. "Mack. Cable."

Jean looked at Cable and mouthed the words "Good luck."

Cold, clear stars hung just out of reach in the mountain night. The car climbed and plummeted so quickly Cable had to swallow against the changing pressures in his ears. The wheels sprayed rocks and grit into black canyons, the headlights leaped against stony walls that Rice avoided by inches. Roads narrowed without warning, dwindled into construction trails, but Rice drove as surely as if he had driven them all before. After a while, Mack, crammed into the back, no longer gasped at each skidding turn, and Cable stopped pressing imaginary brakes. They were safe, indestructible, in a charmed machine with a master of magic.

When they reached the main highway, the Porsche flattened into shrieking speed. Once Cable thought he glimpsed a patrol cruiser's whirling red rooflight, but the trap he anticipated was never sprung. Had they outraced police radio? Had the master of magic cloaked them invisible?

At a gas stop Cable switched on the radio. The deadlock had tightened. The mutineers had tried to telephone a local radio station, but a military monitor had broken the connection. In retaliation the mutineers had fired a machine-gun burst, raking the no-man's land between the compound and the cyclone fence. Ricocheting slugs smashed several jeep windows but no one was hit.

For hours the only sound was the engine's shrieking violins. Near the Nevada border the violins were joined by an intermittent percussive thump, the car's first complaint. But Cable knew the Porsche would go the distance, willed by Rice.

Fourteen

Floodlights pinned them. A giant loomed out of the blaze. His blue-black face filled Rice's window. "Authorized personnel, sir?"

"I'm Charles Rice. Who's in charge here, Sergeant?"

Rice's crisp assurance drove the soldier back a step. "I'll get the lieutenant."

Rice opened his door and climbed out stiff-legged. Mack stumbled out of the cramped rear.

Cable slipped out the passenger side into a shadow between shimmering pools of light. A two-and-a-half-ton truck blocked the road. Jeeps flanked the truck, radios crackling. A picket line of riflemen curved into the darkness. Guard dogs strained at their leads, rumbling. Rice had snapped his way past ten miles of police detours, but he would need more than testy confidence to crack this last perimeter. Cable circled the orange car to join Rice and Mack in a spotlight.

A helmet with a single painted white bar bobbed up.

The lieutenant was a young bantam, nervous behind his Airborne swagger. He waved a slip of paper. "You're not on my pass list, sir. You'll have to turn around."

"I'll speak with your commanding officer."

"He's pretty busy right now."

"Make the call, Lieutenant."

"I know who you are, sir. I have special orders concerning unauthorized personnel who attempt to . . ."

"You'd better cover yourself, Lieutenant." Rice's voice was firm, almost avuncular. "If this site goes up your commanding officer isn't going to take the rap. Are you? For not checking the CP?"

The lieutenant blinked. He wheeled and marched away.

"He looks scared," whispered Mack, empathetic.

"He should be," said Rice.

They walked closer to the truck. The road it blocked continued for another half mile to a high cyclone fence. On one side of the road was a herd of low, dark shapes ringed by sentries. Cable picked out civilian cars and television cameras set in the sand. The military command post was on the other side of the road, higher, harder shapes, two armored carriers, a helicopter, a large tent that partially obscured the concrete missile compound beyond the cyclone fence. Revolving drums of light mounted on the armored trucks swept the compound and glinted off a grove of skeletal towers. There was no sign of life beyond the fence.

Two off-duty guards strolled near. One said, "It's Rice-a-Roni himself."

The sergeant snarled, "Off the road, troop." They drifted away reluctantly.

The lieutenant returned, relieved. "Someone's coming out, sir. I didn't mean to . . ."

"You thought you were doing your job."

A jeep burst out of the command post area and rattled down the road. Sentries saluted as it careened around the truck. A tall colonel hopped out, his holster slapping his starched flank. He wore a black brassard with white letters: IO. The information officer, Cable thought: Rice may be just a minor public relations problem, but at least they think he's worth a bird colonel.

The colonel said, "Look, Rice, we've got a very delicate situation here. I'm sure you can appreciate that. You can help us by clearing the area."

"I can help you by going in and talking to those men."

"I doubt that. Any outside interference can only exacerbate the situation. Endanger lives. This area is off-limits to all civilians. Mr. Rice."

"You've got the news media in there."

"Those damn vultures got in before we zippered up. Look, Rice, you can see what we're up against here. We're chin deep and sucking air. I'm sure you mean well . . ."

"Let me talk to your commanding officer."

"Out of the question."

"Then let me talk to the media. I have no intention of leaving here until I've done what I can to get those men away from those little red buttons. I'm your one chance, Colonel. Are you ready to take the responsibility for stopping me?"

"All right. I'll tell the press you're here. If they want to talk to you, they'll come out."

"That's not good enough," said Rice. "I represent the American people, too. You can keep me on this side of the fence, that installation is under military jurisdiction. But you have no right to keep me out of the press area."

"No right?" But the colonel's lined face was screwed into thought. Cable tried to imagine the debate in his mind: Rice was burned out, but he had enough glamour to divert the newsmen for an hour or two, keep them off his back and give the general some extra time. See the crazy astronaut, a comedy act for all catastrophes. The space clown.

"All right. Lieutenant, escort Commander Rice and his people into the zoo. Tell the newsmen I'll meet with them again at oh-seven-hundred. Rice, you're going to buy me time."

But Rice was already climbing into the Porsche.

The newsmen booed the lieutenant and eyed Rice. Old news. There were about a dozen of them, loafing against their cars, smoking and drinking Army coffee out of metal canteen cups. Cable recognized the TV reporter he had seen on Petty's set, his make-up caked and his toupee askew.

A radio reporter sauntered up. "What's the skinny, Commander." Cable resented the undertone of mockery.

"I want to go in there before those boys get rattled and start popping the no-go locks."

"You really think they'd throw a missile?"

"It's a possibility." He gestured across the road toward the command tent. "They're letting this get out of hand. Unless they're deliberately trying to provoke an excuse for an assault."

The radio man clicked on his tape recorder and stepped closer. Other newsmen surrounded them. TV lights flicked on, and the ring of sentries pressed in. The soldiers' young faces were strained.

"You think they'll try to blast their way in?"

"I hope not. Why didn't they let those men call out?"

"The IO said they couldn't risk the disclosure of classified information."

"They had a monitor on the line, he could have cut them off any time. I think they don't want the grievances made public."

The newsmen nodded and murmured. They had obviously chewed over that all night, and now they had someone to say it for them.

The TV reporter shouldered through with his crew. "Fellas, let me get the network A.M. out of the way, okay?"

The others widened their circle as he adjusted his hairline and posed with Rice. The camera's red eye glowed.

"In the cool, still hours before dawn, tension continues to mount at this once obscure missile installation called Skylancer No. Four. There has been no further communication with the eight enlisted men who control the defense site and its underground silos. We do not know if their hostages—a captain and three sergeants—are dead or alive. Through the desert night, coyotes howled and the lights burned in the command post tent of Lieutenant General Jordan P. Hollowell, a deputy chief of staff. Twice, his helicopter left and returned. Spokesmen refuse to deny or confirm speculation that a special weapons team is being assembled for an assault on the steel-reinforced concrete compound. Spokesmen will only say that Hollowell is in constant contact with his superiors in Washington.

"Meanwhile, here in the desert north of Las Vegas, Nevada, the tension is a palpable thing. National Guard units have been placed on standby alert, local and state police have thrown up a cordon of road blocks twenty miles in diameter. Edgy airborne troopers patrol the area with dogs and automatic weapons.

"One visitor who somehow managed to slip through is here beside me. Commander Charles Rice, the former astronaut. Since his ill-fated appearance at the Astrodome on July Fourth, Commander Rice has been wandering the Southwest, his call for a second American Revolution falling on increasingly deaf ears.

"Commander Rice, I'm afraid I'll have to ask you this question first. Are you here for publicity?"

"I'm here to prevent a massacre."

"Earlier, you told me you were afraid the mutineers might, in your words, pop the no-go locks. Those, of course, are the electronic safeguards against accidental firing. Is it your opinion they might threaten to fire missiles if their demands are not met?"

"We don't even know what their demands are. We may never learn the true story here. If the government decides to silence those men—as they've tried to silence me—Skylancer No. Four will just be a hole in the ground."

"You're referring to the possibility of an assault."

"I'm referring to the fact that every missile in the Skylancer system is remotely controlled by a central black box. If the government decides to destruct those missiles in their silos, we'll never know the truth. We won't even be sure if the government did it or if the men inside blew themselves up, by mistake or otherwise."

The mike trembled in the TV reporter's hand. "Sir, are you accusing the government of premeditating the slaughter of . . ."

"I certainly am."

"Don't you think that's shouting fire in a crowded room?"

"That's only a crime if there is no fire."

The TV reporter signaled his crew. "That's a wrap." The red light went out.

The other newsmen moved in. Cable sensed they were not entirely convinced about the black box, but they would report it. They needed something to freshen their morning recaps, and they had to protect themselves against each other.

The little lieutenant followed Rice and Mack and Cable back to the Porsche with three metal cups of coffee. It was lukewarm and thickly sugared. Rice set his cup on a fender and stared at the compound, a low silhouette against the lightening sky.

"Commander Rice? I never knew all those missiles were hooked up to a central black box."

"Are your men nervous, Lieutenant?"

His chuckle was false. "They're saying there's nothing to worry about as long as the general's still here."

"They're assuming the general's not expendable, too," said Rice.

A soldier's face peered over the lieutenant's shoulder. "How long you going to stay, Commander?"

"Until I get those men out of that compound," said Rice.

They sat on the car and watched a bloody sun rise out of the sand. The floodlights winked out. Orange-red sunlight softened the harsh shapes of night. The vehicles and tents strewn around the cyclone fence were diminished by the sandy vastness. The sun inched higher, its ascent acknowledged by glinting reflections off glass and metal, the windshields of jeeps, the helicopter, rifle barrels, the wings of a small reconnaissance plane that buzzed lower and lower until it barely cleared the antennas and the radar tower, now fiery stalks.

At six A.M. one of the newsmen turned up his radio. Rice's black-box statement led the news.

The sentries were unsettled by the broadcast. They muttered and their hardware jangled. The newsmen, roused from catnaps, gathered. A telephone rang in the command tent, a needling sound that stirred the guard line.

At six-thirty engines roared. Two armored carriers pulled up to the fence, blocking the newsmen's view of the gate and of the missile compound. A fresh guard mount joined the soldiers encircling the newsmen. The colonel appeared and slapped the roof of the Porsche. "Let's go." The reporters hurried over but the colonel ignored them. The ring of riflemen opened for the colonel, Rice, Mack and Cable, then closed to contain the newsmen.

Six officers stood among the portable green metal tables and cabinets of the command tent. They wore sun tans and decorations. One officer was seated. His faded but sharply creased fatigues only bore three woven stars. His face was as hard and spare as Rice's. It would have to be Hollowell.

There was no greeting. "They want to see you, Rice. Alone."

Rice nodded.

"Now hear this. You have no authority to negotiate with them. Your only function is to find out what's on their minds and report back to me. Shall I repeat that or do you understand?"

"I understand, General." Rice's voice was matter of fact, there was no deference in it.

"I don't trust you one inch, mister. That black box crap was the foulest lie I've ever heard. You knew they'd hear the broadcast and fall for it. If this operation turns rancid I'll find nine ways to hang you and I'll pull the rope myself. You're a retired officer. Am I coming through?"

Outside the tent, Rice whispered to Cable, "Keep your eyes open." The fence gate swung open. Rice walked briskly toward the compound's main entrance, a reinforced steel door. There was no drama in his stride, a businessman on his way to a meeting. He was halfway up the sandy path before Cable thought to scan the area.

Two men squatted at a jaggedly clipped hole in the fence, tubes balanced on their shoulders. An officer crouched behind them. Cable started toward them. A wall of sun-tan shirts blocked him. The sentries had pulled back to the armored carriers. The newsmen were out of sight.

The steel door cracked open as Rice reached the compound. He paused. A light breeze flapped the skirt of his blazer. He leaned forward slightly, his lips moved. The words were too low and far away. In the breathless hush Cable heard the officer at the fence hole whisper, "Ready." The gunners steadied their tubes.

The door swung open.

"LOOK OUT."

Cable's scream erupted without struggle. An image flickered: A skidding truck, the driver's face behind the snow-crusted windshield horrified by the sight of the small boy and the woman at the bottom of the icy hill.

Rice dove into the compound.

"FIRE!"

The steel door banged shut.

A dull crump and a rattling clangor were almost simultaneous. Two grenades bounced off the door and gyrated in the sand spewing clouds of gray-green gas. A vagrant fume drifted back to the fence and scraped Cable's eyes.

Hands grabbed Cable and rushed him to a jeep. Handcuffs clicked. He found himself manacled to Mack and to the jeep's roll bar. His own feelings of fury and triumph were mirrored in Mack's round face. There was a defiant tilt to the piglet nose and the wavery eyes shone.

"He did it," said Mack fiercely. "They double-crossed him and he still did it."

The colonel loomed up. "You are in trouble."

"You're in trouble," sneered Mack.

"He's inside, but we've got you." The colonel made a drill-field turn.

"That won't matter to him," said Cable.

The sun stoked the warm morning. Heat reflecting off the sand baked Cable's face. The gas clouds hovering at the compound door finally broke into green balloons that rose into the bleach-blue sky. He thought of Lynn, her knapsack filled with wet cloths and tubes of alcohol, mineral oil, vaseline. She was fearless under gas attack, the last one to run away, itching, choking, blinded. They had never faced this particular gas at a demonstration. He wondered how powerful it was. None of the soldiers near the fence was masked, but they seemed alert for a wind shift.

The officers had disappeared into the CP tent. Non-coms barked their men through unnecessary formations and details, but the soldiers could not be diverted; fear encumbered their feet and drew their eyes to the tent, to the general's helicopter, to the silent compound and its hidden silos. The soldiers flinched at sudden noises, the rattle of cans in the field kitchen, urgent telephone rings inside the tent, the growling return of the recon plane.

A corporal and two riflemen brought water for Cable and Mack. The soldiers held the canteen cups as they drank.

"What's gonna happen?" the corporal asked.

"Don't worry," said Mack. He didn't look worried. For the first time, Cable felt close to him.

"Don't worry? You ever see one of those white cigars go up?"

A sergeant stamped up. "No talking with the prisoners." When the men shuffled away, he said, "Been in there a long time."

"Don't worry. The Commander knows what he's doing."

The sergeant cursed and walked away.

The CP tent flaps burst apart.

"Here we go," said Mack.

Hollowell led the officers out. The IO colonel ran across the road to the press. The armored carriers roared, and bumped over the sand to take up positions on either side of the gate. A sergeant unshackled Cable and Mack. The gate was swung back. The television crew led the newspack scrambling up the road.

The compound's steel door opened.

Rice stepped out. The red tie and blazer were balled in his left hand. The sleeves of his blue shirt were rolled, and the shirt was open to the coppery hairs of his chest. The round medallion of Liberty Two dazzled in the sun.

He waited for the newsmen to finish jostling for position at the open gate. The officers assembled stiffly. Behind them, the soldiers strained at the invisible bonds of their formations.

Rice walked slowly toward the fence. He never looked behind at the double file of men marching out of the compound and following him down the sandy path.

The riflemen cheered and waved their helmets.

Rice halted at the open gate and raised his arm. His thumb and forefinger were at right angles, the other fingers closed. Cable had never seen the gesture before.

Mack trembled beside him. "L for Liberty."

The twelve men behind Rice halted. One of their sergeants ordered them into a parade rest.

Rice's voice was clear and sharp, each word an arrow in the dry, still air.

"The immediate crisis is over. I have inspected the electronic locks and they are all in place. The installation is cleared of all personnel, but the system is functioning on automatic response. The four hostages are unharmed. In a few minutes I will turn the mutineers over to their commanding officer. No deals have been made. They understand that their actions were criminal. There can be no amnesty. They must undergo courts-martial.

"However, the American people must understand that what happened here is no isolated incident. It is an example of the breakdown of a society manipulated by the few for their own power and profit. The mutineers of Skylancer No. Four considered themselves patriots. As did their brothers on the other side of the fence who were prepared to destroy them.

"The mutineers have told me of four months of complaint and protest against eighteen-hour duty tours on sophisticated technology that demands peak concentration. They have told me that they exhausted all official methods of making this situation known, including a written report to the Inspector General. They told me that several members of their unit were disciplined and transferred for contacting their congressmen. Who did nothing. They told me they undertook this criminal action as a last resort in the interests of national security.

"These statements have been substantially confirmed by the hostages.

"And I believe them.

"There is still no justification for military men, bound by very special codes of discipline, to disobey direct orders, to imprison their superiors, to seize an installation.

"These men have an obligation to their government. Even if it is a government that manipulates defense as a vehicle for corrupt patronage rather than for the safety of its citizens.

"It is not evil to claim obedience, or to give it. But it is evil to claim obedience or to give it falsely. The government has lied to us, and we must see it plain. We must be able to understand, without condoning, men who disobey military orders in the interests of national security. And we must be able to understand, without condoning, the general who tried to kill all of us in that compound. He, too, thought he was serving his country.

"This is not a military problem. Our citizens are manipulated, forced to the wall, set against each other at every level and in every corner of our society. The problem will not be solved until the people of America see the earth plain and dare to join me in the second American Revolution."

Rice paused, and Cable felt thrill and terror. Rice could

do it. He could stand on the earth and hold it in his hand.

Rice turned. "Captain, take charge of your men."

The captain stepped out and led the files through the gate. As they passed, Rice raised his arm again in the L salute, then brought it smartly to his side.

The newsmen pointed their mikes at Rice but faltered as he swept past them. They dare not touch him, Cable thought, a force field surrounds him, he has leaped out of man's grasp. Cable marveled at the serenity of Rice's face, the smooth-striding body. He hurried to keep pace with Rice. Only Rice's eyes suggested the energy he had expended, those glittering, possessed eyes.

The silver schoolbus was waiting behind the Porsche.

They drove through a gauntlet of waving arms and open faces. The road to Las Vegas was lined with cars, motor-cycles, pick-ups, dune buggies, Nevada, California, Colo-rado, Arizona license plates. Children were held aloft for a glimpse of the man on the aluminum platform, his legs braced, his shoulders back, his head an ax cocked at the pale smear of moon in the afternoon sky.

Newsfilm helicopters rocked overhead, blades tearing and scattering bursts of shrill cheering. Policemen touched their visors as Liberty Two rolled past. Summer vaga-bonds, perched on their packs and bedrolls, returned the L for Liberty.

"I'm shaking all over," said Jean.

"Do you want me to drive?" asked Cable. "Do you want to take some pictures?"

"Later on, thanks, but now I just want to groove on this. I've never been part of anything like this."

"No one has."

Duwayne Stockton steered the bus down the center stripe. The Sons, bolder by the mile, leaned out side win-dows to flash the L back at the crowds, to cheer them cheering Rice. The crowds thickened as the bus approached Las Vegas, families atop their mobile homes, migrant workers on the backs of flatbed trucks. Big Carley hung on the rear ladder. He started at each staccato crackle of fireworks as if he was expecting gunfire. He seemed poised to leap up to the platform and shield Rice with his body. The new Larry Bruno, thought Cable.

Jean held the Porsche a car's length behind Liberty Two. The newsmen followed, then a lengthening line of spectator vehicles falling into procession.

Imagine them silver, strung out from coast to coast.

At dusk, near the city limits, the motorcycle troopers clearing the way roared back to halt the caravan. Welcoming traffic had clogged the road.

Rice spoke. His words were unintelligible, muffled by engine noise, but the people swayed to the movements of his body and the rhythms of his sounds.

"It's a little scary," said Jean. "The hero-king. He does think he's the hero-king. This is what his grandfather groomed him for. Armstrong got the moon, and he wants the earth."

"Don't go off the deep end," said Cable. "They're all grateful and excited and curious. Today he's a hero."

"It's more than that. The power inside him, all that power and energy and confidence, you can almost see the waves ripple out of him. He's so sure he knows what he's doing, so sure he's right. Aren't people always looking for someone to tell them what to do?"

Cable was ashamed of his faint resentment at the bright interest in her eyes. He said, "I'd like to know if there really is a black box."

"Do you think he'd actually lie about that?"

"Why not? He's sure he's right, isn't he?"

The downtown Las Vegas sidewalks were thronged. A spearhead of motorcycle troopers and two open cars packed with city officials led the caravan to the Strip, a tunnel of blaring music and dazzling lights. Lounge bands stood on portable bleachers and trumpeted them along. The marquee of every casino-hotel blinked twice as Liberty Two passed.

Fifteen A campfire cast dark dancing shapes on the blushing silver schoolbus. A guitar twanged behind Joey's gentle harmonica. The soft night breeze was sweetened by marijuana. A baby sobbed toward sleep against a firm young breast, peach in the flickering light. An aluminum lawn chair creaked as an old man turned to hawk and spit. Beyond the firelight, among the circled cars and campers, murmurs and the clink of bottles. Looking west into a star-pricked sky, Cable imagined them a camp of pilgrims resting in the desert before the final trek through summer-cleared passes to the lush green valleys of California. America had come this way before, he thought, the rootless, the ambitious, the old and young drawn together by the vision of a better place. But the promised land had grown to mock their grandchildren. Behind him, to the northeast, the lights of Las Vegas painted whores' smiles on the night, and jets whined, flying lights brighter than the stars.

He estimated two hundred people clustered around the bus, the most curious, the most adventurous, the least connected of the thousands who had followed the caravan to the sandy flats southwest of the city. They had not let the troopers wave them on to Los Angeles or back to Las Vegas, they had stayed after the television cameras were finally dismantled and packed off, after Rice had disappeared into the bus to meet with city officials. Cable had left the meeting after a few minutes. Rice was in full control. The politicians were intoxicated by the publicity value of his presence. They sent policemen scurrying to fill his orders for portable commodes and garbage barrels and temporary telephones. Cable had suddenly needed to be free of the glittering eyes and the sharp, sure words.

He searched the encampment until he found Jean, shooting, and followed her. Those who had settled for the night formed a community with the easy camaraderie of veterans of the road, of trailer jamborees and music festivals. They built the fire and shared their food. They broke into smaller groups to talk or sing or relive the day on television sets lugged out of campers.

Jean borrowed an old army blanket and spread it near the fire. For all her chatter she could be silent, too. They sat together without speaking. Once, he took her hand and she answered only with the pressure of her fingertips.

Liberty Two's loudspeakers crackled. A song faded in midverse.

"This is Rice. The entire nation, the entire world, is looking to us now for leadership. Those of you who wish to remain in the vanguard of the second American Revolution must prepare yourselves for this leadership.

"In the morning, there will be a complete inspection. Anyone found with illegal drugs or firearms will be turned over to local authorities. Anyone found with liquor or tobacco will be asked to leave."

A groan rose out of the shadows. Jean stirred. "To-bacco?"

"Drugs and tobacco may be disposed of before inspec-tion in the oil drums behind Liberty Two. Pour your al-cohol on the ground. Someone will be available at the door of the bus to take your weapons. They will not be returned.

"During inspection, you will be assigned specific camp duties. Please make known any special skills, experience or interests. At this time, sections will be formed in food preparation and handling, in health and sanitation, in training, information, physical fitness, transportation and internal security.

"If you are not ready to accept the responsibilities, the sacrifices, the hard work of our crusade, clear the encamp-ment before morning.

"For those of you who dare be free, welcome to the Lib-erty Encampment."

The speakers snapped and died.

Jean said, "I can't quit smoking."

"It's a dirty habit."

"I'll gain forty pounds."

Cable rolled against her. "You're too bony anyway."

"Don't be so smug, you don't know what you're talking about. I'll turn into a raging bitch, I won't be able to focus, goddammit, I'm not going to . . ."

"Come on." He jumped up and pulled her to her feet. "Let's go watch the heads and juicers unload. It'll shame you."

"I'm going to tell him I can't do it. I don't have to do it. I'm not one of his . . . his sections."

"That's right. You're a camera."

Car engines started. Cable counted a dozen before there were too many to be distinct. He wondered how many of the two hundred would stand morning inspection. As they

196

walked around the bus, Jean pulled loose to light a cigarette with an exaggerated defiance.

Lines were forming at four smoldering oil drums. The mood was nervously manic. A heavy young girl mimicked a revival tent shimmy. Her unfettered breasts jumped like chubby rabbits under her sweatshirt. "Glory, glory, brothers and sisters, turn your swords into plowshares and your roach clips into earrings."

Her friends clapped. A raw-boned gray-haired woman cackled and pointed at her with a half-empty whiskey pint. A tall boy in an army fatigue jacket held a beer can to his crotch and bumped out the beer in short splashes. Mack stepped forward and slapped the can out of his hand. The boy looked up, blinked at Carley over Mack's shoulder, and grinned unsteadily. "All comes out this end, anyway," he said.

Duwayne Stockton stood at the bus door, breaking open a shotgun. He sighted through the empty barrels, grunted, and handed the gun up to Georgie Trott. Half a dozen men shifted from foot to foot, stroking their rifles.

Rice materialized. "The last cigarette."

Jean grimaced as if the cigarette had turned bitter in her mouth and threw it down. She ground it out with the toe of her blue jogging shoe.

"It's not easy to give up life's little crutches," said Rice softly. There was no trace of condescension in his voice.

"Did you ever smoke?" asked Jean.

"I never did. I drank. With Cissie. For a little while. It was the only way I could communicate with her. I hated what it did to me but I thought I could reach her and pull her back. Of course it didn't work. So I made her stop. But I didn't give her anything to replace it. She graduated to pills."

He nodded at the people lined up at the oil drums. They

had fallen silent as flames licked the inside of the drums, fueled by tobacco and paper packets.

"It's going to be hard for them at first, but liberty is stronger stuff. You don't need anything else. And you can't have anything else if you're going to see the earth plain. You can't lose yourself in diversions, in liquor, dope, gambling, promiscuous sex, fads. Abstract psychological indulgence." He looked at Cable. "Why did you leave the meeting?"

"I wanted to clear my head."

"It was a long day for you. I hope you realize how critical your actions have been these last two days. We wouldn't be here now if you hadn't taken charge when I collapsed. Or if you hadn't shouted to me at the compound."

Cable locked his trembling knees.

"I've ordered three motor homes. I'll use one myself, and one as an administrative office for the Caravan. The third one's yours. You'll need a place to work on the book, and Jean will need a darkroom. You can have as much or as little day to day involvement with the encampment as you choose. I'll be calling on you from time to time, but I recognize the importance of a complete and honest record. What we've done, what we will do."

Cable struggled to make his voice as flat as Rice's. "How complete? What about the black box?"

"I want the truth. By the time your book is published the truth will be history. Do you have a place to sleep tonight? There's plenty of room in the bus."

"It's a nice night," said Cable. "We'll stay out."

"Good night." Rice strode away.

Jean pressed against him as they circled back to the campfire. The light deepened the tunnels of her eyes. "That'll be nice, our own place. You must feel very proud."

"I suppose I should. I suppose I should feel thrilled and

grateful, but I don't. He's so sure of me. Of us. I'm not sure how I feel."

"Is it the responsibility? Of his confidence in you?"

"Maybe." He said it sharply to end the conversation.

"Are you afraid of disappointing him? You shouldn't be, not after . . ."

"We've got a blanket, not a couch."

"Hey, Cable." She took his hand. "Don't tune me out. Just when I need you the most." She sounded falsely high. "I've got to throw hundreds of life's little crutches on the fire."

He picked out stars and tried to fit them into constellations but the lines he drew from star to star formed no shapes he could imagine as archers or bears or dippers. No order in the sky.

"Cable?"

"Hmmm?"

"What are you looking for?"

"Up there?"

"Anywhere."

"I'm looking for my friend up there. When I was a kid I'd go up to the roof of our apartment building, it was one of those tarry roofs, soft and sticky in the summertime, I'd go up at night and look at the stars. I pretended I had a friend on one of those stars, a boy just like me, just as lonely and screwed up, looking down. We'd talk."

"Do you feel lonely and screwed up now?"

"I don't know what I feel."

"Maybe your friend was a little girl. Maybe it was me." She touched his hair. The fire had died and he could not see her face in the darkness. The camp slept around them. "Cable?"

"Go ahead. I'm sorry I said that about the couch."

"That's all right. Jonathan always used to say I was practicing without a license."

"Your husband."

"My husband." He wished he could see her face because he couldn't read her voice. Rueful? Resentful? "Cable? Is it me? You seem different since . . . since we got together. About Liberty Two. You seemed more willing to let it carry you along. You have some very real doubts about Rice now. Don't you?"

Too perceptive, he thought, she was too sensitive to mood. If he could love her completely, trust her, confide in her without reservation, open all the doors and closets of his mind to her, her perceptions would bring them closer. But he couldn't, and her perceptions would push him away, force his mind to become fugitive from hers.

"It was interesting about Rice drinking with Cissie," he finally said. "It must have been after the baby died. Or was killed."

She sighed at the abrupt detour, but followed it. "It must have been a very bad time. I can believe a man can love a woman even if he thinks she killed their baby, but I don't see how there could be any hope for them if they don't talk, if they have terrible secrets from each other. Do you?"

He veered again to safer ground. "Are you a good cook? Now that we're setting up housekeeping."

"I'm pretty good. But I hated it. We got into that damn gourmet dinner thing. Jonathan was very proud of my cooking, of how I looked, of how trendy the apartment was. It was all part of his image of himself. He shouldn't have had to define himself in those ways, he's a good architect. And I certainly didn't want to define myself as just his wife."

"How did he feel about your photography?"

"He encouraged it as long as he thought it was a hobby.

I started out by photographing buildings he was interested in."

"You had no children."

"He was ready. We'd had the trips and the impulse dinner parties and the ski lodge and the rallies. That damn car. He always drove and I always navigated."

"Is that why you kept it? To spite him?"

"I guess so. All I really wanted was my clothes and my cameras and my freedom. But I took the car. I was going to give it back to him, but I'm not so sure now. I think I'm going to paint it silver."

They folded into their separate thoughts. Cable did not know if she fell asleep first.

Sixteen

The day broke clear and bright. The encampment came to life slowly, tired and hung over, blinking into an unkind light that sought swollen faces and rust-pocked cars. Half the two hundred had left in the night, fewer than Cable had figured but enough to give the survivors a sense of having endured and passed a test. The pace of the morning built as the early sun baked limp arms and shuffling legs. A litter detail was formed, the commode doors banged, there were calls for coffee. Liberty Two's speakers piped out relentlessly cheerful tunes from Joey's harmonica. There was a flurry of excitement as a television van rolled in, a lunch wagon, newsmen's cars. Jean spotted the familiar black Ford before Cable did.

"Look who's back." She snapped Jack trotting toward them behind an enormous grin. His face was tanned and his hair seemed even blonder. The Center's sun lamp, thought Cable. He was not glad to see Jack.

They all shook hands and Jean loped off toward the bus. Rice was starting the inspection.

"Barrett's coming in tonight to see you," said Jack. "He'll be at the Holiday Inn at eight."

"Why?"

"Clune went berserk over that Skylancer thing. He wants a full field report from day one. Barrett's on the spot, he figured Rice was burned out after Houston and he let things slide. You're going to have to save his ass."

Rice moved slowly through the encampment, talking and listening as Mack and Carley poked through suitcases and rucksacks, opened car trunks and rummaged through trailers. A demeaning inspection, Cable thought. But the people didn't seem to mind and Rice was relaxed, if distantly friendly.

The heavy girl who had shimmied at the drug dump laughed as Mack examined a bottle of pills he had found in her pack. "Take one, lover, it'll cancel your periods."

Jean lowered her camera. "Those look like birth control pills, Mack."

Mack blushed and Rice waved the bottle back into the pack. He offered the girl a thin smile. "I want to be sure that if anything's found here later on it came from outside the encampment."

"Don't worry, Commander, nobody's going to plant dope on me."

"What's your name?"

"Amy." Her face was pretty despite the fat and a blemished skin. Cable figured she was about nineteen.

"How long have you been traveling, Amy?"

"All my life."

A crowd drifted around them. A television cameraman pushed through. Carley started toward him but Rice motioned Carley back. A padded sound boom was extended over Rice's head.

"Where are you from?"

"I'm Amy from Everywhere." Her bravado dissolved under Rice's eyes. "Troy, New York."

"Cold winters," said Rice.

"Cold people, cold ideas, one big, frozen trip."

A shirtless boy said, "Amy was too hot for Troy."

Rice ignored him. "Why are you here, Amy?"

She crossed her arms over her heavy breasts. "I like to see what's going on." She fought her discomfort. "You don't want me here?"

"I'm very glad you're here. Can you touch your toes?"

"Huh? Sure." She bent over in one swift jacknife and slapped her palms on the sand. She jerked up and winked at the campers. "Would you believe five years of modern jazz dancing? In Troy, New York?"

"You're a strong girl," said Rice. "I'd like you to lead calisthenics tomorrow morning."

"Me?" The idea intrigued her for an instant, then she shook her head. "That's not my thing, Commander."

"Work out a schedule. Ten minutes of limbering exercises. You'll increase it later. You might think about breaking into groups according to age and physical condition."

"What's this got to do with the Big L?"

"Liberty is not anarchy, it's not a letting go, a downhill escape. To be free you have to be strong and disciplined and clearheaded. A new era requires renewed people. People who can't be manipulated. If we're going to shake this world loose from the pirates and the stowaways we have to be better than they are. On every level. I'll be available in the morning."

Rice moved on. Amy did not look entirely convinced, Cable thought, but her mind had been reached; she'd play the clown to protect herself, but she'd probably lead calisthenics in the morning.

A tall old man, paunchy and nearly bald, leaned out of a trailer. A stout woman stood behind him. "Commander, I ain't even seen my toes for twenty years, but I jocked everything on wheels, doubles, semis, tankers . . ."

"He's a big rigger, Commander," the woman said, "and they just let him go."

"What's your name?"

"Henry P. Lane. They used to say the P's for Push. We're going to San Diego, I got a boy in the Navy just like you was, and a daughter married a college professor lives in Los Angeles. Four grandchildren."

"Glad to have you aboard, Mr. Lane. Duwayne Stockton's setting up the transport section, he can use a good man. I hope you'll stay."

Lane gave Rice a snappy L salute.

Young and old, all white, unconnected and disconnected. Predictable, thought Cable. The old ones had their cars and trailers, enough pension money to keep going, but nothing much to do. Probably hope to meet some people and fill dead time and pick up a new story or two to spin through the uncomfortable, useless afternoons in their daughters' houses. Talked with that astronaut, Rice, he says to me, Push . . .

The young ones had everything to do, afraid of missing anything, but they had no tools to shape and use their experience. The Big L, another instant Way. With a guru from space. Wow. They had come from cities, from big suburban homes, from good schools, no schools, but they had all been outfitted in the same Army-Navy stores and rasped by the same roads. . . .

The vanguard of the second American Revolution. Refugees from themselves. The young would move on, and the old would fall behind. And Rice would orbit forever, summoning phantom caravans.

But Clune had gone berserk. And Clune was no fool.

"Commander, this concept of an open Caravan. As I understand it, you say you would welcome the Ku Klux Klan. Is that right?"

"What I said was this: Anyone willing to accept the discipline of the Caravan is welcome. I don't care what they call themselves, Klansmen or Black Muslims or Communists or Republicans. As long as they don't try to drive more wedges between people."

"If, for example, the right wing should find you particularly attractive . . ."

"Those are your labels, media labels, right wing, left wing. All these separate groups are fragments of the whole, arcs of the circle. I want to reassemble the circle in a unity of spirit and purpose. Let me emphasize that this circle will not shut people out. It will bind them together."

"What about violence?" A radio reporter, his mike pointed like a gun.

"What about it?"

"When you talk about a new structure, you're talking about violence. The so-called power structure, the government, the corporations, the very rich like the DuPonts, the Clunes, the Rockefellers, they're not going to sit around while you . . ."

"The first American Revolution was violent because the oppressors were not convinced of the determination of the revolutionaries, or of the righteousness and inevitability of their cause. The purpose of the Caravan is to help all Americans see it plain, to convince the oppressors that they must become the people if they want to survive."

A pencil reporter: "Commander, after all the publicity

over Skylancer dies down, do you think you'll be taken seriously?"

"Only history can answer your question. But you might start by asking all the people around us. They're making commitments. Many of them have already made personal sacrifices to remain here. And their numbers are growing. I've made no appeals for followers, yet more than eighty new people showed up at Liberty Checkpoint before noon today. That was two hours ago and you can see the cars backed up waiting to get in. Our circle grows."

Late in the afternoon, the three Winnebago motor homes rolled in, rectangular twenty-two foot self-propelled boxes. They had been hastily sprayed with silver paint that flaked along the joinings. They all had California dealer plates.

The newspack had decamped for the day. Most of the incoming traffic was returning from food shopping. A new fire was started. Mack sat in the bus, interviewing recruits for the Sons of Liberty. Amy made an announcement over the speakers. At 9 A.M. a bugle would call everyone for the first session of Fitness for Liberty. She sounded very earnest. Cable did not see Jean.

He walked out to the county road fronting the encampment. Liberty Checkpoint was a homemade stop sign nailed to a stake wedged with rocks in a jack-rabbit hole. Jack and Georgie Trott were scaling stones at a road marker. He led Jack out of the boy's hearing.

"Are the Winnebagos bugged?"

"No, not yet. We blew that one, Mr. Cable. They came right out of the showroom, a quick paint job and on the road. By the way, watch for two bearded guys in a yellow Toyota with SCUBA decals on the back window."

"Who are they working for?"

"I'll have to find out. They're free-lancers, I've seen

them in Chicago. This is going to be an undercover con-
vention." He laughed. "We'll end up penetrating each
other. Don't forget, eight o'clock. You can take my car."

"I'll use Jean's."

"She left about two hours ago."

"Where'd she go?"

"I don't know. The big cowboy was with her." There
was a taunting inflection in Jack's voice.

Light faded gradually. Cable circled the encampment
twice, looking for Jean. Yesterday's seasoned veterans
made newcomers welcome. Amy presided over a huge iron
pot simmering on a portable gas grill. She had brushed
back her hair and tied it into two loose tails with red knitting yarn. Women came out of trailers with smaller pots of
meat and vegetables and poured them into the common
pot. Someone brought Amy a spice rack and she made a
little ceremony of adding pinches and dashes from the
glass-stoppered bottles. Two young men with neatly
trimmed beards took turns, stirring with a wooden ladle.
Their noisy gusto seemed forced to Cable. One of them
banged the ladle on the pot rim and shouted, "I pro-
claim thee Liberty Stew." The crowd applauded and the
two exchanged wry glances. The spooks in the yellow
Toyota.

Duwayne had lined up the three Winnebagos nose to
tail on the far side of the bus. He and Lane, the retired
trucker, talked in a mechanic's jargon that Cable barely
understood. After a while, Lane went back to his trailer
and Duwayne handed Cable a set of keys.

"Yours is the one on the end. Some machine. Folks want
to get back to nature so they invent a rolling motel." He
slapped his breast pocket, then shrugged sheepishly. "Been
reaching for my butts all day. Told Carley to bring back
a load of gum. And some clothes. We lit out of Beryl's with

nothing but the clothes we was wearing. I hate to raise my arms around people."

"That night at Beryl's. When you told Rice you had been waiting for him a long time."

"I'm not right sure what I meant." The leathery little face wrinkled into serious thought. "He was looking at me like I was supposed to say something, and that's what came out. Sounds foolish now."

"No, he does that to people. It was just the way you said it. You'd been waiting for him."

"Well, I don't know." Stockton squirmed. "He's just a man, but he's a different breed. Sees things different. Cuts right to the bone of things. I know what he means about seeing the earth plain. You look at those politicians on TV, changing their stories every week, new haircuts, clothes, trying to make you believe they're just like you only a little smarter, a little trickier. Now, he never says what you want to hear, he says you got to wake up and do it for yourself. And he's sincere. I'm just running off at the mouth, I don't have to tell you all this, you been there since the beginning. I better go look at that bus, been stalling."

Cable unlocked the end Winnebago and climbed into the stale chill of air-conditioning. The mobile home was new, the bucket seats in the driver's compartment still covered with showroom plastic. The nylon carpet was a speckled green and brown, coordinated with the brown paneling of the overhead cabinets and the green and yellow curtains and upholstery. A dinette booth, a galley, a bathroom. A long couch across the rear wall that opened into a double bed.

He stretched out on the couch. He wondered where Jean had gone with Carley. He felt uneasy without her. The Winnebago was sealed against the world outside, the voices and clatter of the encampment rarely broke through the hum of the cooling system.

Noise at the front door startled him. Jean clambered aboard with packages. Mack handed up her camera knapsack, her suitcases, Cable's suitcase.

"Hey. I hope you're really hungry. I'm going to make you a great dinner tonight."

"Where've you been?"

"I drove Carley into town, he had shopping to do for Rice. I'll tell you about it over dinner. When we got back I saw the mobile homes were here so I went out again for food. I hope you like . . ."

"I have to go out."

"It won't take too long."

"I have to go now. Can I use your car?"

"Sure. What's wrong?"

"Nothing's wrong."

"When will you be back?"

"When I'm back."

She looked hurt. "I just meant about dinner."

"You better eat without me."

"Okay." She turned her back as he side-stepped past her along the narrow aisle.

Sand opened the motel room door. Barrett sat sideways at the bureau-desk, offering Cable two profiles of his benign face, one directly, one reflected in the mirror. Except for the part in his white hair, Barrett's two-faced head appeared identical from either side. He drummed on the desk top. He seemed edgy, impatient. His mood infected Cable.

There were no preliminary greetings. Barrett said, "Tell me, Cable. Is Rice insane?"

Sand said, "That word has no meaning. It's a legality."

Barrett sighed. "There was a piece in the *Times* this morning, quoting a quite eminent psychiatrist, something to the effect that Rice is acting out the savior myth, the whole ball of wax from Jesus Christ to the Lone Ranger."

"Is this what you called me out for?"

"Look, Cable," there was a steeliness in Barrett's voice he had never heard before, "we're in a crunch. I've got Douglas Clune sitting on my head, I'm not going to have you nibbling at my feet. We've lost touch with this situation, primarily because of you. There isn't much point having a man in the field if we have to get our information from the newspapers. Sit down."

Cable remained standing.

"Let's get down to nuts and bolts, Cable. First of all, Jack's in charge now. That's right. You'll be reporting to him. You'll make it your business to see him at least twice every day, in the morning and in the late afternoon. He'll be in contact with us. Any information you have, any messages we have for you, will be funneled through Jack. You are not to call the Center unless Jack specifically tells you to.

"Second. What's your assignment? Rice. I want you in his pocket, I want you in his skull. If he goes to the bathroom, you'll check the bowl. I want a minute-by-minute diary of Rice's activities, his contacts, his thoughts, his plans. Am I making myself clear?"

Cable nodded. Barrett seemed uncomfortable looking up at him, his head cocked so sharply his ear nearly touched his shoulder. A petty act of defiance, thought Cable, but not without a small satisfaction.

"Third. I want a preliminary report from you. A catch up, actually, on everything Rice has done from July fourth to the moment. I hope you've been keeping notes because I want every scrap, what he said, what he saw, how he reacted, who he was with. There was a time you were quite good at that.

"Fourth. Now sit down, goddammit, right on the bed.

That's better. Look at me. I want to be sure this is all registering.

"The girl, this girl you're living with. Exactly what does she know about you?"

Cable barely controlled his anger. "Nothing at all."

"You're living in some kind of dream world. Have you forgotten who you are, who you work for? What happened on your last assignment? I want you out of that trailer tonight. You sleep alone."

"I only talk in my sleep when I'm drugged and I've had just about enough of your . . ."

"Don't you raise your voice. Cable, I've been very indulgent with you. To a fault. I've respected your skills and I've sympathized with your tragedy. But you've had more than enough time to recover. I think it's time you shaped up. For your own good."

Barrett stood up. Cable had forgotten how short he was.

"Any questions? No. Fine. I'll leave you with Dr. Moore. I'm sure you two have things to talk about. Don't forget the report. Tomorrow night at the latest." He opened a door and walked through to an adjoining room.

Sand said, "Don't let him throw you. He's a master at delegating his own anxieties. Clune's riding him hard. Tell me how you're feeling."

"I'm not moving out of the motor home."

Sand nodded and lit one of his plastic-tipped little cigars. He sat down in Barrett's chair and crossed his long legs.

"I didn't think you would. It's always been your pattern. Attached to a woman, demanding more trust than you're willing to give. For a reason we have to explore, you went further with Lynn than with any . . ."

"You sonuvabitch." Cable jumped up. "Mike Vogel wasn't her brother, was he, you ran him in on me just when you thought I was beginning to get my . . ."

"Who's Mike Vogel?"

"Who's Mike Vogel. Come on, how much of a cripple do you think I am? Right after our little session in Houston Lynn grows a brother who knows all about me. Was he in the closet or did you play him the tapes? I should have seen it right away."

Sand's high forehead contracted into glistening brown furrows. "Mike Vogel. You better lay this out, Cable. It sounds like . . ."

"You're a lousy actor, Sand."

"Where are you going?"

"You figure it out. You know all about my patterns."

"Cable!"

He walked out, tensed against a karate chop, an arm snaking around his neck. But Sand was still seated, brow wrinkled, as Cable closed the door between them.

He drove north of the city on quiet, dark roads. Clune's gone berserk and Barrett's on the spot and Jack's in charge and Sand's a lousy actor. And Cable's living in a dream world. Don't count on it. Cable's waking up. Dirty sonsuvbitches. See it plain. Cable's got a neurotic pattern, is that it, Dr. Moore? Well, let's get down to nuts and bolts and nail that pattern to Cable's back. Let's feed him his mother and his wife and his son right out of those drug bottles of yours, and then we'll run in a staffer to remind him about Lynn, and just for insurance we'll dangle Bonnie Fuller in front of his face. He hasn't managed to kill her yet. Mr. Clune's taken a personal interest in this project, obviously our future funding may be involved, you can see my position. Barrett said that nearly two months ago, before we left for Indianapolis. And now Clune's gone berserk and he's sitting on Barrett's head. That's just too bad. And it's not my problem.

Driving back, he remembered Bonnie talking about her younger sister living in San Francisco, married to a businessman named Archie Gorman. They've been after me to sell this dump and come live with them.

She'd go to them if she was free. If she was alive.

A dim overhead light glowed in their Winnebago. The faint stink of burned food hung in the cooled air. One plate, one coffee mug, a knife, fork and spoon stood upright in the dish drain. In the sink, a pan soaked in green liquid detergent.

Jean slept heavily on her side, her mouth open, clutching a pillow to her chest. The covers were twisted and her nightgown was tangled at her waist as if she had been wrung through a nightmare. He undressed and slipped into bed behind her, fitting himself to the crouch of her body. He worked his hands under the pillow to hold her breasts. He pressed his lips to the nape of her neck.

"No. Leave me alone." Her voice floated up from a well. "Go away, Jon. Just go 'way."

He turned her roughly. "Jean."

"Go . . . Cable. Oh, Cable." She wrapped her arms around him.

She was dry and tight but he pushed into her. They grunted at the rough friction but thrust together until her muscles loosened and fluid spilled. When the tension spurted out of him he held her close and fell asleep on her breast.

A morning newscast dubbed the encampment Liberty City. By noon the name was stuck fast, a handy tag for the media, for the campers a symbol of their existence as a community. Homemade bumper signs appeared: WE'RE FROM LIBERTY CITY. Car antennas sprouted handkerchief ensigns with crude copies of Rice's flag-and-rocket medallion. A bedsheet banner was attached to the stop-sign pole at Liberty Checkpoint. The letters of the new name had been cut from red and blue felt and unevenly glued to the white fabric. Copper wires had been hemmed into the banner to stiffen it out. Cable thought of the American flag Rice had planted on the moon, wired to simulate waving in a windless atmosphere.

He watched Amy's Fitness for Liberty session, a disorganized babble of strident commands and good-natured groaning. The fat girl stood on the aluminum platform, shouting cadences as she twisted and bent. She was oblivious to the jokes and half-hearted response below her. The ranks mingled and broke as campers collapsed with comic sighs. The few serious exercisers, mostly older women and a dozen young men around Mack, faltered.

Rice stepped up beside Amy. She stepped back and crossed her arms as he spoke to the crowd.

"In a few days we will begin a journey never before attempted in the history of our country. We will be looking ahead, not behind. The Liberty Road will be long and hard. There will be no time for stragglers."

Rice wore a fresh white turtleneck shirt that Cable had never seen on him before. Jean and Carley must have bought it for him. The skin-tight cotton emphasized the hard mold of his arms and chest and enhanced the shiny medallion. Tight white flared pants. White patent boots. Rice's sandy hair was longer than Cable remembered it, just beginning to curl over his ears and down his neck. The graying sideburns were thicker, growing down to the lobes of his small, flat ears.

The crowd shuffled into spaced ranks. Rice nodded at Amy and climbed down the ladder. Passing Cable, he said, "Aren't you exercising today?"

Rice walked on without waiting for an answer, but Cable reacted involuntarily, taking a step forward before he stopped himself. I'm not one of them.

He watched Jean swing easily through the knots of campers, shooting, talking to everyone, laying down her cameras to pitch in on a chore. He envied her natural way, and wanted to believe it was a tool of her trade. She was relaxing people so they wouldn't look self-conscious when she photographed them. But he knew better. She was secure inside herself and she was allowing herself to move to the rhythms of the moment. She was becoming part of the life of the encampment, and out of sync with him.

Jack had reinserted himself without effort, the beach boy's beach boy, casual and friendly. He was supervising three new Sons of Liberty inspect and register the continual trickle of incoming traffic, tourists, newsmen, peddlers, the latest immigrants to Liberty City. Jack's in charge.

Mack swaggered. The police chief of Liberty City. He ordered transistor radios turned down, garbage bundled, fires contained, clotheslines restrung in a central drying area. He was fair but ponderously authoritarian, settling the petty arguments over duties or property or living space. He invoked Rice's name as a badge. Joey followed Mack everywhere, basking in his borrowed power. One of the young men from the yellow Toyota, now clean shaven and pony-tailed, stalked behind them. The enforcer. Cable heard Mack call him Paoli, a name from the St. Louis library book. Reborn in the revolution.

Late in the day, while Cable watched, Paoli was forced to action. A girl who had hitchhiked alone to the encampment accused three boys in college fraternity tee shirts of having forced her into the back of their car. She said she had to fight her way out. Mack ordered the frat boys out of Liberty City. They refused to leave. They had been teased on, they said. The girl had wanted money. Paoli glided forward, easily blocking a clumsy punch. He spun one boy around and ran him head first into the car door.

He grabbed another in a cop's hammerlock and levered him to the sand. The third boy jumped into the car and started the engine.

The irony did not amuse Cable. How many campus riots had Paoli helped incite, how many young radicals had he whipped into violence and then fingered for the FBI? He thought of Sand punching the cop to save him from being shot. Or had Jack made up that story? Or is Paoli reporting to Jack, too?

The old role is failing me, my notebook as prop, a disinterested and tolerant mask on my face. He had felt alone in crowds before, but never lonely. His objective had always given him protection and comfort. The newspaper story. The Center report. The connection with a higher purpose that allowed him to feel superior to the people he was observing, recording, spying on.

But this time he merely felt alien.

Toward dinnertime Jean asked him if he would mind eating at the campfire. She wanted to add their food to the Liberty Stew. He did not feel strong enough to demand they eat alone.

He felt displaced at the campfire. His attempt to be convivial made him feel awkward. The others knew he had been with Rice from the start, and they treated him with deference; first at the common pot, nearest to the fire. He could not respond gracefully. A phrase had sprung up, "The spirit of Liberty City," and each time it was uttered, each time the L was flashed, he felt eyes turn toward him for approval as Rice's surrogate. His cheeks ached from a false smile. He pretended to enjoy the stew, which was tasteless to him, he nodded mechanically as Push Lane, then Amy, then a dozen others loudly remarked on how well the generations had integrated around the fire. A fellowship of freedom. The Spirit of Liberty City. He was finally released from public scrutiny when the instruments were dragged out, guitars and recorders and flutes, harmonicas, an accordion, drums. The crowd swayed as it sang folk songs and old show tunes, the standards of a million marshmallow roasts, a Protestant hymn led by the surprisingly fine church choir soprano of Lane's stout wife. Jean laid her head on Cable's shoulder and sang in a confident off key. Her face was flushed with pleasure and firelight.

They walked back to the Winnebago at midnight. They opened the rear bed together and undressed silently in a dim night light.

"You really moved around today," said Cable.

"I loved it. Such good vibrations. I've never seen anything like it. By the time I got turned on to the movement, it was all ego trips and politics."

"You can't compare two days of this carnival to civil rights or the peace movement. Whatever else they were, they had specific goals, there were issues at stake. This thing is a . . . a drive-in."

"You should try to let go a little. Feel what it's about instead of intellectualizing it."

The gentle reasonableness of her voice roweled him. "You know, your responsibility is to the people who are going to look at your pictures. You can't put yourself in those pictures, manipulate them. That's dishonest."

"Cable, if I didn't know you better I'd think you were serious. You're not a shadow, you're not an invisible man. Get out and . . ."

"I'm very tired. Let's go to sleep."

"Poor Cable." She pressed her hands against his cheeks. "It's okay. You can blow up, too. You've earned it. Let Momma tuck you in."

He slapped her face.

She jumped back. Her eyes bulged to their tunnel rims. She touched the red blotch on her cheek.

"Jean, I'm sorry. I'm very sorry."

"No one ever hit me."

"I never hit a woman before." His anger deserted him. He felt gutted.

"Why?"

"I don't know. I just don't know."

"What did I say? What did I do?"

"I'll sleep up front."

"No, Cable, please don't shut me out." She led him to the bed. He turned his back on her and lay stiff. When she began to cry he turned and let her burrow her wet face into his chest. After a while she began to caress his body, gentle strokes that lengthened until her hands reached his limp penis. She stroked harder, urgently, took it into her mouth to give it life. She tried for a long time and he wondered if he could be willing himself dead, to protect himself, to punish her for being able to touch him so deeply.

This time, Cable's own fingers turn the ignition key, long black fingers attached to his arm with electrician's tape. The red Volkswagen explodes and the raining glass and metal bounce off his white space helmet and fall at his feet, windshield shards, silver fender scraps, a single orange camera filter. He kicks them away with his bloody blue sneakers.

Cable awoke at dawn and left Jean sleeping in the Winnebago. Liberty City was just beginning to stir for its third day. The older campers clattered at their trailer stoves. The younger ones turned in their bedrolls fighting consciousness. Near the county road a boy he had never seen before asked, "Liberty business?" He carried a two-foot nightstick Cable recognized as one of the clubs the White Action Force had brought from Cleveland. Now it was painted silver.

"Are you on Liberty business?"

"None of your business."

"All perimeters are secured from sunset to sunrise. Captain Mack's orders. No one goes in or out of Liberty City except on Liberty business."

Cable walked on.

"Halt!"

He imagined his left hand closing around the club, his right smashing the young face. His muscles quivered.

"Halt!" Three sharp whistle blasts brought others out of the dappled early light.

"For Chrissake, that's Mr. Cable." Georgie's voice.

"Sorry, sir. Just following orders."

He wandered back to the glowing ash heap of the campfire. It's a walled city now. Another prison. Boxes within boxes, the Winnebago, the encampment, the Center, my own head. I have to get away.

Duwayne and Carley had unhinged the tailgate from a pick-up truck and rigged it to the front end as an earth leveler. Lane stood in a group of new cronies watching the two men scrape rocks and cacti and scrub growth from a patch of land south of the encampment. Lane saw Cable and gestured with an oversized coffee mug marked *Push*.

"They're clearing a chopper pad," said Lane.

A wiry old man with a clouded eye said, "Take 'em all day with that contraption."

"Don't need much room. Those choppers can land on a handkerchief, right, Mr. Cable?"

Cable nodded. He had seen these old men all over the country, spectators at a thousand construction sites measuring their fading days in steam shovel scoops. They might as well be here as anywhere.

"Gonna have important visitors," said Lane. "You can't make any time on that county road with all them tourists."

"Who you figure's coming out?" asked the one-eyed man.

"Could be most anybody. Some big TV star. Maybe dignitaries."

"The President!" A man guffawed.

"Wouldn't surprise me none. The people's here."

They strolled back for breakfast and to spread the rumor.

The sign of stones was Mack's idea. He led Amy's breathless exercisers out into the desert for the largest rocks they could find. They heaved them up into trailing trucks. Sons of Liberty splashed the rocks with silver paint. Jean walked among them with other photographers, shooting. She forced a smile for Cable but he could not return it. He felt oppressed. Hemmed in.

The stones were arranged into ten-foot letters, WELCOME TO LI, before they ran out. They were rearranged to spell LIBERTY CITY.

Exhausted, the crowd stood for an hour in the suffocating heat before a helicopter finally churned out of the north, turned, and settled down in a stinging sandstorm. A single passenger jumped out. Howard Lefferts in a boldly checked tan suit and cherry-red slip-ons had the jaunty glow of a celebrity, but the crowd did not recognize him and fell back, disappointed. Lefferts walked quickly toward Rice, who was waiting in the doorway of his motor home.

Jack touched Cable's arm. "You better go in there with them, Mr. Cable."

The undertone of command rankled less than Jack's calling him mister. He imagined a condescension in the word.

He followed Lefferts inside.

"I think this should be private," said Lefferts.

"It is private," said Rice. He motioned Lefferts to the dinette booth and sat facing him. Cable sat in the driver's chair, behind Lefferts.

"Liberty City isn't exactly what they had in mind," said Lefferts.

"Liberty City exists," said Rice. "Start from that premise."

"Commander. Since the Astrodome we've resynthetized the basic . . ."

"Say what you came to say."

"Okay. Wendt's staff did a deep demo on three states. California, Arizona and Florida. They're all prime. Here's the scenario. You take up residence in one of the three. You become involved in a local issue with national and international implications. Something compatible with your credibility. A nuclear power plant. A defense site. Technological planning. Eventually you'll be drafted to run for office. At least Congress, probably the Senate. The campaign machinery will be there.

"But first you have to disband Liberty City. Call off the Caravan. It's an unpredictable force. Wendt and Knox feel you would be loosing a mob on the country."

"Is that your feeling, too?"

Lefferts shrugged. Cable imagined his hedging half smile. "Traditional politics bores me. But substantive change only occurs through visionary legislation. As a senator—as president—you could make the second American Revolution a self-perpetuating institution."

Rice said, "The day I announce my candidacy I nullify everything I've said and done since the moon. It all becomes a publicity stunt. And if I do allow myself to be boxed into your system, they'll find a hundred legal ways to disqualify me or defeat me or bottle me up in minor committees. I won't be free."

"You'll have legitimate power, official access," said Lefferts. "We all see you as a charismatic leader, a man who can create a climate for reform. For hope. People respect your accomplishments, your sincerity. You've got no politi-

222

cal debts. You can get this country moving in positive directions."

Rice stood up. "I can do all that without Wendt and Knox. Their time has passed. I don't need them anymore. All I need is those people out there. They believe in me and I believe in them."

Lefferts stood. "If you march on Washington, the best you can hope to accomplish is a weakening of the administrative powers of government. I think you want the same thing Wendt and Knox want. A national administration that's more responsive to the needs of the people, that's willing to regulate the major industries in the people's interests, that has the power and confidence to dismantle the oligopolistic structure, to reshape technological rationality, to . . ."

"Words," said Rice. "New clothes for a rotting leper. I don't think we have anything more to say about this."

Lefferts shook his head. "I'm sorry, Commander. I enjoyed working with you in Houston. I was looking forward to working with you again."

"That's entirely up to you," said Rice. "You did a good job in Houston."

Lefferts smiled, including Cable. There were green hairlines between his gums and his capped teeth. "In that case, Commander, count me aboard. I'll be back as soon as I see Wendt. I have a feeling we might be underestimating his flexibility. Mr. Cable? Will you walk me to the helicopter. I think we should get reacquainted."

The newspack recognized Lefferts and started toward him. Mack moved in with twenty Sons to form a circle around Lefferts and Cable. Mack jumped inside the circle and raised a silver club.

The Sons faced out and locked arms. The newsmen were stopped by the white-shirted chests. Photographers poked cameras between pony-tailed heads.

Mack yelled, "Liberty Step!"

The band of Sons began a shuffling ring dance, turning faster and faster until the circle ballooned out and the newsmen were pushed away.

"Forward!"

The circle buzz-sawed through the crowd. Mack ran around the inner ring, prodding faltering Sons with his stick. Walking in the calm eye of the hurricane, Lefferts said to Cable, "I've seen this before somewhere."

Probably in Cleveland, Cable thought. Where it was probably called the White Action Step.

"Whatever it is, it's damned effective. Look, Cable, you're supposed to be his friend. At least he thinks so. You better talk to him. He's got a ton of charisma but he's no Moses. He's got no solid base, just a bunch of hippies and old crocks. Once those cameras leave, he's dead. Right back where he started, only this time he'll really be old news."

Cable felt strangled by the gyrating formation. I have to get away.

"He's hot right now, Cable. He thinks it's never going to end. Believe me, I know the feeling. But it always ends. And when it does he'll just dry up and blow away. With all his slogans and his salutes and his fancy ice-cream suit."

At the sign of stones, Mack bawled, "Flanking columns!"

The circle broke into two ragged files and Mack ran ahead to lead them to the helicopter. The rotary blades spun. Lefferts ducked into the gritty spray and climbed in.

Cable jumped in after him.

"Where are you going?" Lefferts was alarmed.

"Can you drop me at the airport?"

"Sure. No trouble." He looked relieved.

The helicopter lifted before Cable's pupils dilated to focus in the dim light. There were four passenger seats that swiveled to face each other. The pilot's brown face was obscured in the sunlight flooding his windshield.

"Better strap up," said Lefferts. He leaned toward Cable. So close, the pits of his face were shallower, less severe. "I hate these damn things, but they really move you around. Look at that traffic down there. Must be backed up half a mile. I guess everybody wants to quit smoking and drinking." He glanced at Cable's face. "Just making a bad joke."

Cable barely heard him. The plan seemed fuzzy and fruitless. But it was something for himself. By himself. He was not sure he had enough money for an airline ticket. Jean's money. She had never asked for an accounting.

Lefferts shouted to the pilot, "We'll make a stop at the airport."

"Right, Mr. Lefferts." The pilot's voice was deep, cool, familiar.

Lefferts turned back to Cable. "You will talk to him. There have to be basic constructs, procedures, he should understand that better than anyone. If you want to get to the moon you don't start by jumping off the tallest building and flapping your arms."

Cable's right leg began twitching spasmodically; he clasped and unclasped his hands. The seat belt was a strait jacket. He closed his eyes and willed the chopper down.

"We're landing now."

Cable opened his eyes. The pilot was looking at him over his shoulder, a plastic cigar tip clamped between Chiclet teeth.

They landed with a thump. Cable unsnapped his belt and began fumbling at the hatch door before the helicopter settled. *This time, Sand won't let me leave.*

Sand opened the hatch without looking at Cable.

"You'll talk to him, Cable," said Lefferts.

Cable jumped out. The heat of the rubbery tarmac seeped up through his shoes. Then he was running.

Seventeen

The City lies sparkling in its sheath of waters, waiting in ambush for Cable. He thinks of Susan: She held his hand as they ran up these hills, laughing, pausing breathless at each crest to embrace, so complete together the streets were theirs alone, the achingly bright city existed only for these two, the first to discover the bridge glowing red in the sunset. A hundred candles melting down the neck of green wine bottles had waited for just these two to light them. He and the small blonde girl took vows of returning, the two of them, some day the three, the four of them. . . .

The City stabs Cable. He remembers returning alone: a damp, chilly spring, his cough echoing through gray streets. He stumbled among ruins to land's end. He lay down to sleep in Golden Gate Park. Or die?

The Gorman house on Russian Hill was white and narrow. He circled the block until he was satisfied the house was not under surveillance from the street, then walked past it twice. Plants in the window. A red metal tricycle was parked against the bottom step of a high white stoop. He retreated to a corner. Clouds dimmed the afternoon sun. He felt inconspicuous beneath the overcast. A curtain twitched, a woman's hand appeared with a white watering can. The spout tilted daintily over a plant. He could not recognize it as Bonnie's hand. The hand withdrew.

He had an urge to get it over with, to knock on the door, to charge in. Or telephone. But they might be tapping Gorman's phone, or watching his house from another window on the street.

Men returned from work, hurrying against the darkening clouds. He joined them to pass the house twice more, quickly, as if someone waited for him, too. A man in a gray tropical suit walked up the steps of the Gorman house, a newspaper and a briefcase under his arm. The door opened just as he reached it. Cable could not see into the house. The man came out a few minutes later, without his jacket, to roll the tricycle through a ground-level door. The man ran back up the steps just as the first fat drops of rain spattered on the pavement.

She's in the house, she's always been in that house. The Center knew it all along. They used her as a threat to keep me dependent, to keep me with Rice. I let them use it. I wanted to be dependent on them.

The street was empty. Lights went on behind curtained windows. A roll of distant thunder, then pittering rain.

They strung me along with Bonnie Fuller, they strung me along with guilt-laden dreams.

The rain fell in thin, warm sheets, cloaking him, soothing him.

The red tricycle rolls down the hill through a curtain of steel-gray rain, weaving around trees and hydrants, bumping off the curb into the street, urged on by the small boy on his stomach, mittened hands clamped on the wooden rudders of his Flexible Flyer, cheeks red with cold and the forbidden thrill. His mother told him never to sled down the hill. She comes out of the apartment house shouting at him, but he plunges on, the red steel runners spraying snow into his eyes. At the foot of the icy hill he loses control, turning over twice, sliding on his back, the red steel bumper pressed to his lips, so cold it sticks. He screams for his mother. She is over him now, her brown hair uncovered, soothing him, righting him, scolding him. Over her shoulder he sees the skidding truck plunging down upon them and he cannot speak.

He is in the Teddy Bear room, his father sits by his bed. How do you feel, Davey? My legs hurt. He asks for his mommy and his father begins to cry.

Stuart. They had named their little boy for his mother.
"STUART!" Cable ran down the rain-slick hill. A car swerved to avoid him, honking.
"STUART!" He fell and rolled to the foot of the hill, coming to rest against the curb. Water rushing along the gutter broke on his body.
"Stuart."

He sees the boy clearly, the enormous brown eyes in the round face, the body just beginning to lose its toddler sway. Stuart's going to be a good athlete, he's strong, look at those shoulders, you can tell already he's well-coordinated. Just like his daddy. Maybe he'll be a swimmer, too. David got an early start.

Davey's four. He goes three times a week for physical therapy. Mostly in the pool, for his legs. He's really coming along. The operations were a success, now he has to build up his legs. I don't know how Sylvia did it, she must have been underneath the truck when she threw Davey.

Stuart.

He lay on his back in the gutter, half submerged, and opened his eyes to the pelting rain, forcing them to stay open so the rain could wash the bodies off his sight. He opened his mouth to the rain. Drown me.

"Stuart, Stuart, Stuart, Stuart, Stuart." Another chant, but the name would never become just a sound. It was attached forever to a little boy with enormous brown eyes. He could never wash it away or drown it or chant it into meaninglessness. He could die, or he could try to live with it.

The rain slackened. He sat up.

Stuart. There it was. Out. In the air. Squeezed from a pus pocket in his head. In New York Sand had said, Look, Cable, it's in your head, that shit's got to come out or your head'll split open like a rotten cantaloupe. In Houston, Sand had said, Cable, I told you once, it's all got to come out. We've got to get it out and deal with it. Before it tears your head off. But Sand had driven it deeper. He never wanted it out. He made me dependent to string me along.

Cable stood.

He walked until he found a cafeteria. It was crowded with lonely diners and refugees from the rain. In the men's room he stripped and wrung out his clothes and dried them under a hot air blower. It took a long time.

He brought two cups of coffee to a table still littered with someone else's dinner. He drank one cup quickly and nursed the other. Sand had strung him along with Stuart while Jack strung him along with Bonnie Fuller. To make him dependent, to send him back into the field, to keep him there. It had not really been very hard for them. He had turned himself over to them, he had given himself up for dead.

Stuart is dead. Susan is dead. Lynn is dead. Mommy is dead.

He cried. Without sound or movement, he cried. Tears dripped off his cheeks into the coffee cup. Brown ripples blurred.

"Mister? I'm sorry. We're closing."

The cafeteria had emptied beyond his misted sight. It was nearly nine o'clock.

The storm was passed. The air was fresh and clean. Neon rainbows on the wet sidewalk.

Cable walked. Whores and hippie beggars approached, hesitated, faded. He bumped into a man who whirled, looked into his face, and apologized.

Cable walked. He would cry again, he knew, he had reservoirs of tears, but for the first time in months his mind felt clear of nameless dreads. It's out now. I can deal with it.

He decided not to go back to the Gorman house, not to call. Bonnie might be there, she might not be there, she might be dead. There's nothing I can do for her now. Except cause her more trouble. And her sister and Gorman and the tricycle rider.

Jigsaw-puzzle pieces from the debris of my life.

He remembered other nights in other cities, overtired and overstimulated by the chase for pieces of a puzzle, walking, thinking, stopping to add to a list of people to see, leads to track, a fact to be scratched out of a public document. Once Stuart was born Cable always called Susan by eight o'clock to say goodnight. He cried for the three of them.

He bought a writing tablet and several pens in a hotel drugstore. He sat in a corner of the lobby and began to write. The house detective watched him for a while, but

Cable kept his head down and the man finally lost interest and walked away.

> 4 July P.M.—Leaving Astrodome subj. immediately began charting future itinerary. Rather than being discouraged by alleged power failure he considered it affirmation of his belief govt. needed to silence him to retain national control. Order of vehicles en route Houston–San Antonio: Staffer in lead station . . .

Cable wrote for hours, dredging up the small details that would be Xeroxed and cut and pasted and Xeroxed again and cross-indexed, Wild Rice, Chip, the motel in Odessa that demanded a damage bond, Billy Fox, the color of the gas at Skylancer, Paoli's yellow Toyota, Lefferts' cherry-red slip-ons, the atoms of fact that would pass through a dozen hands in Research, that Barrett would nod over, sure that Cable could have left out nothing, that Cable was saving his ass.

I'm buying myself time. To finish a puzzle.

He wrote around Jean. She barely existed in the report. There was no way he could avoid mentioning that Rice had driven her car to Skylancer, that she had gone to buy the white clothes with Carley. They knew that already. But he did not report that she had boarded the bus after Odessa, that she had driven it off the reservation, that her money had kept them going, that they had become lovers at Beryl Petty's. That he was going back to Liberty City because she was there and he needed her.

Descending into Las Vegas through the early light: The encampment has spread, its southern border now reaches the sign of stones. The sun picks out each silvered rock, the three Winnebagos, the empty platform on Liberty Two.

Wake up. I'm back. I've come all the way back.

Eighteen

A mile from Liberty City the traffic on the county road fused into a glass-and-metal snake inching through black exhaust fumes and the steam of overheated radiators. The taxi driver banged his wheel. "Be another hour getting in."

"I might as well get out here," said Cable. "What's going on?"

"I should of known. My kids left the house at 3 A.M. to get on line for the show."

"What show?"

"Where you been? 'The Bart Pike Hour.'"

Cable paid the driver and climbed out into the smothering morning. The heat enclosed him and the fumes irritated his nostrils and eyes. But he felt cool and eager beneath the discomfort of his skin.

He walked along the sandy shoulder past bursts of noise from the stalled cars. Restless children hung out of side windows. Teen-agers clapped and sang back at their tape decks. He recognized Bart Pike's dungeon monotone. "The Song from Solitary." "Just One of Your Lies." The voice sounded even more mannered to him now than it had at the wheel of Liberty Two. As artificial as the Astrodome grass.

Ahead of Cable, a pillowy fat man trudged from car to car displaying a large square of cardboard festooned with colored buttons: Rice's likeness above the words *Dare Be Free;* a photograph of Liberty Two; the words *See It Plain* superimposed on the earth. The kids in the back seats nagged for the buttons. Women's hands thrust out coins at the fat man. A young father walked around the front of his car tugging a blue Banlon shirt over an early paunch. He picked one of each button off the cardboard and ceremoniously pinned them on the matching blue shirt of a little boy in a car seat. Cable walked faster.

The roadside commerce thickened as he approached Liberty Checkpoint. Cold-drink stands, station wagons crammed with paper periscopes, felt amusement-park hats, toy rockets. Under an awning attached to a panel truck, a middle-aged man with a Marine tattoo was ironing decals of the Liberty Two medallion on plain white tee shirts. Cable thought of the Speedway. The Liberty Carnival had begun.

The crude bedsheet banner at the checkpoint had been replaced with a professionally constructed archway. Twin flagpoles set in concrete supported a silver-coated canvas sign. The archway was high and wide enough for two lanes of traffic. The sign read LIBERTY CITY in orange Dayglo. There were random perforations in the canvas to reduce wind resistance. The sign seemed cheap and fake to Cable, a side-show come-on, but he did not feel personally offended. I know who I am. Now.

Jack did not seem surprised to see Cable. He passed his clipboard to one of the Sons and trotted up, a tall, blond dog, his good nature and energy undiminished by the heat. Cable handed him the folded sheets of writing paper.

"The report."

"Great. I can't wait to read it, Mr. Cable. I know it'll be . . ."

"Let's cut the crap, okay? Mr. Lynch."

The blue eyes were no longer so ingenuous. "Look, Mr. Cable, being in charge means zilch. It's strictly admin. It's just easier for me to move around and make the calls. You've got Rice and Sand's tied up with the bird." He offered his hand. "Okay?"

Cable nodded but he did not shake Jack's hand. "Who's helicopter is it? How did Sand get in?"

"I really don't know, Mr. Cable. Ask him. He's been back and forth with Pike's people. You wouldn't believe the bodies and equipment for one TV show."

"When did all this happen?"

"They started coming in yesterday afternoon. Mr. Cable?" The spurned hand touched Cable's arm. "One thing you should know before you go in. Compliments of Porky's Gestapo. Jean spent the night with Rice."

Cable forced himself to shrug. He walked in.

The encampment had grown denser in the past twenty-four hours, and had split into little neighborhoods. There were more young families now, more small children scampering among late model cars. Fortyish men and women in the kind of determinedly festive sports clothes he had seen around suburban gas barbecues. The pensioners and the summer hippies were still a majority, but the middle was settling in. A sprinkling of young working men in odd pieces of uniform, dusty construction boots, blue garage shirts with first names in woven script above a breast pocket, hard hats. Girls in stylish, inexpensive clothes, carefully groomed and made up.

234

Four or five bodies rested on cots in an open-walled first-aid tent. A doctor was treating a child's leg.

Technicians swarmed over Liberty Two erecting a super-structure of reflectors and amplifiers and perches for cameramen. Cable estimated several thousand on the sand around the bus, staking places for the show. Georgie and Paoli and a dozen Sons patrolled aisles, distributing white paper sun visors, salt tablets and cups of water from canvas buckets.

Mack stood on a car roof shouting orders through a battery-powered bullhorn. He wore a red golf cap with a Rice button pinned to the club's insignia. When he saw Cable he flashed the L salute and beckoned. Cable ignored him and continued picking his way through the audience toward the bus. Mack slid off the car on his rump, handed the bullhorn to Joey and ran after him.

"Mr. Cable. I want to apologize about the incident yesterday. Lieutenant Trott reported it to me and the Son who failed to recognize you has been disciplined." There was a new hardness around Mack's mouth.

"Disciplined?"

"Probation, extra sanitary details and demerits against promotion. It was necessary to make an example. Vigilance is paramount, but disrespect to leadership cannot be tolerated."

"He didn't know me."

"That's no excuse. You were with us when the bus rode alone." The myths begin, thought Cable. There will be a "Horst Wessel Song" for Larry Bruno.

"Sir, I'd like to see you later. Privately. On Liberty business."

"Of course." He wondered if it was about Jean and Rice.

Mack saluted and marched back to his post with a stiff-legged step.

The end Winnebago was locked and curtained. He wondered if Jean had already moved in with Rice. Just as well. I've got to be free now, responsible for no one but myself.

The middle Winnebago, the Caravan headquarters, had been taken over by a motley of pearl-button cowboy shirts and plaid sport jackets, black attaché cases, guitars and make-up kits. Pike's people. In the distance, a helicopter snarled. Sand with another load.

Carley waved him into Rice's Winnebago. Cable looked for traces of Jean. There was a stack of wet plastic dishes and mugs on the galley counter. Had Jean cooked his dinner? His breakfast?

Cable opened the curtain to the rear bedroom. Rice stood on a small wooden platform studying a typewritten index card. A plump little man with a mouthful of pins was crouched at Rice's feet, basting the slack of silver cloth around Rice's ankle.

Rice was wearing a silver jumpsuit. The cloth had a metallic sheen and it was so closely woven it appeared to have the texture of aluminum wrap. Yet it fitted his body so precisely that it wrinkled only when he moved. The silver track of a heavy-duty zipper gleamed like a new scar from his throat to his crotch. His genitals bulged against his left thigh. There were covered zippers, no more visible than fine seams, down each sleeve and from the small of his back down to each heel.

"Gorgeous," said the tailor through his pins. He stood up, his chestnut hairpiece reaching Rice's waist. "I'll taper the other ones this afternoon. Your calf muscles are the problem, they're too big in relationship to your ankles." He backed into Cable. "Excuse me. You got an opinion? Fantastic?"

"Very striking," said Cable. The tailor dismissed him with a damp sigh.

"Cable." Rice looked up from the index card, obviously

pleased. "Has Jean seen you? She wasn't as sure as I was you'd be back." He looked down at the tailor. "Aren't you finished?"

"We'll take it off now, to be on the safe side." The tailor opened the zippers carefully and gathered the cloth as Rice slipped out. The astronaut's body, naked except for the medallion, offended Cable. He imagined it pressed into Jean.

"I'll be back to dress you, Commander." The tailor left, cradling the jumpsuit.

Rice sat on the bed. "Are you all right? You look very tired."

"I had something to do."

"I'd like to have a long talk with you, Cable. But this isn't the time. By the way, I'm not angry."

"That's a relief."

Rice ignored the sarcasm. "This is the setup. Pike's taping his show this morning. It'll be on network tonight. He's introducing a new song, 'The Ballad of Liberty Two.' It isn't exactly 'The Battle Hymn of the Republic, but he's captured the mood."

"Did you contact him?"

"He walked in yesterday. I barely knew who he was. He's appearing in Las Vegas. Lefferts is with his lawyers next door working out the details. What's the matter?"

Cable shrugged.

Rice laced his fingers behind his head. "We can't be rigid. Music is a form of communication that stirs people to action. 'The Marseillaise.' 'Yankee Doddle.' "

" 'Horst Wessel.' 'God Save the King.' "

"Cable, the day we carve the L on the Washington Monument it won't matter how we got there, only that we made it."

"You told me that once. The end justifies the means."

"It's self-evident."

Carley poked his head through the door. "Five minutes, Commander."

Bart Pike was tall and gaunt, his face a marked map of hard travels. When he took a deep breath his ribs were outlined through his brown rodeo shirt and his glazed eyes narrowed with pain. A head, thought Cable. Probably needed a handful of pills just to get up to the platform.

"The name's Barton Pike and this is my hour to howl. I'm standing on a beat-up old school bus, the kind of bus that come bumpin' down to the raggedy hollas of my childhood and carried us up to a place where they tried to teach us to read and figger and write. I didn't ride that bus so often as I should of, but I'm gonna be ridin' this one. It's called Liberty Two and it's got room for all of us. You sit back now. We're gonna ride together."

The cameras swung out to pan the crowd. A make-up man scurried up to mop Pike's brow with cotton balls. A man with a clipboard motioned Rice to the rear ladder.

"Those sun visors are reflecting back. Will you ask the audience to remove them."

"The sun's too strong right now," said Rice.

"Be for less than an hour, Commander."

"If you want them off you'll have to wait for sundown." Rice mounted the ladder.

The man shook his head at Cable. "Your boy makes B.P. look like a charlotte russe."

"Pike's only a superstar," said Cable.

The man winked. The fraternalism of flunkies, thought Cable. Your boy. My boy. It's all showbiz till he carves that L on the Washington Monument.

On a monitor Pike was in rugged profile, staring into a crowd that looked like a vast tide of white-tipped waves. Rice was behind him, slightly out of focus, a shimmering silver statue. A prompter flipped a cardboard page and

Pike began to haul up words from the wellspring of his soul.

"I wrote this song before I met this man. But, like a lot of folks, I feel I've known him a long, long time. I admired him and I prayed for him. To my everlasting shame, I laughed at him. But now, by God, I'm with him. 'Cause I know he's with me.

"I call this song, 'The Ballad of Liberty Two.'"

The crowd took a breath and its sudden hush intensified other sounds: a plane taking off, a baby's cry, the clank of equipment. Pike's face filled the monitor screen with suffering and excess. His voice was deep and clear.

> This lonely rider lost in the canyons
> That swallow my brothers
> Looks up in a night of rockets and yearning
> To hear a voice from the sky.
>
> Silver, lighting up the world,
> Brighter than a star will ever be,
> Liberty Two,
> Oh, Liberty Two,
> Carry me back home
> To a world where I dare to be free.

Rice had not moved. The camera moved back to bring him into off-focus in a corner of the screen. Pike frowned as he plucked a melancholy chord.

> This rider is listening
> An astronaut calls him,
> A man from dark spaces
> With words learned on high.
>
> Silver, lighting up the world,
> Brighter than a star will ever be,
> Liberty Two,

Oh, Liberty Two,
Carry me back home
To a world where I dare to be free.

This rider will follow
The man dressed in silver,
The man with a message.
Rice knows the way.

Chord echoes fell and vanished like snowflakes. Rice
stepped forward and Pike handed him the mike. He spoke
crisply, rupturing the mood.

"In forty-eight hours we will sing this song in the Los
Angeles Coliseum. A liberty hymn for America. In fifty
hours this silver bus will begin its journey across America
to Washington, D.C. Our song will echo across the country. The new national anthem. A call for a new beginning.

"Join us. Paint your car silver and join the Liberty Caravan. Join us in Reno, Nevada; in Salt Lake City; in Chey-
enne, Wyoming; in Lincoln, Nebraska; Chicago; Columbus,
Ohio; Pittsburgh; Washington. Join the second American
Revolution and Dare Be Free."

He passed the mike back to Pike and stepped back out
of focus.

This rider will follow
The man dressed in silver,
The man with a message.
Rice knows the way.

Silver, lighting up the world,
Brighter than a star will ever be.
Liberty Two,
Oh, Liberty Two,
Carry me back home
To a world where I dare to be free.

Lights blinked off in the metal tower and Pike sagged against an aluminum guard rail. He stuffed a small plastic tube into one nostril and inhaled.

A woman's piercing voice rose from the crowd.

"Silver, lighting up the world . . ."

Push Lane's wife. Cable searched for her among the rising white visors.

The director shouted, "Get that. Sound."

The song grew, widened, deepened, covered the desert floor to the horizons and filled the bowl of the sky.

". . . Liberty Two,
"Oh, Liberty Two . . ."

Rice and Pike stood shoulder to shoulder, the astronaut impassive, his eyes beyond madness, the tall singer blinking at tears that formed on his long black lashes and dripped into the crevasses of his face. Your boy has just hit the top of the charts, thought Cable. But the voices touched him, too.

". . . carry me back home . . ."

Cable forced himself to move, to break the spell. He stepped on someone's foot, but there was no complaint. He stumbled around the bus, over wires and electronic boxes. Pike was clutching his pants leg, holding himself together. Rice was a silver statue.

". . . I dare to be free."

He remembered telling Rice there should be exit music at the Astrodome, and Rice had said it would be diverting. He had wanted to leave them in absolute silence facing the truth.

We can't be rigid.

Rice wore a blue terry-cloth robe. The silver jumpsuit hung from the knob of an overhead cabinet. Empty, its long zippers open, the suit was a tawdry cloth, a torn banner.

"Are they still out there?" asked Rice. He was sprawled on the rear bed. One of the secrets of his energy, thought Cable. He can flop and relax like a child, anywhere, any time.

"They'll be out there for a while," said Lefferts. "They have to rechoreograph a few numbers for the platform. Shall we get started? First of all, the advance men. Wendt has people he can trust all the way east to Chicago. After that we'll have to . . ."

"I don't think we'll need any advance work after Salt Lake City," said Rice. "By then the Caravan will be a tangible reality."

"I'm thinking logistics, not publicity," said Lefferts. "Local roads won't be able to handle the flow. The interstate system is also a military highway, so they might be able to hit us with an injunction there. National security."

"Don't overanticipate problems."

"Look, Commander, when they shot you to the moon they didn't just point the rocket and . . ."

"That was a technical exercise, we'd been through it before. There are no analogies to Liberty Two. We're talking about sending an idea around the world."

"Of course, Commander. I understand." Lefferts' earnest voice. Cable realized he disliked Lefferts intensely. Viscerally.

"I hope you do understand," said Rice. "I hope you're not talking about some cars driving cross country. The Caravan is a force of nature. It cannot be stopped or diverted. Let local people handle the traffic flow. There'll always be help for Liberty Two. There always has been."

"I guess you feel the same way about food, water, medical assistance and mechanical support."

"I do."

Lefferts checked off five lines on his yellow pad. "Now here's a shaft of insight into the co-opting character of the free enterprise system. Product endorsements. Naturally, I've declined, but . . ."

"What products?" asked Rice.

"You name it. Tires, breakfast cereals, clothing, soap, toilet paper, shaving creams, aspirins. The indistinguishables, the . . ."

"Get me a complete list," said Rice. "I'd like to think about it. We could set up a rating committee. Liberty Consumers. We could issue an efficiency report on each product when we reach Washington."

"Commander, it can only be construed as commercialism. It's complicating, it's . . ."

"It's a new dimension," said Rice. "The circle includes, not excludes. The Caravan carries all. But Business America isn't going to buy its way into the Caravan. For once they'll have to perform. And be judged by the truth." Rice looked at Cable. "What do you think?"

"Great if it works."

"Your enthusiasm is underwhelming," said Lefferts dryly. He's needling me, thought Cable, to get off the hook for disagreeing with Rice. But the perception didn't mitigate his anger.

Rice asked, "When's Wendt coming in?"

"About an hour or so. Farmer Lew's going to be in disguise. The quintessential pol."

"Who the hell are you working for?" asked Cable.

"Ultimately, the American people," said Lefferts seriously. "I'm representing Commander . . ."

"I think you're a goddam whore, and you've always

been, and you'll lay anyway the customer wants."

Lefferts rose. "I'll come back when you're free, Commander."

"I was just leaving," said Cable. "I don't want to miss the rest of 'The Bart Pike Hour.'"

It was past noon. A thermometer mounted outside a trailer registered 108 degrees. "The Bart Pike Hour" ground on, pausing every few minutes for lighting adjustments, fresh applications of make-up, conferences on new camera angles. The crowd sat patiently, flushed, stoned by the heat. Cable watched two Sons lift Push Lane's wife out of the crowd and carry her to the medical tent. Push held her hand and Jean walked alongside the stretcher shielding Mrs. Lane's face from the sun with a straw hat. The tent was already filled with heat-stroke victims. An ambulance siren whined in the distance.

Cable reached the tent at the same time Jean did. He wasn't sure what he wanted to say to her.

"Doctor?" She was handing him keys. "You can put some of your patients in the end Winnebago. It's air-conditioned."

Their eyes met over Mrs. Lane's body. He had nothing to say to Jean and he turned away.

Jack was barely sweating. "This is my kind of weather. Last winter in New York nearly finished me."

Me, too, thought Cable.

"We checked in nearly twelve hundred cars today. The place is crawling with F.B.I. Those guys are so dumb it's unbelievable. They take off their ties and think they're invisible. Did you know F.B.I. buys stripped-down sedans to save money? And then they slap on some chrome for camouflage?"

"Lefferts is with Rice," said Cable. "Wendt is coming in. Incognito."

"Oh, yeah? That's worth jingling Barrett."

There was something false about Jack's interest. Casually, Cable said, "Is there a line in to Lefferts?"

"Nobody told me."

Too fast, just a breath too fast. The question should have been worth a shrug, a moment's thought. You're not all that slick, Jack. You should have paid more attention in your school. When you were going over my old assignments. The classics.

"I mean, anything's possible, Mr. Cable. But Barrett would have told me. Don't you think?"

"I'm sure he would have."

Jack looked satisfied. Cable wasted some time at the checkpoint looking over the license-plate lists, chatting with the Sons sweltering at the unshaded post. They told him they had logged in cars from thirty-one states. Jack had organized a dollar pool on who would check through the thirty-second.

He strolled back into the encampment. The Center must have reached Lefferts some time after Oklahoma City. Through an intermediary, probably. Lefferts wouldn't know for sure who his contact was. Maybe he thinks he's feeding the government some information for a post-dated favor. He must have leased the helicopter and hired Sand. God knows who he thinks Sand is. And he certainly doesn't know who I am. I shouldn't have called him a whore. Lefferts is nothing, just another plug into Rice for Douglas Clune. Lefferts was just the easiest target for all my anger. I should have been cool, detached. But it felt good.

Mack said, "Mr. Cable," twice before the first time registered. "Can I see you now, Mr. Cable?"

He followed Mack into the middle Winnebago. The "Pike Hour" people had finally left. The motor home was littered with empty Coke bottles, cigarette butts and clumps of greasy tissue.

Mack shouted, "Paoli, get a clean-up detail in here."

Cable sat on a corner of the rear bed. Mack opened a cabinet and pulled down a steel box. He staggered under its weight and almost dropped it. Fire resistant, Cable thought. Mack cupped a hand over the lock as he clicked off the combination. Mack's paranoid, too.

Mack lifted the lid and withdrew a sheaf of papers. Cable glimpsed small metal objects in the box before Mack closed it. An iron cross bearing the letters W.A.F. A gravity knife.

"Could you look this over?"

The top sheet was new, a neatly handwritten title page: *Organizational Manual—The Sons of Liberty/by Captain Alexander Mackintosh.* The following pages were dog-eared and blotched with fingerprints. The typewriting was uneven, a threadbare ribbon and a jumpy carriage. Words, paragraphs, several pages had been carefully inked out. The words Sons of Liberty and the letters S.L. had been careted in on every page.

"Has Rice seen this?"

"No. He told me to check it out with you or Lefferts before I had it printed. I wasn't about to show it to that Commie lawyer." He opened the typescript to the third page.

A handwritten paragraph had been pasted onto an inked-out page. There were lumps under the strips of new paper where the paste had dried unevenly. The paper was wrinkled. Cable thought of the wallpaper strip in the Teddy Bear room. He felt only a mild interest in the curious associations of his mind. He read the paragraph:

> While the Sons of Liberty are open to all—regardless of race, religion or previous affiliation—superior officers must

constantly be on the alert against those whose real loyalty is to foreign countries—i.e., the Soviet Union, Africa or Israel.

Cable said, "This is the old White Action Force manual, isn't it?"

"I needed a model." Mack looked him straight in the eye. "An organization is an organization."

"How would you feel if I told you I was Jewish?"

Mack's eyes did not waver. "If it's true, you've overcome it. It doesn't matter any more. Is it true?"

"If it's true, it doesn't matter any more. Right?"

Mack looked down. "Right."

"How do you plan to use this?"

Mack hesitated, then looked up. "As the Caravan moves east we'll be sending out Sons to organize chapters in each of seventeen primary areas. As soon as he's formed a cadre, he'll move on to a secondary area. Then a third. Eventually we'll have more than a hundred chapters connected by a network of motorcycle couriers. Paul Reveres, I call them."

"For what purpose?"

"The couriers? Information and mutual defense."

"No, the whole organization."

"I don't understand the question."

"Why do you feel it's necessary to create such a large national organization?"

Mack nodded seriously and settled his head into his neck until a second chin formed. The little Nazi is practicing for "Meet the Press," Cable thought.

"Our Commander is a great visionary, a charismatic prophet, the greatest American I have ever known. But there has always been resistance to the Truth. That's a historical fact. The Sons of Liberty will be ready to counteract that resistance. By any means necessary."

"Does Rice know the extent of your plans?"

"He's aware of our loyalty."

"I'll go over this right now."

"Thank you, sir. I'd appreciate any corrections you make. Grammar, spelling. I'm no writer."

"Sure." Neither am I. Any more.

Mack made the L salute and curtained Cable into the stern of the motor home.

He had read the manual before in a dozen versions. Only the names had been different on the smeary mimeographed sheets he had studied at the newspaper and at the Center. He scanned for topics that had once amused him.

> Women have always posed problems for red-blooded Patriots; a real Man needs female companionship. But if Paul had listened to Mrs. Revere he would have stayed by a cozy fire that night of 18 April 1775. You have to make your wives and girlfriends understand that Liberty always comes first.

He had never taken the groups seriously, psychos, fat boys, self-haters, bullies, sadists puffed up by press attention and liberal revulsion, paranoids nourished by street beatings and assistant D.A.s who bent civil-rights laws to sweep them out of sight. The Sons were scraped out of the same scum pot. But they were marching behind Liberty Two.

> Appearance is second only to discipline in public demonstrations. Never wear sweaters or coats over the uniform. Never wear hats. In severe cold weather wear your "warm johns" under the uniform. The psychological effect will be terrific. Your shivering enemies will quake at your strength and determination and your friends will be favorably impressed (including your secret friends among liberty-loving policemen).

Old stuff. They probably wore sheepskins under their togas in Rome. Every Fascist, Communist, Nationalist handbook ever written had that paragraph. But none of them ever had Rice.

> Ammonium nitrate, a common farm fertilizer, and No. 2 diesel fuel or kerosene, in a 95 to 5 percent mixture, requires a one-pound stick of at least 60 percent dynamite for detonation. Close confinement is essential for maximum explosive force. For example . . .

Cable pushed through the curtain. Rice had to know about this now. Paoli was sitting in the dinette booth cleaning his nails with a car key. He stood up.

"If you're going out I'll guard that for you, Mr. Cable. Captain Mack doesn't want it to leave headquarters."

Cable dropped the typescript on the dinette table but Paoli's eyes didn't follow it. He watched Cable carefully. Professionally. A spook, Jack had said. Whose spook? M.I.? F.B.I.? The Center?

They exchanged L Salutes. Ironically?

Carley was blocking the door of Rice's Winnebago. "I'm sorry, Mr. Cable. I can't let anybody in. Not even you. There's somebody in there with him and the lawyer."

A big man sauntered up with a fixed smile. "Problem?" He opened his suit jacket.

"No problem," said Carley. "This here's Mr. Cable."

The big man nodded amiably. "How's it going, Mr. Cable? Hot enough for you?" His thumb picked at his belt buckle. Wendt's bodyguard, Cable thought. The helicopter waited out in the desert.

Cable walked away. See Rice later about the manual. He remembered he had not slept for nearly thirty-six hours, and he suddenly felt tired, heavy-armed and weak-legged. He climbed into the end Winnebago before he remembered that Jean had turned it over to the doctor.

Push Lane was dozing in the passenger seat of the driver's compartment. The bunks were filled and a double-decker cot had been jammed into the aisle. He asked the nurse to get him fresh clothes from the rear closet. She had to climb over bodies.

Lane roused. "Mr. Cable. That was real fine of you and the missus to give us your place."

"How's your wife?"

"She'll be fine; don't need to go to the hospital. The heat and all that excitement just knocked her out. I'll tell you something, Mr. Cable, we been married forty-one years last month and I thought I knew that woman. She's no wallflower, she's got a mind and she speaks it, but when she stood up there and started singing, I nearly swallowed my teeth. And then my old ticker started beating so hard I thought it was going to break my ribs. Say, uh, they said I could stay here with her overnight. You might like to use our place, ain't so fancy as this but there's a fan over the bed and clean sheets in the closet." He unsnapped a leather key ring from a belt loop and took off one of a dozen keys. "You know it? Says Shady Lane on the door."

"Thanks." Cable took the key. The nurse gave him an armload of clothing and his vinyl toilet kit from Indianapolis.

A steady stream of cars moved out to the county road, but the traffic was much lighter leaving the encampment than it had been this morning coming in.

The Lanes' camper, mounted on a pick-up truck, was small and neat. A bed in the back, a tiny galley, two chairs and a table folded into a wall. The bathroom was a closet with a chemical commode and a shower head on a flexible steel pipe. A portable TV. Fringed nylon curtains. The air was hot and stale. He debated turning on the exhaust fan. It would be useless unless he left the door open, and the air outside was no cooler or fresher. An excuse to keep the door locked. I don't feel safe in this place. Armed body-guards and homemade bombs and Jack lying to me about Lefferts.

He took off his shoes and stretched out on the tufted blue bedspread. Family photos behind clear plastic on the wall. In an overhead rack a Bible, a stack of trailer magazines, a sewing bag. Forty-one years together compressed into this metal room. He decided to rest for a few minutes before he showered and shaved.

"Silver, lighting up the world,
"Brighter than a star will ever be . . ."

At first he thought he was dreaming, but the sound buffeted the camper. Cable peered out into the dying light. Torch flares studded the shadows and spark showers fell back into campfires. A hundred TV sets turned to full volume cast blue and rainbow glows. Bart Pike's Hour to howl. He must have slept for four or five hours.

He switched on the Lanes' set. It hummed for a long time before Rice appeared on the screen delivering his call. He seemed very tall. Looming. The old Alan Ladd angle, Cable thought. Ladd on a box, the girl on the ground and the cameraman shooting up from a trench. The NASA publicity photos of Rice before his moon flight had been shot from the same angle. Rice had looked like a giant.

Cable left the set on while he used the bathroom. No power failure compounded by an engineer's error this time. They let him announce his revolution on prime time.

Why?

They were too smart to think they could control him.

So they must be planning to kill him.

The thought absorbed Cable. He approached it coldly, detachedly. From their point of view. They would have to kill Rice soon. Once the Caravan was on its way to Washington, an assassination might loose a mob on the country, a headless silver body thrashing in grief and frustration. Riots. An insurrection. Other leaders to spur the frenzy in the dead astronaut's name. It would be suppressed, but not without death and disruption. Unhealable scars. Pockets of underground resistance. The Sons of Liberty. Rice would have activated a metastasizing cancer that could never be entirely burnt out.

Kill him soon. How? The country had grown too wise too quickly. So many conspiracies, so many botched cover ups. The country might not buy another crazed loner bursting out of a crowd with a Saturday Night Special. A contrived accident? Too tricky for a man without regular habits, a man under such close media scrutiny. A stroke-inducing injection? Rice is too alert to let someone get that close.

It would have to be a dramatic finale that kills Rice and somehow discredits him. Simple. Open and shut. No investigation necessary. No Commission creating more questions than answers. Nonpolitical. A passionate murder. Cissie. Larry Bruno's mother. The brother of a Galloping Ghost. Someone, anyone with a personal reason to kill Rice. Primed to do it and set up to take the fall.

Cable shaved closely and showered until the water ran cold. He emerged in time for the end of the "Pike Hour." A reprise of "The Ballad of Liberty Two." The cowboy musicians hummed and gazed skyward as Pike crooned the song as a spiritual.

Cable snapped off the set, rechecked the door lock and changed the sheets on the bed. He climbed between them naked.

They would have to kill Rice soon.

They. The all-purpose They. We've been addled and terrorized by warnings and whispers. They. All the creepers in the night. The Jew-Communist International Conspiracy and the Roman Catholic Church. The Radical Right and the Bearded Left. They're gonna getcha if you don't watch out. The Haves, the Have-nots, the Faceless Bureaucrats and the Establishment and the Blacks. The Third World, the Fourth Estate, the Fifth Column. The Men in the Trojan Horse.

Raddle our minds with fragments of absurdity, with real shards of false fears and false grains of truth.

But somewhere out there, right now, are people with a plan.

A key scratched at the lock.

Fear paralyzed, then released him, a frozen hand closing and opening. He slipped out of bed and felt around the galley until he found a large meat knife. Its wooden handle was too slender for a secure grip and its heavy triangular blade weighted it clumsily. He did not know how to use it. Stab or slash? He had never been in armed combat. Just throw the damn knife and rush after it. He wished he was wearing at least shoes and undershorts.

The door opened, the trailer shifted on its springs under a light step. The light went on.

"Hey! Cable."

He threw the knife on the galley counter. It clattered into the sink.

"What are you doing here?"

Jean closed the door. "Push Lane gave me the key. He didn't tell me you were here."

The missus, thought Cable.

"Well?" said Jean.

He felt vulnerable without clothes, no pockets for his hands, no shoes to tap, no coverings to posture behind.

"I'll get dressed and get out," he said.

"Do what you want. You always do."

"What does that mean?"

"It means I think you're just so into yourself there isn't any room for me or anybody else."

"So that's why you spent the night with Rice."

"Who told you that?"

"What was he like? I need to know for my book. It'll add a new dimension." He could not squeeze out all his anger, and his body shivered.

"I didn't spend the whole night with him." The deep eyes narrowed. "The only person who saw me go in and out was Jack. He relieved Carley at the door."

"Was it good?"

"Look, Cable, you don't own me. You don't even want me."

"Did you find what you were looking for? The right thread to pull all your pictures together?" His voice seemed to him to be coming from a cold and distant place.

"You got on a plane and flew away. Jack told me that. You got on a plane and flew away. Just like that, you flew away. You didn't tell me you were going, you didn't say a word." Blotches appeared on her chest and neck. "You didn't even talk to me when you came back."

He walked past her to the bed and began dressing. He remembered the day he had stomped away from Lynn so he could call the Center, sure her pride wouldn't let her follow him out of the park. He realized he wanted Jean to follow him out of the park.

"Cable?"

He could not find clean socks. They were not in the pile of fresh clothes the nurse had collected for him. He decided to wear his soft suede shoes on bare feet rather than put dirty socks back on. Dizzy, he had to sit on the bed to put on his shoes.

"Cable. Talk to me."

"About what?"

"About what. You're still turning away from me, you still

don't trust me with what's in your mind. You never ever answer my questions. What right do you have to ask me questions? Where did you go? Why couldn't you tell me?"

"I had something to do."

She started to leave. She opened the door, one foot was poised to step out, before she hesitated. She rooted in her knapsack until she found an exposure meter case. She withdrew a crumpled cigarette and lit it with a shaky match.

"Cable? Do you really want to hear about me and Rice?"

"It's your story." A knotted shoelace defeated his trembling fingers. He had pulled off his shoes without untying the laces.

"I didn't go to bed with him, if that's what's bothering you."

"Why not?"

"It just never happened. I would have. I was very angry at you. You hurt me. I took a lot from you, Cable, I was prepared to take a lot more. But I'm not going to stand around like a fool while you walk in and out on me without a goddam word."

"So you went over to screw Rice."

"I showed him the new batch of pictures. He liked them very much. He never even touched me. He talked about you."

"That must have made you happy."

"Oh, Cable, think of somebody else besides yourself for just one minute." She slammed the door shut and sat down beside him on the bed. She took the shoe out of his hands. Her long fingers easily untied the knot.

"What did he say?"

"I didn't really listen, I was so angry. I didn't want to hear about you. He was sure you were coming back. He said you must have had something very important to do, but you'd be back. He asked me if I loved you."

"What did you say?"

"That I wasn't sure you would let me. He said you were still working out a lot of things for yourself, and when you worked them out you'd be back and I could love you and he could trust you."

"He was right," said Cable.

"Where did you go?"

"I can't tell you. I can't even tell you why I can't tell you. Jean? Can that be good enough for now?"

"Cable, hold me."

He awkwardly put his arms around her shoulders. She looked for an ashtray, then made a face as she ground out the cigarette on a metal window sash. "That was my first cigarette in four days."

He squeezed her against him. She turned in his arms and pushed him down, pressing him into the bed with her body, kissing his lips, his eyes, his cheeks, pulling off their clothes, rousing him with her hands and mouth, her eyes closed, her body already thrusting. She mounted him frantically, her head thrown back, her big teeth bared, her hands behind her on his knees. He reached up to hold her breasts, and he stared at her face. She was lost in her own music. Susan had screwed for warmth and pleasure, and Lynn for release and domination, and Jean was screwing for reassurance that they were really connected. He felt a momentary resentment at being used, then a curious detachment during which he thought, Of course, if we can't use each other when we need to, what's it all about? and then he was swept away by her driving rhythm, spent dry by it, but he moved with her long after he had come, gratified by her happiness.

She collapsed on top of him. She surrounded him with her legs and arms.

Later, in sleep, they joined again. He rolled on top of her and they moved slowly and sweetly. They fell asleep without finishing, still connected.

Nineteen

The rainstorm woke Cable, wind-driven water marbles bouncing furiously on the camper's metal roof. Jean's eyes opened. Her face was calm, scrubbed clean of expression.

"Hi."

She smiled. "Hi."

Neither of them moved. Water splashing against the windows obscured the world outside their metal box.

She said, "I forgot where we were."

"In Lane's trailer."

"No, I mean in Liberty City. When I woke up I just thought we were in our own place somewhere. Does that scare you?"

"No."

"Cable? This place scares me. Rice. All these people. What's going to happen to them?"

"He's going to lead them out of the desert. And carve an L on the Washington Monument."

"I think something terrible's going to happen. There's a kind of mindlessness out there. You were right. It is a carnival. A drive-in. Mack's become some sort of a monster, he's got his own little army, they go around intimidating people. How does Rice let it happen? And all the new people coming in, the vibrations are crazy. When Mrs. Lane started singing it was absolutely thrilling, but later on, when I thought about it, she wasn't really here, she was back in her church. Nobody's really here."

"They all brought other places here, the places they're running away from. Didn't we?"

"All sorts of things are happening and nothing makes very much sense. Everybody's just sort of waiting to find out what Rice has in mind, and sometimes I think he doesn't have anything in mind. He thinks it's all going to work out just because he says so."

"What do you think's going to happen?"

"I think the government's going to try to stop him. Any way it can." She sat up. "Look, we've been here five days, right? Who owns this property? Where are the local police, the health inspectors? If this were a rock festival there'd be a bust every hour. We're next door to the most corrupt city in the world, screwing up their traffic, maybe even taking people out of the casinos, and no one's said a word. There hasn't been any noise about that missile-site thing. Where's the Mayor, the Governor, the President? We're still in the United States, aren't we? I think they're all keeping a low profile until they figure out how to stop him once and for all."

She was smarter than he had ever realized. He felt proud and uneasy. "Maybe we could make it. You're a paranoid, too."

She let him divert her, laughing, "Now that ain't called for," poking his stomach as he pulled her close. They wrestled, tickling and pinching each other until their play swelled into passion.

"Hey. You know what I'd like to do today? Go swimming. You still have that suit?"

"You are crazy."

"We'll go swimming some day, won't we, Cable? Promise?"

"Promise."

"I want us to have a future. Outside all this."

The rains quit in midmorning and the wind shifted, pushing the emptied clouds away. The sky was a pale blue and the sun was strong, drying the moist patches the sand had not absorbed.

The camp uncovered and stretched in the comfortable dry warmth. A line of cars waited to be checked through. They bore new bumper stickers, GOD BLESS CHARLES RICE and LIGHTS ON FOR LIBERTY TWO. A circle of uniformed Sons guarded the helicopter. Sand sat in the open hatchway, his legs dangling, his face tilted to the sun.

Rice was holding a news conference, by far his largest. Cable counted eleven television cameras. He didn't bother to count the radio tape recorders. A hedge of mikes in front of Liberty Two with call letters Cable hadn't seen in years. BBC. TASS. ADN, the Germans. EFE, the South Americans. Miles of black cable tangled on the sand, the silver school bus is plugged into the world.

". . . reaction to the announcement that Salt Lake City has just passed an ordinance banning processions of more than ten vehicles except for military parades and certain funerals."

Rice in a silver jumpsuit stood behind a wooden podium that bore a metal Liberty Two medallion as large as a car tire. It looked like an official seal.

"We expect that kind of repressive reaction. At first. But I'm sure the people of Salt Lake City will not allow their elected officials to block their access to Liberty."

"Commander, there've been some reports from around the country, people preparing for the Caravan by selling their homes, withdrawing life savings, quitting their jobs. Do you approve of people throwing up everything to . . ."

"Throwing up everything?" Rice's voice was mild. "Do you consider waking up from a drugged nightmare throwing up everything? Is daring to be free . . ."

"Mr. Cable." Mack tugged his arm. "You didn't make any corrections. It was all right."

"It was all right." And it doesn't matter. When they hit Rice you're dead, too. But Mack's face demanded more, so Cable said, "It was a little heavy-handed in spots, but I didn't want to tamper with your style."

"The emotional stuff. Believe me, Mr. Cable, you need that garbage to appeal to the masses. I didn't write it for you or me or a bunch of college professors. It's for the man in the street. The guy in the tavern. You can't reach those people with quotes from Spengler. I can hardly understand that kind of stuff myself."

"Then it's fine, Mack, just fine." He forced himself to pat Mack's shoulder. Satisfied, Mack marched back to his post near Rice.

The astronaut's voice was hard, commanding. He was setting a line.

"I think some of you people in the media are trying to use history to prejudge the Liberty Caravan. You're wasting your time. There are no precedents, no clues. The Caravan is an original. A first. I am an original, a first. You have an obligation to history to report what you see and hear and smell and touch and taste. That will be faulty enough. Don't report what you think is going to happen based on your preconceptions.

"I have some announcements.

"This morning a group of Zuni Indians rode into Liberty City. They represent an advance scouting party representing many tribes of the Southwest. A week ago I visited their reservation. They rejected me as another white man's trick. They didn't understand that the second American Revolution is neither color-conscious nor color-blind, but a revolution for all Americans who dare be free. The Zunis have seen it plain. Other Native Americans will follow.

"Today I received a telegram from Major Alvin K. Rombacher, Jr. You'll remember that Ken was in the back-up crew for my moon flight. He's joining the Caravan in Reno. With his family.

"A mobile hospital unit from Fort Sam Houston has left the base and is en route to join the Caravan.

"I would like to read you a statement I received from the former Secretary of Agriculture, Lewis Wendt. I quote: 'Like a prophet of old returning from the mountain with a new and better way, Charles Rice has come back to us from the vastness of space with a message embedded in the very foundations of our republic. The second American Revolution is an alloy of our heritage and our future. I urge all Americans to see it plain.'

"You people of the media, the eyes and the ears of the world, have a tremendously challenging responsibility in the days and weeks ahead. It will be your . . ."

Cable edged away. Rice is on the launch pad now, and counting. Once he leaves Liberty City he's going to be hard to turn around, and once he leaves Los Angeles he's gone. In orbit. The administration waited too long, they must have kept assuring the President that Rice would burn himself out and because the President needed to believe that, nothing was done. Hands off Rice. Leave him alone, no harassment, no inquiries, no trespass violations for Liberty City. But Rice isn't going to burn himself out.

Rice is getting bigger, stronger. They're marching out of Army forts, and Wendt's finally jumped on the band-wagon, and another astronaut's on his way and Bart Pike's song is going to be the new national anthem. The people are painting silver. Rice isn't going to burn himself out, and it's much too late for anything but murder.

"Didn't you hear me call you?" Jean grabbed his arm.

"What's the matter?"

"Is there something between you and Jack?"

"What do you mean?"

"He was with a lot of people just a few minutes ago, Billy Fox and Amy and Paoli, and he pointed at you talking with Mack, and he said it looked like you were plotting something. He didn't know I was there, and he kept talking, and he said he didn't really trust you, you were always acting strange, and coming and going, he said he thought you were resentful because Rice's gotten so big, you can't have him all to yourself anymore. And then he said, Oh, God, Cable, I got so mad, but I kept my mouth shut because, you're going to think I'm really crazy, but it was sort of . . . sinister, and I thought you'd better know, and maybe he shouldn't know you knew. I'm all mixed up."

He pulled her around the crowd to the far side of the bus. The corridor between Liberty Two and the motor homes was deserted.

"Go on, it's all right."

"He said you really flipped out when Rice took your girl."

They're setting me up to take the fall. The nonpolitical murder. Rice killed by a man who was with him from the beginning. Over a girl. Perfect. So much for the second American Revolution. The country is saved from following a man who can't control himself or his closest aides.

"Listen, Jean, you've got to make me a promise. If I ever tell you to leave, to go away, to go hide somewhere, you'll just do it. No discussion, none of your questions. You'll just go. Promise."

"Not unless you tell me what's going on."

A technician walked around the bus uncoiling wire. He looked at them curiously. Cable lowered his voice. "This is very important, Jean. You've got to promise me that if I tell you to go, you'll go. No bullshit."

"Only if you go, too," she said. "Now you're mad at me."

"I guess so." He touched her cheek. Without thought, naturally, he said, "I love you."

Liberty City grows. More cars and campers, some of them painted silver. Bumper stickers—I HAVE SEEN IT PLAIN and RICE KNOWS THE WAY. The newspack swells into a restless crowd within the crowd, in constant movement, descending suddenly to gang-interview Billy Fox or Captain Mack, surging away to the temporary telephone installations, hanging up in midconversation to join the pack chasing down Lefferts or Duwayne Stockton or a flamboyant newcomer, a motorcyclist with a Liberty medallion freshly tattooed on his chest, a television starlet festooned with silver spangles from her nipples to her thighs. The newspack gorges quickly, rushes off to regurgitate. The tattooed biker is no Hell's Angel, not even a Galloping Ghost who has seen it plain; he is a simple-minded bartender from San Bernardino. The starlet is nervous. Her press agent nods as she repeats, "I've spent so much of my life in a fantasy world, I know Truth when I see it." Once she has spoken, only the photographers are still interested.

The pack surrounds Jack, who delights them, the surfer-Ghostkiller, modest but merry and open as the sun. They snare Sand, who plays moody and cool: Yes sir, the Moon Man makes sense to me. Now I'm talking just for myself, not for my Brothers. I was in a war where the only heroes were the studs who ejected quick enough to get to sit it out in bamboo jails. What about my buddies who came home in rubber bags with smack sewed inside their bellies?

The pack traps Cable, but he plays them shrewdly, mumbling, shrugging, blinking at their cameras. Just writing Commander Rice's book. Don't get to see him too much now, he's so busy. I'm clipping your stories for background. The pack dashes off; a black preacher with a diamond star in his front tooth leads in his swaying flock, women in pastel gowns shaking tambourines. Cable is relieved but disgusted; pride in his old trade fades.

Once interviewed and dismissed, Cable is free to roam unmolested; he is consciously ignored, as if they are afraid he will badger them for more of their precious time. He moves among the pack listening for the asides they continuously exchange; the journalists are excited, given to extravagance. Cable hears one say, This is true Populism, and one laughs, they must be pissing in their pants in the Oval Room. A woman reporter says, Charisma, it's the only word, we should have saved it, God, look at those people. A national correspondent, irked by sand in his shoes, answers, Those people, you can't make chicken salad with chicken shit. The younger reporters wink behind his back.

Jean is spared and Cable is grateful. Loping along with her cameras, she is mistaken for one of them. Her complicity will not be evident on miles of microfilm and videotape. He thinks of the holes in his report.

The pack brings in more news than it gathers. Each time they call in, their editors order them to get Rice's reaction to newswire bulletins. *The New York Times* has editorially asked Rice to see himself plain: Demagoguery has often disguised itself as Deliverance. Citizen's groups in five towns on the Caravan route have asked their councils to change the town name to Liberty. A teen-aged couple in Los Angeles painted themselves and their baby silver from head to heel; the baby is in critical condition. Lieutenant

General Jordan P. Hollowell has been transferred to an overseas NATO post; the Pentagon denies that the new assignment is in any way related to his performance at Skylancer. Chicago passed a parade ordinance similar to Salt Lake City's. A member of the Senate Committee on Aeronautical and Space Sciences has called for an investigation into what he calls the illegal procedures of Rice's medical discharge. The President cancelled a news conference, presumably so he would not have to answer questions about the Liberty Caravan. The American Civil Liberties Union has offered its services to Rice to contest the parade ordinances. Military policemen sent after the AWOL hospital unit have apparently joined them. A man caught robbing a bank in Miami says he needed the money to buy a car for the Caravan. Wall Street reports a nervous market. Gun sales are up. Cissie Rice has announced she will join Ken Rombacher and his family to await her husband in Reno.

Paoli joins Carley at the door of the lead Winnebago to fend off the pack. One pool photographer allowed to enter reports that the Commander is working on tomorrow night's Coliseum speech.

Beryl Petty and his plump, blonde wife roared into the encampment in a double-bottom, a truck tractor towing a semitrailer and a refrigerated unit. The tractor was splashed with silver paint and on the roofs and sides of the trailers were giant red letters, LIBERTY CAFE. Petty honked his way through the crowd as close to the bus as he could get, waving out the window, finally dynamiting the brakes and jumping out when he saw Cable and Jean.

"Where is he? I'm coming along. I sold the place, I got every cent right in here." He opened the refrigerator unit for the TV cameras. Ribbed carcasses beaded with congealed blood hung from the ceiling, and slabs and haunches of meat were stacked on the floor.

Carley, attracted by the commotion, grabbed Petty and shouldered a path back to Rice's Winnebago. They returned in a few minutes, elated. Carley boosted Petty up to the cab roof.

"Folks, folks, get those fires started. I just talked to the Commander. We've gonna have us a Liberty Roast."

Cable slipped away. Paoli made no move to stop him from yanking open Rice's door. The astronaut was leaning back in the passenger seat.

"I've got to talk to you. Right now."

"David Cable, my biographer. You've met General Knox."

Tyler Knox stood in the aisle between the galley and the dinette booth. He was taller, more imposing than Cable remembered from the brief meeting in Oklahoma City. In troika with Wendt and Lefferts the General had not emerged distinctly in Cable's mind. He had appeared stiff then, slightly blustery, a movie general fighting a rear-guard action against time. But now, alone, there was energy in the thrust of his big, flat body and even his out-of-style seersucker suit seemed like a statement of spiny integrity.

"Are you sure you want this man to hear what I have to say?" asked Knox. It was more of a challenge than a question.

"Go ahead," said Rice. He waved Cable to the driver's seat. To the right of the throne, thought Cable. Knox, a rebellious duke storming back to court from the occupied provinces.

"Before it's too late, Rice. Send those people home."

"They've come here to reclaim their home. I'm going to lead them home."

"Send them home before they get out of hand. Don't delude yourself. That's a mob out there. Just because there are women and children out there, just because you've gotten them off booze and cigarettes for a few days, don't start thinking you can keep them in line. That's a mob out there. The government knows it's a mob. They've got Guard units on stand-by alert. They're issuing riot gear to the Airborne."

"The Army will lay down its arms and join us." Rice's face was tranquil. His body was motionless in the large black vinyl recliner.

"You're living in a dream world. A goddam dangerous dream world. You're going to lead that mob right into a confrontation that could rip this country apart. A Civil War. A Civil War, man. I've seen 'em. No rules, nothing. It's not war, it's just bloodshed. You think of that. Leave us wide open. It'll be a horse race to see who can mop us up first, the Soviets or the Chinese."

"You're a soldier, Knox. Your only frame of reference is war."

"I've been in three, Rice, from first shot to the conference table. And some little ones you never heard much about. I can talk straight to any man alive. You haven't seen anything, you've spent your life playing with toys. You listen to me. I don't want anything from you, I'm not one of your flunky yes-men." His sharp glance pecked at Cable. "It's nut-cutting time. Face facts. You got lucky. You bamboozled a few people. You panicked Lew into a public statement."

"Wendt came to me."

"Running scared. A goddam pragmatic liberal, I call him a velvet hand in a tin-foil glove. To his face. He was scared of getting left behind. And Lefferts. A lawyer." The word seemed to tighten Knox's throat. It came out harshly. "Lefferts'll go any way the action is. And cover his fancy ass. Don't start thinking you've got any kind of a mandate just because the press is having a field day and those people out there think you're the Candy Man.

"I'm talking straight. I think you're behaving irresponsibly. Look, I was in the military for thirty-three years, and I know this country. I've been a hero and a villain and a johnny-get-lost. I've seen this country from every angle.

"The pansies were always afraid the Army'd try to take over. Maybe we should've. But we never even tried. You know why? Because we believed in the regulations. Like the Constitution and the Declaration of Independence and the Bill of Rights. When things went wrong we knew it wasn't the system, it was the guys in the black hats bending the regs. And sooner or later the system would take care of them.

"Now, I'm not saying you haven't got some good ideas. And I was willing to go along with Wendt running you for Congress. Shake people up, get 'em thinking, get 'em up off their hands. But I'm not going to back a half-baked, tin-horn Messiah."

"A tin-horn Messiah," repeated Rice. The phrase seemed to amuse him. "Knox, I've never said I was anything more than what I am. A messenger. All I've tried to say is this: The system is no longer functional, the institutions act only for their own perpetuation. The rules are just fences to keep people contained. See it plain and change the system. Dare be free.

"It's too basic to argue. You can't shoot holes in the wind or the tides or the pull of the moon. There's no body of theory to attack, no *Mein Kampf* or *Das Kapital*. No Gospels. Nothing to force people to become allies or enemies, nothing to play their fears and prejudices, nothing to divide and destroy them. I represent Truth. You can't be for or against Truth. It exists. It's what you see when you see things plain.

"Truth is not a roll-call vote, it's not an instrument to revise the regulations or reverse the decisions or justify human misery. Truth is not a game plan, General."

Knox shook his head. "You're talking about blind faith." He was winding down. He braced himself against the galley counter. He had come with a forlorn hope of being heard out, thought Cable, and now that he's made his pitch he has little in reserve.

"Blind faith," repeated Rice. "The great trap. When I was in the hospital after the moon shot, I had a midnight visitor. One of the richest, most powerful men in America. He was a major NASA contractor through a network of interlocking corporations, very few people knew how involved he was in the program. He got into my room when they were still keeping my wife in the lobby waving to me over close-circuit.

"This man, I'm sure you know the name, Douglas Clune, sat on the edge of my bed and asked me if I had felt the Hand of God on my shoulder when I stood on the moon. I said, No. He asked me if I had heard the Voice, if I had seen the Vision. I told him it was far more profound than that. I had had a rational experience. Clune was very disappointed. He wanted to finance an evangelical crusade. He wanted me to lead this country back to decency and righteousness and the fear of a moral God."

Cable felt no surprise, only a faint drumming excitement. The pieces were snapping into place.

Knox asked, "Do you believe in God?"

"I'll tell you what I told Clune. I don't believe in an accessible God. I do believe there are forces in our known Universe which we call supernatural because we don't trust each other enough to harness them. These are forces of energy that can power existing technology to free all men, make all men equal. These forces would transcend borders and governments and nations and economic systems."

Knox looked bewildered. It was getting too thick for him. But he tried. "You mean like atomic energy? Solar energy?"

"Not at all. I'm talking about the powers that move time, the powers that hold the stars in their courses, that give and sustain life. I told Clune that a religious crusade was a manipulative device, that I had come back to cut strings, not to pull them. He called me a fool for missing my chance, but he was afraid. That man, and men like him, have tried to stop me at every turn. From the motorcyclists at . . ."

"We checked that," said Knox. "The exhibitors paid those hoodlums to harass you."

"At every turn there were attempts to stop me and at every turn I was encouraged and strengthened. When they pulled the plugs at the Astrodome my voice grew louder. When they tried to trap me at Skylancer, the whole country saw . . ."

"You turned that into a circus," said Knox. "That black box crap could've killed a lot of people."

"Are you sure there is no black box?" asked Rice.

"Never heard of it. It makes no sense to centralize a defense system. Just one group of . . ."

"Then you're not sure."

Knox sat down.

"They will try again and they will fail again. They cannot stop me until my mission is completed. And then I will hold the earth in my hand."

"You're crazy," said Knox. "You are crazy." He stood up. "I'm walking out of here, Rice, and I'm going straight to Washington and I'll talk to anyone who'll listen until I find someone who'll find a way to blow you to hell."

"You're a brave and honest man, Knox. Some day you'll see it plain and walk beside me."

Knox swayed in the aisle. Words failed him. A ropy blue

vein divided his forehead and threatened to burst. He made a sound, deep and wet, and marched stiffly out of the motor home.

"He'll be back." Rice swiveled his chair to face Cable. "You want to talk to me?"

"Yes. I . . . I have to tell you something." At first the words were dry and painful, as if they were pushing through valved passages, and then they came with a confessional rush. "Clune sent me. To spy on you. From the beginning. Jack works for him. So does the helicopter pilot. His name is Sanderson Moore, he's some kind of psychologist. Lefferts is probably tied up with them indirectly. There may be others in the camp. They may be working with other agencies. I'm just beginning to figure it all out. I never knew they were operational. I think the Center will try to kill you."

"They can't kill me. I've come from too far and I've got too far to go." The chair reclined farther and Rice's eyelids fluttered.

"You've got to listen." Cable was on his feet, in front of Rice's chair. He sensed it was useless, that Rice was beyond his reach, that he was talking only for his own salvation now. "You've got to get out of here. Right now. Find another way, go underground, take Wendt's offer . . ."

"This is the way." Rice's eyelids closed and he smiled. "When you came to me, Cable, you were running away from life. I've watched you work things out and grow strong. Give and take friendship. Give and take love. Assume responsibility. Assume command. Now you're running toward life. I want you with me tomorrow, I want you beside me when I step out of my silver helicopter onto the Coliseum field."

Rice's eyes did not open and he did not speak again. Cable imagined him in the rocket's barber chair, counting to lift-off.

Cable walked alone into the desert. He thought of Clune sitting on Rice's hospital bed offering him the nation as congregation. Teach them the fear of a moral God. The nineteenth century trying to buy the twenty-first.

Another image nagged: Rice leading his Caravan across the country, his eyes fixed east as the silver stream behind him overflowed the banks of his control, a gathering flood of violence and anarchy. Maybe not civil war, but certainly civil disruption. Rice carves his L on the Washington Monument, a symbol without a system, a call to the people to respond. To what? A vision without structure. A tinhorn Messiah without a game plan.

Why should we have to choose between a Clune and a Rice, between two desperate kings, between political and economic manipulation so complex and powerful it absorbs government, and a mindless liberation that might destroy it?

I don't have to choose. Get Jean and leave this place now. Let Clune and Rice fight it out. I don't belong to either one of them. Any more.

Twenty
The Liberty Roast began at twilight. Smoke from cook fires thickened the dusk. Cable circled the encampment. He estimated nearly four thousand people from the silver school bus to the county road. White-smocked Sons cranked the roasting spits. Flames leaped up to lick away glistening fat. Two documentary film crews moved from fire to fire.

Rice will die tonight. The certainty calmed him. There is nothing I can do. He'll die with me or without me. If I'm gone, if they can't frame me for the murder, they'll just find another way.

Cable remembered Jack in Houston, three-foot dolls and Teddy bears, Georgie Trott saying, You really missed it, Mr. Cable. Jack wiped 'em out. The greatest shooting you ever saw. Jack winking, When you're hot, you're hot.

At nightfall, when Rice mounts the aluminum platform to speak to Liberty City for the last time, he will be high, well-illuminated, relatively stationary. The perfect target, Cable thought.

Get Jean. Leave this place.

Rice was right. I came to him running from life, afraid of living, and now I am running toward life, afraid of dying.

I owe him something. If I can help him, if I can save him, even if only for an hour or a day . . .

And yet, what moral right do I have to pay a personal debt with the lives of those who will be caught in the madness I have prolonged by an hour or a day?

Liberty Two stood empty, waiting for Rice. The bronze desert darkened. At nightfall, a man could move unheard and unseen across the sand and slip into the shadowy corridor between the bus and the Winnebagos. Cable strained through night sounds of the desert. Rats and badgers foraging around the garbage dumps, a coyote howling, lizards scraping over the sand. Rabbits.

A single shot, the muzzle flash lost in the dancing firelight, the sound unheard in the shouts and laughter, the clatter of pots, the whine and sputter of trailer generators. As the crowd surges forward toward the fallen silver figure, Jack would drop his rifle and join the screaming confusion.

A machine gun rattled, jabbing his heart. Fire crackers. Cheers and applause. A Roman candle rocketed into the dark sky and blew into a wheel of sparks. The campers boisterously lined up for hunks of hot meat. Mack shouted through his bullhorn. Push Lane proudly led his wife toward a roasting spit, a film crew walking backward ahead of them. Amy talked to Billy Fox of the black button eyes. Half a dozen young Indians squatted near a highly polished old pick-up truck.

He felt pity for all of them. In a little while each would

be alone again, thrown back into a world in which they had found no place. Graduates of Liberty City, older, wiser, and lamed forever by a silver sliver of hope.

He did not see Jean. He should have talked to her, he should have told her everything. Ignorance would be protection for her, yet he wished she could have known who he was.

"Don't turn around."

Paoli's voice. A hard object poked his side.

"Walk behind the bus. Very casual. We're talking. That's it. Nice and easy. Some night, huh? Never get used to how cool it gets here at night."

They walked behind the bus into the shadowy corridor. The bright festival was hidden.

"You can turn around now." Paoli held a short-barreled revolver. Probably a Magnum, Cable thought, sawed down into a belly gun. Inaccurate at distance, a punishing recoil, but it could blow a deadly hole. He was pleased at the matter-of-fact processes of his mind. He wouldn't panic. He wouldn't force Paoli to shoot him ahead of schedule. Clune's schedule. Jack shoots Rice. Paoli shoots me. I'll be found with a rifle in my hands. A jealous lover. Open and shut.

"What's this all about?" asked Cable.

"We're waiting for someone," said Paoli.

"The Ballad of Liberty Two" crooned out of the speakers. The lights on the aluminum platform blazed.

Paoli was alert, poised. His eyes never left Cable's face, the gun was steady in his hand. Cable measured the distance between them. He would be dead before he grabbed the gun. A useless gesture. No one would hear the shot.

The "Ballad" swelled, a hymn into a chorale, Bart Pike's voice a thunderous summons. Fireworks crackled, sprays of darting color, red and yellow and blue flowers that lost their petals and drifted away.

Cable felt hollow. We'll never swim. No future outside this place. I'll die here and she'll never know the truth. Will she believe I killed Rice? Got to get that gun.

"You're the patsy," said Cable.

"You can do better than that," said Paoli. But Cable sensed an uncertainty in his voice.

A shadow twitched between the Winnebagos. Someone was there. Probably one of the Sons on patrol. Get his attention. If Paoli can be diverted for just one second . . .

"Use your brain, Paoli. I'm staff, you're just a pick-up." Cable tensed to move.

"Come off it." Paoli cocked his head toward a faint sound behind him.

"Put down that gun and . . ."

"Lower your voice."

Paoli turned, too late. The shadow was upon him, and dark hands like cleavers chopped him down. He fell in a broken heap.

"Sand!"

"Let's get out of here."

Cable dove for Paoli's gun, expecting a crushing blow, but Sand stood motionless as Cable came up with the revolver in his hand.

"Look, Cable, it's a trick deal all around. I'm folding. I just came back to get you."

"Why?" He pointed the gun at Sand.

"You'd never understand. I'm not sure I do. Let's go."

"I asked you why. You're one of them."

"Don't press me, man." He could not see Sand's face, but the deep voice sounded labored.

"Don't move. Where's Jack?"

"It doesn't matter. If Jack doesn't hit him, someone else will. The Center's spread, and it's deep. Look, we don't have time. You don't have to trust me, you've got the gun."

"Why did you come back?"

"I had something, Cable. I was into something fine and they took it and they twisted it and they made me into a . . ." He stopped. "I never figured they'd turn around and set you up. And I never figured they'd kill that kid so wantonly."

"What are you talking about?"

"Vogel."

"Mike Vogel?"

"You didn't know. He was Lynn's brother. The Center killed him. After you mentioned his name at the Holiday Inn, I told Jack. He said he'd run it through Research. The next day the kid was found in his car, outside Boulder. An overdose. I just found out about it, I've been out at the airport, they're spraying the bird silver for tomorrow. It was in a Denver paper. Vogel's father is a big shot from New Jersey. He's out there conducting his own investigation. The old man says the kid wasn't doing drugs anymore. So do the other kids in the commune."

Cable lowered the gun. "They killed him because he knew who I was."

"Let's get out of here."

"They killed Lynn. They blew up that whole house, all those people. They figured that someone in that house wired my car because he knew who I was, so they killed them all."

"Let's go. If we get out of here right now we'll be all right. I've got friends in San José."

The sky was suddenly empty of flares and the "Ballad" died in midnote. Rice mounted the platform.

"We've got to find Jack. Stop him."

"For what?"

"For me. Help me."

"No way. I'm bailing out."

"Bailing out? After the Teddy bear room, the dreams, after what you did to me?"

"I'm sorry, Cable. I thought it was valid treatment. I thought I was supposed to get you back into the field, to help you come to terms with yourself. They used me, too."

"You take one step and I'll blow your head off."

"Good luck, Cable."

Cable watched Sand disappear back into the shadows. The sonuvabitch knows I'd never shoot him.

Rice shimmered on the platform. He spoke.

"This is our last night together in Liberty City. But long after our footprints have faded from this sand the world will remember and honor what happened here, how the spirit of Liberty City leaped out of the desert and soared across America. How people from every . . ."

Cable rolled Paoli's body under the middle Winnebago. Paoli had brought him here to be near Jack, to shoot him after Jack killed Rice. So Jack would come here. He would probably fire from one of the Winnebago roofs, shoot Rice in the back, then slip away, into the crowd or out into the desert. He would leave it to Paoli to put the rifle in my hands, to wait with my body. Paoli might even have some police credentials. The Center was spread, and deep. Cable pulled off his shoes and pressed himself against the motor home's metal side. He searched the night and listened to the desert. He would have to remember to hold the Magnum very tight, to squeeze off bursts as it kicked against his palm.

". . . make every city a Liberty City, every man . . ."

A rubber sole squeaked on a ladder rung.

A figure rose on the lead Winnebago's roof, then dropped into a huddled shape. Cable moved out a few steps and glanced at the figure from the corner of his vision until his night eyes focused and clarified the outline.

Jack was locked into a sniper's sitting position, knees up, elbows braced against the inside of his thighs. He was ten feet higher than Cable, perhaps thirty-five feet away.

Cable was no marksman. At this distance, with this gun, he could not be sure of hitting him.

". . . at dawn the Sons of Liberty will direct your vehicles into two columns for the drive to Los Angeles. You will . . ."

Jack took a deep breath, exhaled, took another and held it. He pressed forward against his thighs.

Cable rushed toward Jack. As soon as he stepped into the patchy light he knew he had made a mistake. He was ten feet away from the lead Winnebago when Jack shifted, lowered the rifle and fired. A weight slammed into Cable's chest. He fell backward. His head struck first. No pain. He didn't move. Jack turned back to Rice.

". . . tomorrow's sun will rise behind our Liberty Caravan for the last time. When we turn east . . ."

The sand is cool and comforting. The pain will come later, when the shock wears off. If I live that long. Now rest. Sleep. I tried.

"I can see it plain, a world of silver . . ."

Rest, Davey. Close your eyes. Feel the breeze in your hair. Sleep.

"The Universe has spoken to me. I have been chosen to lead the way . . ."

Wake up, Cable. Open your eyes. The Coach's great flat feet slapped across the sand. Pull, Cable, you'll never know who you are till you get to the other side. You got to come the distance to find out who you are.

The gun was still in his hand.

". . . for I know the way, and I will show it to you . . ."

I love you, Davey. David. Dave. I killed you all, I let you die.

He heard the pop of fireworks through the booming in his ears. The "Ballad." He turned his head. Rice, legs spread, arms outstretched, a blazing silver eagle. Rice threw back his head to the thunder of the crowd.

The gun was heavy, too heavy, but he raised it, an inch at a time, struggling for breath, until he could see only the top of Jack's head over the short barrel.

He squeezed the trigger, again and again and again, until the barking, bucking metal clicked and fell out of his hand.

Twenty-one

He searched for the golden Teddy bear with the wrinkled smile but someone had torn down the wallpaper strip. White walls, a pale face.

"Don't talk now, darling. Just rest. You'll be all right. The bullet went right through, it didn't hit anything important. You're going to be even better than new, you've got some of my blood inside you now."

"Rice?"

A white jacket. "Better let him rest now, Miss Stryker." His arm was pricked.

"Rice was here, he'll be back to see you in the morning."

He awoke to pain. Sunlight without warmth through a sealed window. Jean dozed in a chair. Her hands were open on her lap, cupped like tulips. Her lips twitched.

The hammering pain high in his right chest quickened. Rice is alive. I am alive. Jean.

The sudden flush of exhilaration exhausted him.

Rice's hand on the back of his neck. A chain of cool metal touched his neck. "This is yours now, Cable. For all men to see."

Rice held the Liberty medallion to Cable's eyes before he laid it on the bandages across his chest.

"The Center. Be careful."

"I'll send for you when you're strong enough to travel." Rice took Cable's hand between his hands, pressed it and was gone.

Jean fed him lunch. Broth, bread, diced meat.

"They'll let you out in a few days. I made a deal with the doctor. He'll treat you as an outpatient if we stay nearby. I thought we could just relax and get some sun and . . ."

"What about the police? I killed a man."

"You're a hero. Jack was an assassin. He tried to kill Rice. He shot you and he killed Paoli."

"Sand killed Paoli."

"Sand?"

"The helicopter pilot."

"He's gone. Rice said he was going to fly the helicopter to Los Angeles himself."

He pushed the tray away and tried to sit up. If I can sit up I can think, but he overestimated his strength and the pain, deep and constant, pinned him to the propped pillows. The medallion rested on his chest.

When he woke again his mind was clear. The pain had settled into a bearable ache and the feverish throbbing was gone. He flexed his toes and fingers. He pinched his body. He was weak, but he felt connected.

Jean was tuning the television set mounted on the wall.

A photograph of the moon filled the screen, its peaks and craters slowly replaced by the features of Rice's face. "The Ballad of Liberty Two." A title appeared: THIS MAN FROM THE MOON—LEADER OR LUNATIC?

A commercial for a diet soft drink.

"Hey, you're up. Just in time. They're doing a special on Rice. How are you feeling?"

"Fine. What time is it?"

"Six. Your dinner's here." She sat on the bed. "What's the Center?"

"Why?"

"You've been saying it."

"It's just an expression."

She was unsatisfied, but the commercial faded and the announcer claimed her attention.

"He has been called a madman, a moon-struck Messiah, a liar and a demagogue, but few men in modern history have captured the imagination of the American people with such sudden intensity. Is he a brief shooting star or a force that will change our lives? Is this man from the moon a leader . . . or a lunatic?"

A rocket rose from a nest of vapors.

"The nation had become indifferent to such perilous journeys. In fact, it seemed almost unaware that Americans were on the moon in early March until one spoke to them."

An astronaut lumbered toward the camera, pitched forward under his backpack, faceless behind a visor that reflected the spidery lunar module. There was a crackle of static and then a voice, distant and uneven but unmistakable.

". . . This is Commander Charles Rice, speaking from the surface of the moon. Tonight I have seen the earth plain. I have seen . . ."

Pictures flashed across the screen, the haunted face that

had startled Cable at Bonnie Fuller's, the colossal Rice astride Larry's body in the Speedway infield, Rice riding silently out of the Dome, marching out of Skylancer No. 4, growing, changing, becoming the silver Apollo beside Bart Pike. Rice's somber face as a bloody body was lifted out of an ambulance and rolled through the doors of a hospital emergency room. Cable's face on the stretcher.

The camera swept across the abandoned encampment, then zoomed in on tire ruts and footprints. The sign of stones. Garbage barrels and the archway of Liberty Checkpoint. Oil stains on the sand. The ashes of dead fires.

A man in a silver jumpsuit walked briskly to a silver helicopter.

"In a few minutes, Commander Rice will leave for the Los Angeles Coliseum where a crowd of nearly one hundred thousand awaits him. During his flight, we will provide live coverage of the preparations in Los Angeles, and a live discussion from our Washington studio where a number of prominent figures in government, journalism, and the academic and religious fields will assess this phenomenon and speculate on its impact.

"For Commander Charles Rice, perhaps for all Americans, a most dramatic countdown. The helicopter blades are whirling. Photographers and newsmen at deserted Liberty City are scurrying away from the swirling sand. Rice gives his now-famous L for Liberty salute through the cockpit window. Now the silver helicopter rises into a pale blue sky on its way to what may be an appointment with destiny."

The silver bird filled the television screen, then gradually grew smaller until it was no bigger than a dime.

Then it blossomed, yellow and red. The television picture tilted. The hospital window rattled.

The announcer shouted, "My God, oh, my God, he's blown up, he's blown up . . ."

Jean covered her face.

Cable struggled up to a sitting position. "The bastards did it. They must have planted the bomb while the chopper was at the airport."

"Oh, Cable."

"We've got to go. Now."

"We can't help him. He's dead."

"But we're alive. Is your car downstairs? Do you have any money?"

She nodded. "Some travelers' checks. Why?"

"Help me get up."

"You can't, you've been shot, you . . ."

"The Center. They killed him. Jack was Center. So was Paoli. Sand. And me."

"I don't understand," said Jean.

"We'll have a head start. Everything's confused right now. Help me. Hurry." He swung his legs off the bed.

Numbly, she draped his left arm across her shoulders and supported him as he stood. The effort made him dizzy, nauseated.

"Where are we going? You need a doctor."

"Get to a motel. You'll buy me clothes, sell the car. They'll be looking for an orange Porsche. Sand's in San José. We'll find him. He'll have to help us. He owes it to me."

They walked into the corridor, a cacophony of shouts and cries and moans. White tunics rushed past them to the TV set at the nurses' station. Patients stood in the doorways of their rooms, asking questions with stunned eyes.

The announcer's voice, ". . . flaming debris scattered for . . ."

The elevator operator had a transistor radio pressed to his ear. He looked at them and said, "You hear what happened? He's dead . . . just like that he's dead . . ."

Cable leaned against Jean as they pushed through the

lobby. The volunteer at the information desk was crying, the telephone operators, their headsets on, joined clumps of murmuring visitors. The doorman looked at Cable and Jean and shook his head. His eyes did not register Cable's hospital pajamas, his bare feet.

He was staggered by the heat of the parking lot. Sirens crisscrossed, became one continuous scream. To the south, a column of black smoke rose out of the desert.

She opened the passenger door and he fell into the bucket seat, breathless and spent. It took her a long time to strap him in, to close his door, to open her door and start the engine.

"This is crazy. You'll die on the road. You'll . . . You're bleeding."

A pink stain widened on his bandages beneath the Liberty medallion.

"It's just seepage. I'll be all right."

"I won't do it, Cable. I want you to live."

"I want to live. I want to swim with you, I want a future. We're dead here. We've got a chance out there."

She eased out of the parking lot onto a main street. Cars had pulled to the curb. Drivers stepped out and clustered to watch the smoke. Police cruisers raced past.

"The Center. He's dead, Cable. What would they want with you now?"

"I know what they are."

"Are you going to be hiding from them the rest of your life?"

"I couldn't hide from them the rest of my life. They'll find me. Sooner or later. But I need time now. To get well. To decide what I'm going to do next."

"Even if we get to San José. And find this Sand. Then what?"

"Can't you go faster?"

"Are you going to expose them?"

"They're spread and they're deep, but they're not omnipotent. If they were, they wouldn't have to kill so many people. They wouldn't be so afraid of people finding out about them."

"How are we going to do it?"

"There'll be a way. There's always a way."

"He said that." Jean glanced at Cable. "That's exactly what he said."

"I know," said Cable.

She gunned the Porsche into speed.